No 2 and a Coloured Picture Gratis with No. 1

PRICE ONE PENNY.

# Joe Sterling

## BY JAMES GREENWOOD
### THE AMATEUR CASUAL

## OR A Ragged Fortune.

EDWIN J. BRETT, "BOYS OF ENGLAND" OFFICE, 173, FLEET STREET,

# JOE STERLING;

## OR, A RAGGED FORTUNE.

"THE JEW LARTED TO THE DOOR, WITH A PISTOL IN HIS HAND."

# JOE STERLING;

## OR, A RAGGED FORTUNE.

### CHAPTER I.

#### IN WHICH THE READER IS KIND ENOUGH TO SEE ME HOME TO MY LODGINGS IN RATS' CASTLE.

It is the 24th of December of the year ——, but the year is of no consequence to the reader, so we will say that it is Christmas Eve of all times of the year.

It cried aloud in the streets.

It beckoned you from the shop of the grocer, blazing with gas, and stuck full of plums and currants.

It chirped from the green and ruddy holly stuck in the butcher's fat beef.

It made itself heard even in the shivering wail of the Christmas-carol singer, who, with her rags flaunting in the biting blast, and her poor, blue, cold toes buried in the snow, recounted the various joys that Mary had.

Not that it particularly concerned me.

I was out of season. Out of luck.

Out at elbows and knees as well.

Out of a bellyful.

Out, in short, of everything worth caring for.

There was six inches of snow on the ground, and it was snowing still, and my old boots gaped at the soles, and my toes were as blue and benumbed as the carol singer's.

Why, then, didn't I go home? the reader will naturally ask.

Why did I not on such a wretched night seek the warmth of a fireside, and such comforts as my parents were able to provide me?

I may as well settle this question before I go any further.

I had no home.

According to the ordinary acceptance of the term, I was as homeless as any outcast mongrel that ever curled himself for a snooze on a baker's doorstep.

As for my parents, the little glimmer of recollection I had of them is not worth mentioning.

Somehow, however, it seems to me that I was not always a "waif" of the streets; not always a poor little fugitive wretch thrown on his wits to pick up a living or go hungry.

Nevertheless, at the time I take the liberty of introducing myself to the reader, although I had no "home," I had "lodgings."

A fine mansion, six stories high at least, with a magnificent water frontage, and commodious cellerage, and all the rest of it.

I was shuffling home as fast as I could, when I heard the shivering Christmas-carol singer.

Perhaps the incredulous reader who does not believe in my magnificent lodgings, will accompany me.

Tread carefully !

Out of the gas-flaring market street into a network of dark, winding alleys that lead down to the Thames.

This way.

Into the narrowest turning yet, where the broken pavement is treacherous to the feet, and the foul ooze of the river may be smelt, and the keen withering wind grips at your ears sharp as cat's claws.

But we are not there yet. Still this way.

Out at the jaws of the filthy little landing way, used seldom but at night, and then by river thieves and smugglers.

Now step down.

Here we are on the bleak river shore, where the charitable snow is striving hard to cover a decent white sheet over the black mud.

Mind your steps !

The pottery folk and the men of the glass works are in the habit of casting their slags and jagged furnace clinkers hereabouts, and, unless your shoes are sounder than mine, nothing is easier than to get an inch long gash in the sole of your foot.

I have done so, many a time.

Come along!

Follow the slimy, green-coated river wall, until we arrive at a clump of water-worn piles.

They are three in number, and bound about and clamped with rusty iron bands to keep them together.

Up with you!

To the top of the reeking, frozen piles!

Aye, that's the way. See how I do it!

But now I come to think of it you had best not try.

There are jagged nails in the old piles, and the frost to-night has got hold of them and they are slippery as glass.

Good-night, my friend. Make haste home to your soft pillows and cosy blankets, and leave me to find my way to my cupboard.

But there is no cupboard atop of the old piles?

Oh, dear, no. I am not yet at home. I am only at the threshold of my abode.

There it is, just before me!

You can't see it. All that you can make out is a black, blank brick wall.

Your eyes are not so sharp as mine, or else you would discover a gap in the wall, a hole that once was a window.

As I crouch like a water rat, making ready for a leap atop of the piles, the gap in the wall is just before me; a width of not more than four feet divides us.

Make ready!

One, two, three, and the trick is done.

The hole in the black wall swallows my ragged little figure, and I am at home.

# CHAPTER II.

### IN WHICH I MAKE A TERRIBLE DISCOVERY.

At home in Rats' Castle!

I cannot see my hand before me, but I have been there too often not to know exactly where I am.

It is a spacious room, I dare say once handsomely fitted and furnished, and merry and cheerful with light and life.

Now a dismal, dismantled place, without even a glazed window, and with walls painted in all the colours that mildew can bestow on them, and with an inhospitable yawning chasm where once was a stove for holding a jolly, crackling fire.

All these deficiencies are nothing to me, however.

Mildew and damp may play what tricks they please with the walls, and the wind may bellow down the yawning chimney as loud as it has a fancy to, provided it keeps out of my cupboard.

My cupboard is in the corner.

It is a comfortable, dry, good, old-fashioned cupboard, with shelves wide apart from each other, and of a depth from front to back of three feet at least.

It is a handy cupboard, with a stout button to fasten it on the outside.

I find it useful for other purposes besides those of a bed-chamber.

Some days I am lucky enough to pick up scraps more than enough for to-day. I know that I can stow the remainder away here, and it will be safe from my enemies.

These are not of the biped sort.

Nobody besides myself knows of my snug lodgings.

If they did I am not sure that they would find courage to occupy them.

No; my enemies have four legs and a set of teeth in their jaws, that at first, used to be my terror.

Rats!

I never knew such an awful place for rats.

Nor could I ever arrive at a satisfactory reason why they haunted the river-wrecked old mansion in such swarms.

True, there were cellars below.

Cellars that were excavated deep under the river bed, and wormed their way beneath the houses on shore; but there was nothing in the cellars.

Nothing but mud; that is, at least, as

far as I could discover by peeping down through the gaps and chinks of the parlour flooring.

Possibly, at a remote period of their history, the great old cellars may have been filled with tallow casks, or cheese, or sugar, and the rats of the present generation had a sort of reverence for the tradition their grandfathers had related to them, and so remained there on the speculation of those fat, toothsome old times being one day restored.

Anyhow, there they were, monstrous fellows, lean and long, and savage as bulldogs.

I was not afraid of rats.

From my very earliest recollection I had been accustomed to " roost " where rats were no novelty. I must acknowledge, however, that at times I found the companionship of the rats of Rats' Castle the reverse of pleasant.

I verily believe that the rapacious villains would have eaten me had they found a likely opportunity.

One night—I had not known them long then—I thought that they would do my business.

When fortune favoured me, I used to bring home something savoury for my supper.

On the occasion in question it was a red herring and a lump of bread.

The rats were awfully artful.

They seemed to have discovered that I was in the habit of bringing food home.

Further, that it was my greedy custom to sneak into the cupboard and consume it without offering them so much as a mouthful.

So what did they do on the night in question but billet themselves all about the cupboard, and there lay in waiting for me.

It was pitch dark in the room, and I dare not light a bit of candle, even had I been possessed of such a luxury.

They scented the herring as soon as I leapt in at the window.

It was stowed along with the bread in my old cap.

I carried the cap in my mouth, otherwise I might have found it awkward to take my flying leap from the top of the piles.

I approached my cupboard, my teeth watering for the sumptuous supper in store for them, when all of a sudden the rats came at me.

As before mentioned, I carried my cap in my mouth, and all of a sudden I felt at least a dozen of their warm, furry bodies assailing it.

I held fast, never fear.

I couldn't see them, but I felt their claws against my face and throat, and I fought for my supper.

I was as hungry as they were.

I hadn't eaten a crumb since I left home in the morning, and I didn't mean to give in easily.

There must have been scores of them.

I could feel them about my feet, and hanging on and endeavouring to climb up the rags of my trowsers.

Once in my struggles to free myself from them, I slipped down, and they thought, I'll be bound, that it was all over with me. But I scrambled to my feet again in a twinkling.

They did not bite much, they only scratched and tugged at the cap, while I, still holding it in my teeth, hit out desperately with my fists, now and then catching one of the thieves by the tail and dashing him down on the boards.

At last, a wary old villain found his way into the cap, and incautiously betraying his luck by a triumphant squeak, in an instant the cap was full of them, fighting and snapping for my herring and bread.

I was glad to drop it and escape into the cupboard and fasten the door against them.

Once within its closed, heavy, oaken door, I might defy them and find amusement in their ceaseless scampering and squealing.

It was not cheerful amusement, but it was better than the charnel-house stillness that otherwise reigned in the mildewed old place.

Better than the melancholy, monstrous plashing of the rising tide against the shiny wall.

The tide was my greatest enemy.

I was, as regards my snug lodging, at it's mercy completely.

Poor, little, motherless, fatherless wretch, outcast and with never a friend in the world ! Many and many a time have I dragged my small and weary legs towards my river-side roost, to find the tide " in," and the way barred as effectually as though a detachment of police with drawn staves opposed me.

I could not swim; and even though I could, the prospect of being saturated to the skin on a winter's night, and afterwards to sleep in my wet rags, was too alarming to be faced deliberately.

So, on such occasions there was nothing left for it but to skulk about, or to sit shivering on the cold steps, creeping down after the water, ebbing so cruelly slow.

But I have wandered far away from my starting point, which will be ever memorable with me, should I live till my hair is as white as the snow that then was falling.

All the preceding day my luck had been "dead out."

I hadn't picked up so much as a penny.

I had not a single crust with which to treat my friends, the rats.

You must know that ever since our fight for the herring I had come to a kind of compromise with them, and usually brought them home a tit-bit which at last they learnt to expect, and, all in the dark, would come squeaking about my feet for.

But, on the night in question, tit-bits were scarce, and my friends, after sniffing about me in vain for a few seconds, scuttled off through the broken flooring.

As for me, I crept into my cupboard, as miserable a boy, I hope, as London that night contained.

I had no doubt that I was alone in the ruined old river-side house.

The question that it might be otherwise never once occurred to me.

True, I had never ventured beyond this front chamber.

I never had occasion to do so.

All that I required, the room so difficult of access provided.

It was quite by accident that I discovered a way into the place, and that snug, dry cupboard, and I was grateful and content to pry no further.

It was something to be grateful for, this never-failing shelter from the wind and rain, when so many of my gutter-prowling acquaintances were glad to huddle, like houseless dogs, in doorways or under the black and reeking Adelphi "arches."

But somehow the consciousness of my good luck did not afford me complete consolation on that Christmas Eve.

I couldn't sleep.

Providentially I had left a crust of bread in the cupboard that morning, and, all in the dark, I munched that, moistening it with my tears, till I began to doze.

Then twelve o'clock struck out, and the bells set off with such a merry jingling and clanging that I was startled to wakefulness again, and I could hear the alarmed rats scuttling away to their burrows.

Suddenly, however, a sound made itself heard, clear and distinct, above the noise the bells were making.

It was a human voice, and it uttered the one piercing cry—

"Help!"

It seemed so close that I started up with a suddenness that brought my head in painful collision with the shelf above that on which I was lying.

Did it come from the river.

I was wide awake, and I had heard no splash before the cry.

Should I get up and have a look out at the loop-hole that faced the black, rolling waters?

Half resolved to do so, I pushed my cupboard door open just a little (I had a stout cord attached to a screw by which I held it inside), and as I did so came the sound again!

"Help! murder!"

Then the fall of a heavy body.

Not in the river though.

In the house; in "Rats' Castle," and in a room somewhere overhead.

I was terribly alarmed.

As before stated, I had not the least idea but that I was the one solitary tenant of the ruined house.

Now I discovered that I shared it with somebody else, and that somebody else was either being murdered or committing murder.

My first impulse was to leap from my roosting place, and fly from the place.

But in this I was baulked.

Since I had retired the tide had risen, and as I could tell by the plashing of the water against the piles, there was water enough beneath the window to cover my head, and half a yard to spare.

There was a door in the room, leading possibly to some passage that opened into

"'TAKE THAT FOR FOLLOWING ME,' SAID I."

the street, and in my desperate fright to get away I tried to open the door.

It was locked.

Should I cry out of the window for assistance ?

There was no one abroad on the river ; and even had there been, they would have been unable to hear me in the row and clatter the bells made.

Perhaps I was mistaken.

Possibly, the terrible sounds I had heard were not in the old house at all, but in one closely adjoining.

But this comforting supposition was speedily knocked on the head.

Not only were there people in the house—they were coming down the stairs.

The footsteps of two men, as I could make out distinctly ; and as they descended and came nigher, I could hear their gruff voices whispering together.

Should I call out through the door, and tell them that there was someone above calling for help ?

It was well for my life's sake that I did not.

Closer came the footsteps.

Closer and closer, and then they paused at the door.

At *my* door.

One of the men spoke.

" Well, what do you say ? Shall we be off at once, or stay here for a spell ? "

" We ain't in no hurry that I know of."

" P'r'aps it will be as well not to turn out just yet."

" Yes, yes, I think so ; somebody may have heard the old 'un holler, and be on the look-out."

" That settles it : in here then."

## CHAPTER III.

### I OVERHEAR CERTAIN STARTLING REVELATIONS.

As the speaker uttered these words he laid his hand on the handle of the door.

" It is locked," he exclaimed, with an oath.

" But you've a key vat will open it, my tear ! "

" Yes ; we'll thundering soon open it, if that's all."

I waited to hear no more.

Spellbound in terror, I had stood close to the door, listening to this strange conversation, unable to move or cry out.

The last exclamation that met my ears roused me, however.

With as much agility as the nimblest of my four-footed friends of the cellar could have displayed, I leapt back into my cupboard.

As I have already mentioned, to its inner side, attached to a stout nail, was a strong cord, which I had fixed the better to guard against the incursions of the rats.

This cord I wound tightly about my hand, and in breathless terror crouched down.

Presently I heard a noise of wrenching and rending, and then the door flew open with violence, creaking on its rusty hinges.

There were two men and one of them carried a light.

Fortunately there was on one side of my cupboard door a chink, and on the other side a knot-hole, so that I had a view almost of the entire room.

The man who carried the lantern was the sort of person that, once seen, is not easily forgotten.

A dwarf-like, hideous-looking creature, with shoulders of enormous breadth, and a head that seemed fixed to his trunk without the intervention of a neck.

He had short, bowed legs, and his broad, flat face, with it its hooked, beaklike nose was rendered more repulsive by a beard of many days' growth.

Seen in the dim lantern light, his eyes shone with a pinkish hue like those of a ferret.

The other individual was exactly his reverse, as regards stature.

A tall man, with a black, close-fitting cap and fiery red hair peeping from beneath it.

What his features were like, however, at present it was difficult to say, for he wore a woollen muffler wisped about his throat and face as high as his ears almost.

He carried in his hand a short, bright crowbar (the implement with which he had forced the door), and a bag of some dark coloured stuff, crammed full of something of which he seemed mighty careful.

The dwarf-like man who carried the lantern proceeded to a rapid examination of the room, and at once discovered the open casement.

"Phew! this won't do!" he observed, with a twang in his voice that once betrayed his Israelitish origin; "give me the bag and put the shutters to, Redpole, my goot friend. He! he! The Golden Glazier should mend his windows. But it is the old story, my tear, the shoemaker always wears bad shoes!"

With a muttered imprecation against his companion's flow of genial humour, the tall man obeyed, and with some difficulty dragged to the heavy and long disused shutters, and adjusted the bar that secured them.

"We'd ha' done better to have stopped up in *his* room," he grumbled; "there was a fire and a cheer to sit on up there."

"*You* would have done better, you mean, my tear," returned the Jew, with a grin; "you forget poor me as was vaiting on the stairs in the dark, anxiously vaiting, as you know, you rogue!"

"Well, you might have come in too," growled his companion; "who hindered you?"

"Pisness reasons, my goot friend, pisness reasons; it wouldn't have done at all," and the Jew chuckled hideously as he peeped into the bag. "Close the door, Mister Redpole, if you please; our little settlement will not be the better if it is interrupted."

"Redpole," as the dwarf called him, made the broken door fast by making a wedge of a splinter that had been torn from it.

"There is not much chance of *his* coming down to interrupt us, Aaron!" he remarked.

"No! did you tie him so fast, my tear?"

"If he get's away till somebody releases him, I'll forgive him."

"But would he forgive *you*, hey! Ha! ha! Dat ish another matter, hey!"

"You are a devilish sight too jocular to be pleasant to-night," the fiery-haired man growled impatiently, "wot's there to be funny about? Hang me if I can make out."

"Yes, yes, hang you! dat is just what I was thinking about, Mister Redpole. If Master Ketch fixes the noose round your throat——"

"You'll make me swear in a minute."

"When your time comes, my goot lad," the Jew hastened to correct himself; "when your time comes, of course I mean, as every goot fellow's must. All I was going to say is that if the hangman trusses you as neatly as you trussed our friend, Sampson Tuff, you will have nothing to complain of."

But the individual addressed did not appear to fully appreciate the other's pleasantry.

"There you are wrong, Aaron Doomstone," he replied, in a surly tone. "I should grumble most confoundedly."

"Why should you, my tear?"

"I'll tell you why. When it comes to my time for dancing to St. Sepulchre's music, I shouldn't like to be gagged like Sampson is."

"He! he! you'd like to make a speech, hey, Redpole? you'd like to give the people some goot advice, and implore them to shun bad company."

"No, I shouldn't waste my time in that way," returned Redpole, between his set teeth. "I should tell 'em who was the greedy old vulture who had hunted me and many a better man to the gallows, and to beware of him."

The voice in which the tall man uttered these words appeared to astound his companion.

With a muttered exclamation he raised the lantern, so as to get a glance of Redpole's face, as though to convince himself whether he was joking or not.

I, too, saw the face.

But there was not the ghost of a joke visible on it.

Unless murder is a joke.

I was much too young to know anything about such matters at that time, but as the foxy-haired man clutched the steel bar, and looked down on his toadlike companion, it seemed that he would have required little inciting to have cracked the other's skull into it.

As the Jew lowered the lantern again there was a devilish leer on his countenance, as though, rather than otherwise, he felt his vanity tickled by the compliment the other had paid him.

He affected to resent it, however.

"A vulture, eh? dat ish a bad name to bestow on any but your enemy, my tear!"

And he wagged his enormous head solemnly, as though his feelings were much hurt.

"I beg your pardon. I couldn't think of a harder one," sneered Redpole.

"The vulture, my good sir," continued Aaron Doomstone, not heeding the interruption, "is a bird of prey, vat cram all the flesh—all the goot meat into his maw, and leaf only the bones to the jackal. Now, I am petter as the vulture. These are not bones, my tear! These are fat yellow boys, every one of 'em, with twenty shillings' vorth of goot picking on each."

And as he spoke he plunged his great hairy hand into some secret recess near his breast, and withdrew a leather money bag.

Turning his back for a moment, as though fearful lest the bag's contents might tempt his companion, he withdrew from the bag several gold pieces which he handed to Redpole.

The tall man took them, and after examining each one carefully at the lantern light, he slipped them into his pocket.

The touch of the gold seemed to mollify him somewhat.

"That's all right and square, and you ain't such a bad sort after all, Aaron," said he; "but still——"

"Still vat?" the Jew asked, as the other hesitated.

"I don't like the job, cuss me if I do," returned the tall man, heartily.

The Jew shrugged his shoulders.

"He would have done as goot for you, my tear!"

"Not at *your* bidding he wouldn't."

"No, my tear, not at my bidding," replied the Jew, bitterly; "the Glazier is too clever, too independent, to do anyone's bidding; but he has done worse, rot him!"

"Ah, it's all very well for an infernal old Jew like you, who hasn't got a spark of Christian feeling," rejoined Redpole, his ferocious mood returning; "but I ain't got no spite agin Sampson, and it goes agin my grain to hurt him. Dog worry sheep is all right enough, but dog eat dog!"

And to show his disgust for such cannibal propensities, the red-haired man took a flask from his pocket and took a long draught from it.

"I don't think that I shall ever find courage to look him in the face again!" said he with a sigh, as he replaced the flask in his pocket.

"It may happen that you may never have the chance!"

The Jew spoke these words as though he was communing with himself, rather than replying to an observation.

"What do you mean?"

"Hey!"

Mr. Doomstone uttered this ejaculation suddenly, as though startled out of a reverie.

"What do you mean by saying that I might not have the chance?" the tall man repeated, suspiciously.

"Vell, you know, my goot friend," returned the Jew, with a devilish twinkle in his beady eyes, "life is very uncertain, and the Glazier is not so strong as he was. He might drive the blood to his head in struggling against his cords, and I might find him out of his misery next time I come to see him!"

A slight noise overhead at this point interrupted the mysterious conversation.

Now, I should wish it to be distinctly understood, that, although this edifying discourse between Mr. Aaron Doomstone and his friend has occupied five minutes or so in writing, actually it occurred in less than a fourth of the time.

Much too rapid was it for me to follow with anything like perfect understanding.

I could hear every word; I could see the speakers; but what did it all mean.

That some terrible deed had been, or was about to be committed, I could not for a moment doubt.

Who was the man "upstairs?"

Was it "Sampson Tuff," or the individual alluded to as the "Golden Glazier?"

Or was the Golden Glazier and Sampson Tuff one and the same?

Why had he been gagged and bound as they had said?

What was in the black bag that the hideous Jew carried, and why was one ruffian so measly, while the other was on such good terms with himself?

As I crouched in the cupboard in a sweat of terror, these perplexing questions crowded my mind, but could find no solution.

But I had yet more to listen to ; more to set me wondering and trembling.

Hearing the noise above, the Jew had darted to the door, and, with the lantern in his left hand and a pistol he had hastily produced from a handy pocket, he opened it a little way, and listened intently.

In my eager anxiety to learn what he was listening for, and favoured by the darkness caused by the withdrawal of the lantern, I ventured to open my cupboard door a little way.

"It is nothing," Aaron Doomstone remarked, as he closed the door again. "P'r'aps our friend Sampson does not find his bed comfortable, and he ish tossing about on it."

"The infernal old den is haunted, I believe," rejoined his companion, uneasily. "I can't stand this dog-kennel; it's as dark and cold as a church vault. Need we stay here any longer ? "

"It would be safer, my tear."

"I don't know so much about that."

"Take a little more rum, my good friend; we must not go yet." Then, as though something previously forgotten had occurred to him, he repeated—

"Yes, we must stop here yet awhile." *Must !*

"Because you see the snow would betray us. It has covered the footmarks we made in coming; it would be a pity to go trampling over it again, and spoiling its good intentions."

"What, d'ye mean to say that we must keep in this miserable hole till a thaw comes ? "

And the red-haired man clapped his cap on his head as though nothing on earth should induce him to stay where he was for so uncertain and protracted a period.

The Jew made no answer, but softly unbarred the window shutters, and looked out.

"No, my tear, not so bad as that, but we must stop till the tide falls ; then we can drop on to the shore from the window, and no one be a bit the wiser."

The other grumblingly acquiesced, but added—

"Can't we make a fire ? There should be wood enough in this tumble-down den to roast an ox."

"There's a cupboard," responded the Jew, whose good humour was certainly superior to that of his companion; "p'r'aps that's where the Golden Glazier keeps his stock of winter coals."

I could almost fancy that I felt the hair rise on my head as I heard these words.

That mine was the only cupboard in the room I well knew.

What would be my fate if I was discovered, I could only dismally conjecture.

"If there isn't coals, there's shelves, I'll warrant," Redpole remarked, and approached the door with the short crowbar in his hand.

I had wound my cord round my hand, all ready for a stout tug, if need be.

Now I was glad to avail myself to the full extent of the precaution.

Planting a foot against the inner side of the door lintels, I leant back as I sat on the middle shelf, and pulled might and main.

"Hang it, it's locked !" said the ruffian, trying it. "Come open, can't yer !"

And as he spoke, he inserted the taper end of the crowbar between the door and the doorpost, and gave a wrench.

I gave myself up for lost, when the Jew saved me.

"There's no need to tear the house down, my goot man," he exclaimed. "See, here is wood enough."

And he dragged from a corner the remains of some ancient partition.

With this a fire was soon made in the yawning, rust-eaten old grate, and the two worthies crouched over it.

I could not now see their faces, but my faculty of hearing seemed to have grown marvellously acute, and not a word of their whispered talk escaped me.

I could hear, too, the jingling of metal, as by the flaring, smoky firelight, the Jew groped with his huge, claw-like hands into the depths of the black bag.

"A fair swag, a very fair swag !" muttered Mr. Doomstone. "He ! he ! Sampson is a good judge ; he knew the sound fruit from the crabs ! A saving man, too; careful against a rainy day !"

And I could hear the hideous fellow chuckle.

"Ah! it wasn't 'ansum, though; it wasn't the hact of one pal towards another," said Redpole, remorsefully.

"Phoo! there are pals enough in your line, my tear."

"In *our* line, you mean."

"Well, well, in our line, if you like it better."

"I shouldn't care so much if the poor beggar hadn't been ill."

"You wouldn't have been here at all if he hadn't been ill my tear."

"How do yer mean?"

"Listen, and I'll tell you."

"All right. Go on."

"You are plucky as the best of 'em, but you wouldn't have tackled the Golden Glazier if he had been well and hearty; he'd have doubled you up and pitched you down-stairs, my goot friend."

"And do you think he won't wipe off his score against us when he gets his strength back again?"

The Jew's tone suddenly changed.

"But he never shall get his strength back," he whispered, his voice trembling with passion. "Mark me, Redpole, he has used his strength, his wonderful strength, which is that of a dozen men possessed of devil's, for the last time, unless——"

"Unless what?"

"Unless he discloses to me the secret of it."

The Jew seemed to mutter these last few words through his set teeth, and in so low a tone that I could scarcely catch them.

The tall man laughed.

"The old sore," said he; "it's a pity that you didn't live in the old times when people believed in witches and demons."

"Why?"

"Then you might find somebody who would listen to that precious nonsense you are always harping on."

"It is a pity that there are fools in the world, and that I am plagued with the acquaintance of some of 'em," returned the Jew.

"Oh, birds of a feather flock together, you know," remarked the tall man, sneeringly.

"Call things by their proper names, you dolt," continued the dwarf, growing each moment more excited, "and I'll tell you that there are still witches and demons amongst us."

"Gammon!"

"Demons who can restore the pulses of the dead, and give life to their limbs, who can make a slave of the lightning, and bid it carry their messages a thousand miles a moment. Yes, yes, my goot friend, I believe in that demon and his name is Chemistry."

The red-haired man yawned as he took another pull at the rum bottle.

"But what's all this to do with Samson Tuff?" said he; "*his* name is not Chemistry?"

"No, no, that is the name of his friend; his close, bosom friend. A goot, faithful companion, my tear, who lends him such strength that iron bolts are no more than dried reeds in his hands; who so charms his sinews and muscles that forged links and hardened steel are no more than paper against them."

The Redpole expressed his contempt for the outburst in a sound that was half a grunt, half a growl.

"Listen, my friend!" continued the Jew, growing quite hoarse in his excitement, "we might be rich men if we could only persuade Samson Tuff to make us familiar with this sly demon of his. We might cry 'open sesame' at every bank door in England. There is not a treasury —not a repository for wealth in the land, that would not fly open at our bidding. Think of that, my tear friend! Think of what might be if this blockhead, this brainless miser, could be made to speak."

"I can think without you holding on by the collar of my coat," I heard the tall man say; "p'r'aps when you have done with your cranky raving you'll pass me the rum; mine's out."

"I have it, my friend," the Jew continued, as though quite unconscious of the other's cool incredulity. "I'll have his secret. I have him now at my mercy. I need no help. I've got him, and I'll hold him."

"He'll do without your holding," remarked Mr. Redpole, parenthetically.

"I'll draw it out of him, this secret of his," Doomstone pursued; "I'll draw it out of him as they draw the temper to maul and rend out of savage beasts. I'll starve him. I'll keep him where he now lies, gagged and helpless, Redpole, and when I get him low, quite low and ferocious only for food, then I'll tempt him. I'll have rich meat to hold before his famished eyes, that shall set his teeth chattering a beggar's petition. I'll have cool water mixed with wine, and I'll tickle his dry lips with tiny drops of it."

It was a queer sight to watch his toad-like figure and his face, as he delivered himself of these blood-chilling threats.

He was squatting by the spluttering fire when he commenced, but, as he proceeded, he started to his feet, and paced across and across the room, as a wild animal paces his den.

The terrible excitement he exhibited, however, was not contagious.

His companion, with no more than a sulky allusion to his friend's crankness, betook him to smoking a short pipe, breaking the monotony of that occupation skivering up the old partition with his clasp knife, and feeding the fire.

Nor did the hideous Jew have anything to say after his frenzied outbreak.

He returned to the fire-place, and there squatted, gnawing his nails, and muttering and mumbling.

By-and-by the tall man rose, and opening the shutter a little, peeped out.

"The tide is away from the wall," said he; "we'll get out of this if you've no objection—unless," he continued sneeringly, "you'd rather stay and execute your amiable desires against poor Samson."

"No, no, my goot friend, not now, not now; we must be patient, my tear!"

"*He* must be patient, you mean!"

"We, I said, Redpole, we. You know when a man has to undergo a painful surgical operation the doctors physic and prepare him. So we must treat the Golden Glazier, d'ye see? We must diet him. He! he! We must bring him low, so as he won't feel the blood letting, my tear."

What it was that the foxy-haired man muttered in reply, I did not catch.

Then the shutters were placed open in their former position, and the Jew, still clutching the bag, dropped from the window-sill on the ooze below.

As he did so, his companion ground his teeth and shook his clenched fists vindictively.

Then he too vanished, and I was left alone.

## CHAPTER IV.

### I MAKE THE ACQUAINTANCE OF SAMSOM TUFF, ALIAS THE GOLDEN GLAZIER.

LEFT alone!

In my dismal retreat, that is to say.

Not in the house.

It is many, many years since that terrible night; but to this day I cannot dwell on the recollection of it without experiencing a sensation of horror creeping over me.

I was now convinced beyond a doubt that the ruined old house was tenanted by someone besides myself.

Not only were the repeated allusions to the occupier of a certain room upstairs unmistakable, I had heard myself that noise overhead that had so alarmed the Jew dwarf, and led him to make the observation that perhaps it was the Golden Glazier turning in his uneasy bed.

But somehow I dare not stir.

I had heard the retreating footsteps of the two men, and listened till they were lost in the distance.

I knew that there was no danger of their immediate return, but I was afraid to descend from my cupboard.

Afraid even to move or to breathe more freely than I had been doing during the last three hours.

The string that I had bound round my hand so that I might pull the harder against anyone who attempted to open the door, had choked the circulation of the blood, and my fist felt like a lump of lead.

But I was so benumbed with terror, that now the danger was past I did not think to unwind the string.

How long I should have remained in that condition of helpless stupor is more than I can say.

I was roused from it presently.

As before mentioned, the two ruffians had made a fire in the wide, unguarded old fireplace.

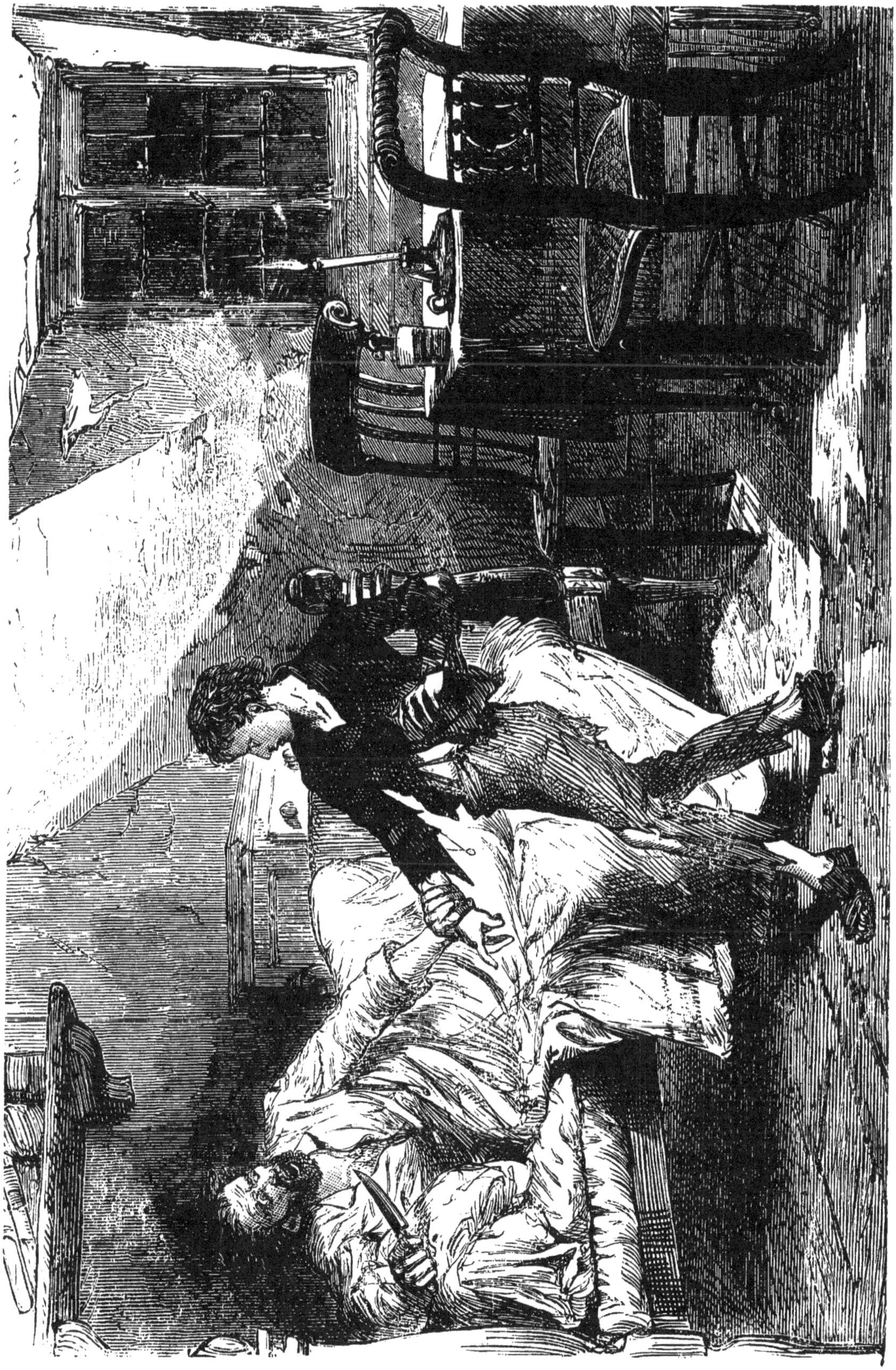

" HE EXCLAIMED SAVAGELY, ' WHO SENT YOU HERE ? ' "

For an hour or more the foxy-haired man had been engaged with his great clasp knife in skivering up the old partition, and the dry and tinder-like chips were strewn all about.

When the Jew opened the shutter to see how the tide was, a gust of wind blowing in must have sent whirling the red-hot embers on the hearth, and some of them had lodged, unperceived, amongst the chips.

A trifling incident in itself, but one that might have ripened into a serious calamity.

At that quiet hour of the morning, on the bleak, deserted river, the fire would have obtained strong mastery ere it was by chance discovered.

The broken windows, and open doors would have fed the conflagration as blast holes feed a furnace. But destruction by fire was not to be the fate of Rat's Castle that Christmas morning.

It was the crackling of fire that roused me from my lethargy.

Starting up, I pushed open the cupboard door, to discover that the floor boards round the hearthstone were all of a ruddy glow, and that, if the wind blew a little longer on them, they would burst into flame.

Jumping down from my perch, and regardless of one or two nasty burns, I swept the smouldering embers together with my old cap, and precipitated them through one of the many holes in the rotten flooring.

There they were instantly extinguished in the muddy residue that was always there deposited.

After some difficulty, I succeeded in quelling the fire that was attacking the floor boards.

Then I bethought me of the poor wretch so mysteriously hinted at as lodging upstairs.

The man of many names.

The "Golden Glazier," *alias* Samson Tuff.

The possessor of a wonderful secret, who, to suit the purposes of the hideous Jew, Aaron Doomstone (the singularity of the name at once impressed it on my memory), was at that moment lying gagged and bound.

Who and what was the prisoner?

That he was ill, the conversation of the two ruffians put beyond a doubt.

As before stated, up to this time I was strange to the ways of crime, yet my knowledge of vulgar slang was sufficient to tell me the meaning of the term "pal."

It meant companion, confederate, acquaintance.

And both men had acknowledged that the mysterious person in question was their "pal."

He was a robber then, a criminal of the most ferocious type, like Aaron Doomstone himself, or Mr. Redpole.

Reflecting on this for a moment, it seemed that my best course would be to be off.

To wash my hands, so to speak, of the ugly business with all speed, and seek fresh lodgings, and keep to myself all that I had seen and heard.

But there was another side to the question, which, young heathen as I was, I could not overlook.

It appeared to me that a certain inexplainable something had ordained that I should be made aware of what I had been.

Already I had probably been the means of saving the life of the poor helpless wretch confined in his room upstairs.

Had I not been lurking in the cupboard, in all probability the smouldering fire would rapidly have grown into huge devouring flames, and so an end to the "Golden Glazier."

An end also to that wonderful Secret of his of which the Jew had shown himself so covetous.

Should I leave him to his fate?

Should I take myself off without so much as warning him of the terrible designs the Jew had against him?

At least, there could be no harm in going up and having a peep at him.

He was bound, and could not hurt me.

It would be easy for me, if he was angry, to run down the stairs again.

I would chance it.

Mustering all my courage, I first of all looked out at the ruined window—it was still blowing and snowing at a pretty rate—to see if the coast was clear in that direction.

Then I ventured out at the room door, and groped my way to a flight of stairs I found there.

It was no easy task to ascend them.

It was still pitch dark, and in many

places the stairs were rat-eaten and decayed, and only the rails remained to tell where the banisters had once been.

It was a house of many floors.

Every landing that I reached I listened eagerly at the door, but not a sound was to be heard within.

So up two, three, four flights, and the topmost rooms were reached.

Now I knew that my search was at an end.

Nor was it fruitless.

A glimmer of light was plainly perceptible through the keyhole of a door.

Applying my eye thereto, I could make out a flickering fragment of a rushlight standing on the mantel-shelf.

But I could hear no sound.

I had ascended the stairs as quietly as a cat, and the possibility was that if any one was in the room they were as yet unaware of my being outside.

Was the door of this room locked?

I did not dare try it.

I applied my knuckles gently to the panels and my ear again to the keyhole.

Not so quickly, however, as I withdrew it again.

There was no verbal response, but plainly enough I heard a strange, rasping sound.

A sound as of nails, or claws, scratching against wood.

A cat, sharpening her talons against a plank, makes just such a noise.

"Is anyone here?" I called.

Again the odd, scratching sound, but much louder.

With my heart in my mouth, but with an irrepressible curiosity to ascertain from whence the singular sound proceeded, I turned the handle of the door.

It was locked.

"Shall I come in?" I summoned courage to call again.

More than the scratching this time.

A mysterious and terrible sound, as of a man, whose mouth was stuffed with wool, endeavouring to speak.

There could be no mistake.

Whoever it was within the room could neither come to the door nor reply in ordinary fashion to a question asked.

Undoubtedly this should betoken gagging and binding, if anything should.

"Shall I burst the door open if I can?"

I was pluckier as a boy than I am as a man, I fancy.

"Yes, yes, and set about it quickly, if you please," so the vigorous scratching, seconded by the husky wheezing, seemed to say, plainly as possibly.

Exerting all my strength, I flung myself against the door, and it at once flew open.

Then such a sight presented itself to my frightened gaze as I am not likely to forget in a hurry.

It was a large room, with a low, slanting ceiling.

It was furnished with some pretension to comfort.

There was a carpet on the ground.

I noticed this particularly, because the first thing that caught my eye was a great, jagged rent in the centre of it, disclosing a square hole in the floor boards.

There were a table and chairs, and a chest of drawers.

But most conspicuous was the bedstead.

A bedstead of the strong, old-fashioned "truckle" kind, with a head and foot board.

It was not standing on its four proper legs, however.

It was tilted over, so that it rested partly on its side and partly against the wall.

There was a man tied to it.

So dull was the flame of the rushlight, however, and so nearly was the man concealed beneath the overturned bedstead, that I doubt if I should have been aware of him but for his eyes.

Wide open, staring eyes, glaring with pain and fury.

It was evident at a glance what had happened.

He had been bound to his bedstead, and in his desperate attempts to release himself, had capsized that article of furniture.

Doubtless it was the noise that this catastrophe had occasioned that was heard below when Aaron Doomstone made the facetious observation about the Golden Glazier turning uneasily in his bed.

He had turned over bedstead and all, poor wretch, and in doing so had nearly put an end to his existence.

In binding him every precaution had been taken to prevent his escape.

The strong cord not only secured him at the wrists and ankles, but was passed round his neck as well.

In his wriggling and twisting he had so tightened this ligature, that I verily believe he would have been strangled had he been left to himself ten minutes longer.

The gag still held its place over his mouth, so that he could make no other sound than the stifled one previously mentioned, but he raised his head a little and made a sign with his eyes for me to approach him.

He was not an inviting object, but it seemed almost as bad as killing him to leave him in this desperate plight.

There was a table-knife lying handy, and, catching it up, and gulping down my terror, I crossed the room, avoiding the hole where the carpet was torn back, and with one stroke severed the cord that secured his wrists.

Then I noticed that the fingers of his great hairy hands were all bloody.

The mysterious scratching noise I had heard was responsible for this.

His hands were secured above his head, and with his finger tips he could just reach the head board, and he had torn and splintered his finger-nails in his attempt to make me understand that there was somebody in the room.

It was no trouble, as the bedstead was tilted up, to push it back again into its proper position.

His first act, on regaining the use of his hands, was to tear the leather gag from his mouth.

He was no better off than before, however, as far as speaking was concerned, his mouth and tongue were so parched and dry.

There was a jug with water in it, and he pointed towards it.

I handed it to him, and he drained it to the last drop.

As he set the jug down he caught me by the wrist with a tight grip.

"Who are you?" he asked, fiercely.

He looked so ferocious that it was some seconds before I could answer him.

"Joe Sterling, sir," I presently replied, quaking with terror.

"Who sent you here? What do you want?"

"Nobody sent me here, sir; nobody knew that I was here; I only——"

He interrupted me by catching up the knife with which I had released his wrists of the chords that bound them, while, with a sudden jerk, he pulled me closer towards him as he lay on his back with his legs still bound.

"Shall I cut your throat or will you tell me the truth?" he exclaimed, savagely. "Once more, who sent you here and what for?"

No wonder that I grew suddenly self-possessed and cool, I felt so suddenly froze with fright.

"Nobody sent me here; I sleep here; and if that isn't the truth you may cut my throat," I answered him.

"Sleep here?"

"Ever so long; in the cupboard down in the parlour. I came up here because I heard 'em talking about you."

"Heard 'em! Who d'ye mean? No lies now?"

"The two men that——"

"That is a lie," he exclaimed, glaring at me in a manner that made me think my last moment was come. "D'ye tell me there were two men? Now, quick! d'ye tell me that?"

"Two men; a tall one and a short one."

"A short one!"

And a strange expression shot into his ferocious eyes.

"Like a dwarf they keep at the penny show, only uglier and broader. It was him who carried the lantern and the bag with the jingling things in it and who——"

"What, Aaron!" and as he uttered the name his eyes assumed an expression of aghast incredulity. "D'ye mean to tell me that Aaron knew of this—that it was he who set that treacherous sneak, the Redpole, on to me?"

"Yes," I replied, "those were the names; Redpole, and Aaron Doomstone."

The sick man's amazement was so great that he left go of my wrist and sank back on to his bed.

"You are sure of this?"

Although I managed to speak with tolerable calmness, I need not say that all this time my heart was thumping in my bosom at a fearful rate.

All that I wanted was to be off.

The shortest way to effect this object, perhaps, was to relieve his mind of the suspicion that I was deceiving him.

I related to him what I had heard Aaron Doomstone say about waiting outside on the stairs while Redpole robbed him. I told him also of the money I had seen the Jew pay over to the toxy-haired man.

It was terrible to witness his rage.

"The crawling viper! the man-selling old Judas!" he exclaimed; "that was the aim of his friendship was it? That was his kindness—his pity for a poor wretch stretched on his bed and crippled with pain! Ha! ha! to think of the pit I have been hanging over this month and more! It's a miracle that I'm alive. It's a wonder that the black-hearted toad hasn't put poison in what he has given me to eat and drink. Oh, Aaron, I should like to have your windpipe under my thumbs just now! By——! for such a treat I'd give my——"

I grew each moment more alarmed at the furious passion he was working himself into, and retreated towards the door.

He suddenly checked his passionate outburst.

"Where are you going?" he exclaimed, fiercely.

"I don't want to stay any longer, sir."

"Hang you! come here. D'ye hear? You know what I promised you, and, by——, I'll do it to if you dare move another step."

If anything was required to expedite my movements it was this reminder of my throat's recent and uncomfortable acquaintance with the table-knife.

I made a bound for the door, and was about to dart down the dark stairs.

The sudden and piteous alteration in his tone, however, restrained me.

"Don't go! don't go!" he almost screamed; "don't leave me to be murdered by them! They will be back again; they are sure to come back. Lord sake, young 'un, don't leave me to be murdered!"

He was not so sure as I was that they, or at least one of them, Mr. Aaron Doomstone, was coming back.

As the miserable man in the bed, looking so muscular and strong, yet so helpless, as he shrieked out his alarm, I could not but think off the terribly ominous words that the Jew had uttered.

"I'll tame him as they tame wild beasts. I'll starve him till he licks my hand for crumbs."

And that this was not the worst, in order to effect his purpose, that the Jew was capable of perpetrating, it needed but the remembrance of the diabolical expression of his countenance to convince me.

It seemed awful to leave a human creature to such a fate!

"I can't stay here any longer," I called out from the stair-head.

"You can't? Why not?"

"Because I'm afraid. But you shan't be left. I'll tell the first policeman I meet, and send him here."

But this was making bad worse.

"No, no, no! you musn't do that, you infernal young——no, I don't mean that. I don't know what I'm sayin'. This rheumatism gives me such awful pain. I'm sure you'd pity me if you knew the agony I'm a layin' in, young 'un!"

I struggled a step or so back towards the door.

"My knees is like dried sticks," continued the robber in a pitiful voice. "I can't bend 'em in the least. I can't so much as turn. Don't be afeard of me. I won't hurt yer. I *can't* hurt yer. I couldn't walk across the room, no, not if the use of my legs would be the reward of it. And they comes and ties me down, and robs me! My old pal, too!"

This last reflection seemed to afflict the Golden Glazier almost as much as his rheumatism; his voice was husky with emotion.

As already stated, I had as yet steered clear of what the law in its wisdom declares to be crime.

I had gone hungry many and many a time, but my hands were at least clean of the guilt of stealing.

I could have no doubt as to the sort of trade this man followed.

Like the "Redpole," he was a thief.

The former had confessed as much. I had seen him receive the wages of his handicraft. "Dog eat dog" could have but one meaning.

But it was nothing to me how this poor wretch got his living.

That wasn't for me to consider.

He was sick and helpless. Should I leave him to the diabolical fate designed him by Aaron Doomstone?

He noted my hesitation, and followed up his advantage.

"I don't know who or what you are," he continued, "but I'm clear now that you don't belong to their gang, curse 'em! You saved my life just now. I should have been choked to a dead certainty if you hadn't come in just in the nick of time. Come here, my boy, and I'll show you that I knows the walue of a good action."

As he had said, he couldn't hurt me even if he would.

There could be no harm in ascertaining what he meant by rewarding me.

I stepped back into the room.

"Now shut the door," he eagerly exclaimed. "You burst the lock; but the bolts are good. That's a brave boy. Mount on a chair and shoot the bolts top and bottom."

It was evident from the size of the bolts, and the massiveness of the staples into which they shot that the occupant of the garret of the ruined house had an eye to security when he fixed them.

I did as he requested.

"That's the sort," the man on the bed exclaimed with satisfaction; "they can't break in on us sudden, anyhow. Now, come here and put your hand under the mattress, just where my head is."

To do this it was necessary to approach him quite closely, and I would rather have avoided that; but it was no use funking now.

I thrust my hand between the bed and the mattress as he desired.

"D'ye feel anything?" he asked.

"Yes, sir."

"What?"

"Something that feels like a bag with money in it?"

"That's the sort; pull it out."

I did so.

It was largish for a money bag; as big as one of his own great hairy hands, I should think.

I gave it to him, and with his teeth he untied the string that secured the mouth of it.

Then he paused, and keenly regarded me.

"I want you to tell me what was the most money you ever had in all your life," said he.

It did not take me long to remember the exact sum, and the particulars of how I had become possessed of it.

The largest amount of money I was ever able to call my own was half-a-crown.

I picked it up on the river bank at a very hard-up time, and went hungry all the same afternoon because I was afraid to change it lest my posession of such an enormous sum might provoke suspicion.

I told him about it.

"What do you mean?" he exclaimed, opening his eyes in amazement; "what was it you was afeard that they would be suspicious of?"

"They might have thought that I'd stolen it," I replied.

His stare contracted into something like a frown as he looked more and more puzzled.

"I didn't ask you what was the most money you ever had that was come by honest," he exclaimed; "what's the most that you ever had that was come by *anyhow*, that's what I want to know."

"I never had any that was come by anyhow."

"Gammon!"

"No, it's quite true. I never have anything to do with money that hasn't been come by honestly," I answered, at the same time, I am afraid, glancing significantly at the bag that he held in his hand.

"Oh!" he remarked, sneeringly. "How's that?"

"Because I never had a mind to it. It never does you no good. I might have had lots of it like other chaps that I know, but I always found that I could get on very well without it."

There was not much in the words, but I suppose that I spoke them with all the earnestness I felt.

At least, that was the reason I assigned at the moment for the sudden startled look he gave me.

It would be hard to describe the varying expressions of his countenance.

As mentioned at the outset, my appearance was scarcely one that denoted prosperity.

My jacket and trousers were curiosities as specimens of patches and tatters, and those two articles of raiment constituted my entire rig.

Shirt I had none, and stockings were as foreign to my use as pocket-bandkerchiefs.

"So you get on very well, do you!"

he remarked, regarding me from top to toe.

"Oh, yes, take it altogether, you know."

"What, togs and all, you mean, of course?" he remarked, with a strange grin on his gaunt, unshaven face.

"Take it all round, and one way and another, that's what I mean," I replied, quite seriously.

Samson Tuff regarded me with an odd mixture of pity and incredulity.

"He means it, too!" he muttered, as though to himself. "Dashed if I don't believe every word he's sayin'! He's one of them 'ere connumbrums wot it's no use tryin' to guess at. Look at him! Just about as starved and ragged a little crow as you'll find in a week's march, and yet he says 'he's doin' wery well!' It must be *in'ards* I suppose—it ain't out'ards, that's wery evident."

"There isn't much in'ards," I ventured to remark; "I haven't had a blessed bit to eat since yesterday afternoon."

"What made you run away from home?"

"I haven't got a home—not a regular home."

"But you've got a father or a mother?"

"I don't know anything about them—it's so long ago."

"How did you get your name, then? There must have been a old Sterling, don't you know, since there's a young 'un!"

"Not that I know of. I only had the name of Joe once. It was the boys who gave me the other."

"The boys? How d'ye mean?"

"The boys I used to know under the 'Delphi arches. Sterling Joe they used to call me, 'cos—well, I dun'now—'cos they liked me, I s'pose. That's how the name of Joe Sterling came. There wouldn't have been much 'Sterling' about it if I had stayed much longer at Mother Palmer's."

The latter part of this last observation I uttered only half aloud; indeed, it was but an involuntary expression of a very bitter recollection that at that instant crossed my mind.

But, curiously enough, it was not lost on Samson Tuff.

As I stood there by his bed, with the sickly-yellow light of the winter's morning feebly struggling through the tat-tered window curtain (the flickering flame of the rushlight had by this time given up the ghost), I observed a sudden change swiftly overspread his countenance.

"What name did you say—what name?" he inquired, in an altered voice, and speaking very eagerly.

"Sterling."

"No, no. The woman—the woman who——"

"Mother Palmer?"

"Aye. Tell me, where did she live?"

"Snow Fields, over in Bermondsey."

I think that I should have kept my mouth shut respecting Mother Palmer's place of abode could I have guessed what would be the effect on the Golden Glazier if I mentioned it.

It seemed for the moment to thoroughly cure him of his ailments, to take the stiffness out of his knees, and give him the use of his limbs generally.

He even made an attempt to rise to a sitting posture, but failed.

"Burn my body!" he exclaimed, his cadaverous face flushing red, and his features twitching spasmodically; "it is the very thought that came into my head as soon as I heard his voice. But how is it possible? It would be like the dead risin' out of their grave. Risin' *here*, too! No, no, it isn't possible—it can't be!"

He was not idle, while in a trembling, almost awful voice, he uttered those strange, disjointed exclamations.

Whatever was the nature of his suddenly conceived suspicion, he straightway proceeded to put it to the test.

Making almost superhuman exertions, to my inexpressible fright and amazement, he pulled me towards him.

Fairly into his shaking arms.

"Now we shall see! now we shall see!" he muttered.

My old jacket was short of buttons. It was fastened at the throat with a bit of string.

For an instant he endeavoured to untie this. Only for an instant, however. Failing in the attempt, with an exclamation of impatience he burst it asunder.

His aim appeared to be to take the jacket off.

This, however, I resented.

I thought of the knife with which he had so recently threatened me; it was still lying on the bed within his reach.

I crossed my arms over my breast, and screaming "murder" strove might and main to wriggle out of his grasp.

But he was too desperately determined on his purpose to be baffled.

Finding, despite his frantic exertions, that the jacket was not to be got off by fair means, he did not scruple to adopt a less ceremonious method.

Clapping one hand over my mouth to stifle my cries, with the other he made a grab at the left side of the jacket, and tore away a big handful of it, leaving my body at that spot quite bare.

But I need not have alarmed myself about the knife, or Samson Tuff's murderous intentions.

All he did, having exposed my naked breast, was to pull me still closer towards him, and bring his hungry eyes to bear eagerly on the spot.

The scrutiny was not of five seconds' duration.

One thing was certain, however ; what he had expected to find and had searched for, he had discovered.

Muttering incoherently, his fierce hold on me relaxed.

The red flush faded out of his face, and he sank back on the bed ghastly pale, and looking like a man falling into a deadly swoon.

"Some water !" he gasped ; "give me some water, for Heaven's sake ! "

## CHAPTER V.

### THE BLACK CROSS ON MY LEFT BREAST.

THERE he lay, senseless and helpless.

Now was my opportunity for escaping if I had a mind to.

Now, also, had I been a thief instead of an honest boy, I might have added yet one more to my previous delinquencies, and that of a magnificent character.

I might have appropriated the Golden Glazier's bag of money.

When, having uttered the imploring words with which the last chapter concluded, he sank back in a dead faint, the bag slipped off the bed, and fell, with a promising chink upon the floor.

There was nothing to hinder me.

I knew my way downstairs, and to the familiar old parlour, from the casement of which I might have carried away the booty, and no one the wiser.

Be it thoroughly understood, however, I do not write regretfully about what I might have done, and did not.

All that I mean to convey is that it was a temptation that might have overcome a ragged, friendless, poor little wretch such as I was, and I tremble to think what I should have lost had I been overcome.

It was but another instance of that simple and respectable truth that has stood the test of mankind's experience since the world began—" Honesty is the best policy."

But the money bag lying there was really no temptation to me.

As already stated, I knew nothing of the ways of thieving. Nor did I have the least idea of making off empty handed.

I was too much amazed and bewildered with the behaviour and the strange talk of the man into whose society I had so strangely fallen.

Something beyond amazed, I think I may say.

By what motive was the man called the Golden Glazier actuated when he so ruthlessly ruined my already sufficiently tattered jacket ?

What was he in search of ? What had he found ?

I knew already, unless I was strangely mistaken ; though, to tell the truth, I had previously thought so little of that said something that it was not a little strange that it should at that moment have occurred to me.

What Samson Tuff had discovered was a certain odd-looking and peculiar mark that my body bore.

A black cross plainly defined, and situated on my left breast, just over the region of my heart.

It was so small that it was by the merest accident that its existence had been made known to me.

Two tiny jet black lines, not more than a sixteenth of an inch in length, and crossing each other, making a figure not unlike the letter X.

Although, as I say, I had observed it long ago, it had left little or no impression on my mind.

Now, however, it set me wondering.

There could be no doubt that it was this mysterious mark, whatever it portended, that Samson Tuff suspected.

There was substantial evidence that it was so.

At the identical spot he had pinched the flesh between his two fingers and thumb, leaving it quite red, and causing the little black cross to show itself with unusual distinctness.

What did he know about it?

What could he, if he had a mind, tell me about it?

What did he mean by his singular exclamation—

"It is like the dead rising from the grave."

In far less time than it has taken to set them down here, did these perplexing questions present themselves to my mind, and resolve me as to how I would act.

I would not run away.

For the present, at least.

I would remain in hopes that he might, when he returned to his senses, have something to say to me concerning the black cross he had recognised so unmistakably.

There was a pitcher with water in it in the room, and I got some and sprinkled his face with it until he opened his eyes.

He looked as though he had been awoke out of a bad dream.

"You have not gone, then?" he exclaimed, catching hold cf me again as though he was mightily glad to find that it was so.

"No; I didn't like to go until you come to yourself."

"Good boy. I should never have believed that there was a bit of truth in it at all if you had gone," he continued, as his anxious eyes furtively glanced towards the hole he had torn in my jacket, "I should have thought that it was all a delusion; that I was drawing nigh to kicking the bucket; and that it was a shape from t'other world, such as they say visit dying men. You won't go will you? You won't leave me?"

Even had I been otherwise resolved, young as I was, it would have been difficult to resist the imploring look that accompanied his words.

"I'll stay here a little while if I can be of any service to you," I replied.

"Thanky, my lad, thanky," he returned, squeezing my hand, gratefully; "you will not be sorry; mind, I promise you that. 'Taint a pound out of the bag that shall reward you now that I know——"

At this point, however, he suddenly checked himself as though he had let slip something he had not intended, at the same time bestowing on me a keen glance as though to observe the effect.

There was no effect to observe, however, and he continued—

"As I was going to say when that infernal pain stopped me, I don't mean to limit your reward to a paltry pound now I know what a staunch little trump you are. You shall have a new jacket in place of the one I tore, Har——what did you say your name was?"

Here was another queer slip of the tongue.

"Joe," I answered, "Joe Sterling."

"To be sure; I must not forget that. Joe Sterling, eh? Sterling Joe. Yes, Joe, you shall have a new jacket and trousers, and all the rest of it—as stunning a rig out as money can buy, if you'll stay—if you'll only stay. Where is the money, Joe?"

I picked up the bag from the floor and gave it to him.

"The dunce!" he exclaimed, as he took it. "The coward! he was afraid of my grip, cripple as I am, or he would have made a dip under the mattress for this. Worth all the rest — twice as much."

The Golden Glazier did not say who the "he" he alluded to as a coward was, but I knew that he meant the ruffian I had heard spoken of as the Redpole.

Presently my companion asked me abruptly—

"There's a hole in the floor, isn't there, Joe?"

I replied that is was so, and described how the carpet was torn away where the hole was.

"Is it empty, Joe?"

"Quite empty."

"Ah, ah! the fools!" he chuckled, ferociously. "They think that they've cleared me out. But they're mistaken, Joe. They wouldn't have ruined me if they had robbed me of my bag of shiners as well. *What is the loss of a few golden eggs to him who is master of the pretty bird that lays 'em!"*

The first part of the above quoted sentence he uttered aloud, but the latter part, that which is underlined, he spoke in a lower tone, and as though talking with himself rather than addressing me.

I was that morning doomed, it seemed, to be bewildered by mysteries, or rather hints and clues to mysteries crowding one on the other.

Who and what was the pretty bird that layed the golden eggs?

Did his words have any reference to that strange charm, or secret, or whatever it was, that I had already heard spoken?

The priceless talisman, armed with which a man might grow as rich as ever he pleased.

Unless I had altogether misunderstood the ravings of the hideous Jew dwarf, Aaron Doomstone, this was its chief virtue.

"They're cunning," Samson Tuff continued; "they are as cute as the devil himself, but they are not cute enough. Clever Aaron, too! the treacherous wolf, he'd have my heart out if he so much as suspected that my golden bird was hid in it. But, it's safe, Joe; and, listen, good lad. Soon as I grow strong again, if you will stay and nurse me, Joe, we will go together, and my bird shall try its wings, and you shall see what it will bring us."

I was almost afraid to hear him talk, he spoke and looked so strangely.

I had heard of mad people, though I had never seen them.

Was *he* mad?

That was the terrible thought that crossed my mind at the time, and even to this day I believe that his senses must have been wandering.

I felt that I ought to say something; and, as ill-luck would have it, I said just what I should have held my tongue about.

"Yes," I remarked; "I heard 'em talking about it while I was hid in the cupboard."

"About what? Who?" he asked, quickly.

"The Jew, Aaron Doomstone. He was trying to make the other man believe about it. He didn't call it a bird, though."

"Talking about it? Aaron talking about it!" the sick man repeated, his face assuming a look of terror.

Then, with a quick, inarticulate cry, he flung his hand up to his mouth—into his mouth as far as his fingers were concerned—and then withdrew them, at the same time grinning through his set teeth.

"All right!" he exclaimed, with a terrible oath, "all right, Joe; but one never knows what these infernal Jew conjurers may do if they catch you dozing."

Mystery on mystery!

It was such a preposterous performance this last one of his, that even I thought that he was mad.

I had yet to learn the truth.

When in due time it appears, it will be seen that what seemed so ludicrous, this thrusting his hand into his mouth, was no more than a simple act of precaution such as the most sensible man in the "Golden Glazier's" place might have performed.

"Tell me, Joe," said he, excitedly, "tell me what Aaron said that the Redpole would not believe."

I had no object in concealing what I had heard; and, as with mouth agape and eyes staring, he listened, I told him all.

## CHAPTER VI.

### I SET A TRAP FOR A BIRD WHO IS MUCH TO WARY TO BE TAKEN IN IT.

A JOLLY good fire to sit by, as hearty a tuck in of eggs and bacon as a famished boy could desire, are windfalls that do not commonly fall in the way of a little London gutter prowler.

These, however, were the blissful advantages I found myself in possession at dinner time of the day (the Christmas day, be it borne in mind), in the early morning of which I so strangely made the acquaintance of Samson Tuff.

From which signs and tokens the

reader may infer that by this time I had come to a perfect understanding with the person whose hospitality I was availing myself.

This, however, was very far from being the case.

There were matters on which he would talk freely enough.

About his ailment, and how long he had lain on that bed a martyr to rheumatic-fever.

About his odd nick-name even.

He was a glazier by trade, he informed me, but he had many years since " gone into another line."

He did not explain what this other line was, but, with an ugly grin, he gave me to understand that it was one that admitted of his indulging in so much leisure, and was so profitable, that his acquaintance in sheer envy had fastened on him the appellation of the Golden Glazier.

But not another word would he say concerning those two subjects of which, as the reader will easily understand, I was chiefly anxious.

Once or twice I endeavoured to recall his attention to the little black cross, but as often he immediately began to speak of something else.

Respecting the talisman which had so provoked Aaron Doomstone's covetousness, he was equally reserved.

" You stay with me, boy," he repeated, over and over again, "stay with me till I get strong again."

As for me, I dare not trust myself to reflect on the strange predicament in which I had become involved.

The best that I could do now was to go on repeating to myself the comforting assurance that it was only for a little while, and that, after all, I was not a prisoner.

Even if he had possessed the inclination, he had not the power to detain me when I felt inclined to go.

But who knew one minute from the other what might happen?

Had not Aaron Doomstone promised to come back ?

Bent on the devilish purpose he had avowed, was it likely he would fail ?

This I had hinted to the sick man on the bed.

" No, no, we are safe enough on that score, Joe, my boy," he answered. "Beasts of prey, such as he is, hunt only by night. And when he comes, we will be ready for him, eh, Joe ?　We will have such a trap for the old fox that shall teach him how rash it is to come poaching into other men's houses !　Ha, ha ! I'm bound to laugh, though it makes me grind my teeth in pain to do it.　I long for you to set about the trap, Joe.　I think that I shall feel well a'most when you can tell me that it's all right, and ready, and waitin' for him ! "

" What about a trap ? " the reader may ask.

It was the very thing that was causing me most anxiety, and making me a most miserable boy the whole time I was regaling on my Christmas dinner of eggs and bacon.

There was to be a trap set for Aaron Doomstone.

I was to set it.

It was to be the first job I set about the moment I had finished my dinner.

As I have previously stated, the Jew was in possession of the key of the outer door of " Rat's Castle."

It was by that legitimate means that Aaron and the Redpole had made their way into the ruined old house the night before.

How and under what conditions they made their exit the reader will need no reminding.

Anticipating the Jew's sinister visit, the door, of which Aaron Doomstone held the key, was to be fast bolted against him.

Of course it was the Golden Glazier who suggested the trap, and, feeling no love for the hideous Jew, and with all a boy's disregard for everything else when a " joke " is to be played, I confess that at first I was nothing loth to go in for it.

This was the " joke."

" When he discovers that the door is fast, Joe, my boy," said Samson Tuff, " he will naturally think of the broken casement through which he and the Redpole escaped this morning.　The night will be dark, and he will bring no light with him ; trust him for that !　He will come in the dark, Joe, and somehow he will climb up to the old window and jump in that way—just as you have been used to.　But he musn't find a floor to jump on, Joe ! "

"I SAW IN THE CORNER TWO BLINKING EYES."

"Musn't find a floor!" I repeated, in amazement.

"Not so much as a cat might walk on," returned the bedridden robber, with a diabolical grin.

"But who is to prevent him finding the floor?"

"You, Joe."

"Me!"

As I uttered the word, a vivid picture of the Jew's tremendous shoulders and bull neck rose before my mind's eye, and I thought that if he was only prevented entry into the house through the window by me, he would encounter no very serious obstacle.

"Yes, you, Joe," the robber repeated, grinning harder than ever as he observed my perplexity.

"I shouldn't like to try it; he's a strong 'un, anyone can see, though he isn't a bit taller than I am. Why, he could take me up like a walking stick in those big hands of his, and pitch me out into the mud."

"He could, of course he could; and, what's more, he would; after he had throttled you, mind, not before. He'd do that, and worse, if he had the chance, but he shan't have the chance. We'll steal a march on him, Joe."

"How do you mean?"

"Look in that cupboard and you will find the key to the riddle."

I did as he desired, but could find no sort of "key;" nothing, indeed, but a few odds and ends, such as a workman might use, including a hammer or two and a handy-sized saw.

I told him so.

"That's it," said he; "the saw. It's a good 'un and a sharp 'un. It 'ull work of itself a'most if you only show it a plank. There's a six-foot hole for it to cut in the flooring just under the hole where the parler winder used to be, and I'll wager that, in a fist no bigger than yourn, it being a willing fist, the job may be done in half-an-hour."

It was in this way that the Golden Glazier conveyed to me his ideas of the sort of "trap" that should be set to catch his arch enemy, the treacherous Jew.

I could not forbear laughing.

"It would serve him right," said I. "How deep would he fall? Because, you know, I shouldn't like to——"

"Certainly not. I shouldn't like to," interrupted Samson Tuff, setting his teeth in a manner that gave the lie direct to his assertion; "but it isn't deep enough to break his bones even. About twelve or fourteen feet, not more, I should think."

"He won't hurt himself in falling?" I remarked, with a mischievous relish for the practical joke to be played on Aaron Doomstone. "It's all mud at bottom. I've looked through the holes in the floor and seen it often."

"You are quite right, Joe; only mud, nothing but mud," returned the Golden Glazier, with a wink, the meaning of which at the time I did not comprehend.

Had I done so, most decidedly I should have declined the task.

Even though thereby I had offended Mr. Tuff, and for ever missed the chance of discovering what the little black cross meant and who it was that had so branded me.

It was not a little strange how this last-mentioned matter remained in my mind since its discovery had so strangely affected the man, who, to my knowledge, I had never before set eyes on.

I have no doubt that it was my yearning to discover more concerning it that induced me to listen to the Golden Glazier's proposal.

He was extremely anxious that I should set about the said task, the preparing of the trap that was to be Aaron Doomstone's undoing.

"You'll have it growing dusk before you are aware of it," he remarked, impatiently. "The afternoons this time o' year are very short, don't you know?"

This was quite sufficient to set me on the alert.

"I haven't forgot the reward, don't you know," continued he, encouragingly. "Soon as ever you come back and tell me that you've done the trick you shall have it. My eyes! I reckon that the amount of it will make you open your young eyes."

But, as already intimated, it was not the inducement of earning a reward of money that caused me to bring my dinner to a hasty termination.

Since the unpleasant task had to be performed, the sooner it was set about the better.

Each moment it became more apparent to me that it was not only dis-

I would do that, and then I would make off, half naked as I was.

Anything, anything, was better than assisting at a murder.

Full of this suddenly-formed and desperate resolve, I hastily sprang to my feet, but at the same moment a hand was laid on me.

A pair of hands!

Out from the gloomiest corner of the room, with a growl such as a wild beast might have given utterance to, sprang a shape, and in an instant it had me in its clutches securely as a big, six-legged spider grapples a fly.

I could not cry out!

I could not move!

While one great hand and arm twined round me and pinned my arms to my sides, the other hand gagged my mouth, covered my face, indeed, so that I could get a glimpse of my assailant only between his hairy fingers.

Does the reader need be told who it was that had seized me?

It was Aaron Doomstone.

I have said that I had started to my feet.

In an instant, however, he hurled me down, and held me hugged in his arms as though I had been no stronger than a baby.

"Ah, hah! ish the vork done, my tear?" he chuckled, with his hideous face close to mine. "Vill you go up and tell Mishter Tuff that the trap is all ready and vaiting for the old fox? Vill you, eh?"

I strove my hardest to wriggle out of his grasp, but an iron vice could not have held me tighter.

"Vill you go up to the Golden Glazier, my tear, and fetch your reward? Ah! hah! I vill reward you for the little job you have done on my account, my tear schild. The little floor-sawing job. I vould let you go, don't you see, but you are too clever for this vorld!"

Again for my life I struggled hard to free myself from his deadly grasp, and did even succeed in getting a grip with my teeth on the thick part of his hand that covered my mouth.

But I might as well have attempted so to make an impression on a rhinoceros's hide.

He did not seem to be aware of the bite even, though I daresay the tremendous rage he was in would prevent him feeling pain that would sting him at ordinary times.

He held me out from him, sheer over the yawning hole!

"You shall taste of the sauce of your own making, my tear," he whispered close to my ear. "Eh? I vonder vat the rats vill think when *you* flop down among 'em. Look down into it, tevil's imp! Smell of the sweet ped in which you shall presently sleep your long, last sleep. A nice soft ped! Not deep; oh, no, not very deep! Down with you!"

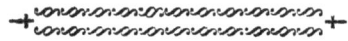

## CHAPTER VII.

### I SAVE MY LIFE AND MAKE A MURDEROUS CONTRACT WITH AARON DOOMSTONE.

"Down with you!"

And, as Aaron Doomstone uttered, or, rather, hissed the terrible words, his hideous face wore an expression I shall never forget, and which defies my powers of description.

By this time the interior of the room was nearly dark.

Nevertheless, I could make out the Jew's features quite distinctly.

His deadly white face, with the scrubby beard bristling black on it, and his eyes glaring with that same strange light that had betrayed them as he lurked on the stairs, but ten times intensified.

He held me fairly over the noisome pit, and next moment most assuredly would have dropped me down into it.

To do this, however, it was necessary for him to remove from before my mouth the hand that all along had been gagging me.

I did not, however, waste so much as a hundredth part of that moment in shouting for help.

Of even less use would it be to appeal to the furious wretch for mercy.

The trapper who, unaware, is pounced on by the tiger he would have snared, might as well ask it.

"'COME OUT, YOU BIG, HULKING RUFFIAN!' SAID THE BEADLE."

There was only *one* way by which I might hope to save my life.

Providentially that way came into my mind swift and sudden as though it had been shot there.

"Stop! I know his secret! Samson Tuff's secret!"

I need not dwell on the despairing energy with which the words were shrieked out.

They produced the desired effect.

I could almost imagine that as he held me over that black gulf his hands were relaxing their hold, when my words stayed them.

At least, a brief respite was secured to me.

Had he been about to cast away the precious "secret" for ever beyond his reach, he could not have stepped back from the brink of the hole with greater precipitancy.

"His secret!" he whispered, in a voice hoarse and trembling with suddenly aroused anxiety; "you know it, you say? *you!*"

I had struck the right chord.

"Yes," I boldly answered, "I know it."

To be sure it was as barefaced a falsehood as ever was uttered, but I think that the appalling fate that threatened me may in some degree stand as my excuse.

Aaron Doomstone, however, was not the man to be betrayed by sudden emotion into a rashness that was irrecoverable.

"Vell!" and though he affected to speak firmly and resolutely, his hands, that still were clasped about my naked body, trembled violently, "the secret! vat ish it? Quick! tell me, or——"

And he made a short, quick step towards the hole.

"The secret I mean," I answered, gaining a little courage, as I perceived the fluster he was in, "is the one that you so badly want to find out."

"Ah, ah! yes, yes, dat ish it. Blessed Mosesh! if I had it, if I had it!"

"You never will have it, if you kill me."

For a few moments he appeared irresolute.

Only a few, however.

Of the two conflicting passions that were wrestling within him—vengeance and avarice—it was long odds on the latter.

"Are you sure that you know it, and that it is vorth so very much? Are you sure, my goot lad, that you are not deceived—that you are not deceiving me?"

And as he uttered these last words, the ferocious glare returned to his eyes, and he clutched me the tighter.

"No, no, that you would not *dare* do!" he continued. "You are a prave poy, an uncommon poy; you must be tor *him* to trust you: but you don't dare deceive me. Look you!" and he released me to extend his arm straight before him, "that is not how far I can reach! I have agents—spies, my tear, that would lay vait and catch you, and bring you back to me, though you vas a tourand miles away—though you vas on the seas, down a coal-pit, anywhere!"

It must have been my desperate extremity that endowed me with such sudden courage and shrewdness.

"He should best know the value of his secret," I remarked; "he was speaking of it only this morning."

"Yes, yes; and vat did he say, vat did he say, my tear?"

"He said," I replied, "when we were talking about—about you know what—that the loss of a few paltry golden eggs did not trouble him much, so that he still owned the bird that layed 'em."

Aaron Doomstone gave a gulp as though my words had brought "his heart into his mouth" as the saying is, and he was swallowing it down again.

"He said that, he said that to you!"

And his hoarse, trembling voice became quite hysterical.

"I only repeat his own words."

"And the pird—the precious pird—as he calls it. Ha, ha! it is his vay to be funny, my tear! He showed it to you, eh? He brought it out, and you handled the pretty pird? Tell me about it, my goot lad—my tear, clever poy."

And shaking as does a man afflicted with palsy, the hideous dwarf patted my naked shoulders caressingly.

This was a poser.

Really and truly I knew no more of the nature of the mysterious talisman than did Aaron Doomstone himself.

Not so much, probably.

He was such a cunning villain.

Perhaps he really knew the shape and

make of Samson Tuff's wonderful secret—the priceless charm, possession of which ensured the owner boundless wealth, and was only trapping me into a confession of my ignorance.

That would never do.

I had better put a bold face on the matter.

"What would you give me if I got it for you?" I bluntly asked him.

"Your own price, my tear," he responded, promptly and eagerly; "I vill make a young shentleman of you! You shall have monish—gold, mind—gold and silver to sphend like a young lord. You shall come home and live with me, and never vant as long as you lif! There's a splendid chance! Don't vait, my tear poy, don't delay so much as a minute. Go up and get it now, go up and get it now, my goot lad!"

And embracing me tenderly, he urged me towards the door.

"First of all I must find out where it is," said I.

The benignity of Aaron Doomstone's countenance changed instantly.

His fawning caress became again a clutch, and his wheedling voice thickened hoarsely with passion.

"You must find it!" he repeated, with a grin of rage. "Oh! I see dat is how we shall pargain. I must vait till you find it, eh? Look at me, dog! whelp! look at me! and tell me that it is so."

I did look at him, and at a glance read in his hideous countenance, further distorted by fury, what would be my fate unless rare fortune favoured me.

"It is in the room somewhere, but I don't quite know where that is what I want!" I tremblingly answered; "I might soon find out."

Aaron Doomstone's wrathful mood again changed.

At least, it seemed to do so.

Daring actors are quick thinkers, and it might suddenly have occurred to him that if the coveted treasure was to be obtained through my instrumentality persuasion would be better than force.

"To be sure, to be sure. Don't mind my hasty vay, my tear. It ish not likely that he would let it lie about on the mantel-shelf like a tobacco stopper, or the shange of sixpence! Ha, ha! you

are right, my goot lad; you must find it, eh?"

"Yes."

"You mean to say that you think you know vhere it is; but you are not sure—not *quite* sure?"

"That's it," I replied, desperately.

"And if it was not in that von place, the place that was the right von could not be far off, eh?"

"It won't do to be in too much of a hurry to hunt about after it," said I. "It might make him suspicious."

"But he *trusts* you, my tear!" And the unscrupulous villain grinned his ugliest. "You forget that. It ish ven we are most trusted that we should make the best of our chances."

Here was more "dog eat dog."

Not loathingly, as had been the case with Mr. Doomstone's tool and catspaw, the Redpole, but with a smack of the lips and a relish as though, of all meat, it was that which best suited his cannibal maw.

He was quite right in one respect, however.

However wicked might be the bed-ridden man upstairs, he had "trusted" me.

He had been kind to me.

Without the least hope of a return (as far as I could see) he had given me a meal and a seat by his fire.

Because he had shown me friendliness and generosity in his rough way, I was to betray him!

"No, you black-muzzled rascal," I said to myself, "give me the black hole and the rats rather."

But I affected to fall in with his views.

"You are quite right, sir; he does trust me," I replied. "I have no doubt that I might soon light on what you want."

"How soon?"

"That would depend. He might have it about him."

This was a view of the case that Mr. Doomstone had not previously entertained.

I could quite distinctly hear his teeth grate as he ground them together.

"Dat ish true; curse him, dat ish very true. I believe that he would swallow it if he thought that he was going to die. Oh, Mosesh, if he *should* swallow it and it ish buried with him!"

And on the mere supposition of a calamity so terrible, the black stubble on the Jew's cadaverous face seemed to bristle with anguish.

He pondered a few minutes, keeping a hand on me the whole time—never fear!

"Yes," said he, presently, and speaking in a still lower whisper, "p'r'aps that way would be the best after all."

"Which way?"

"The shortest one, my tear—the shortest and the safest!"

And, as he uttered the words, with his great thick lips close to my ear, his face assumed an expression that was truly demoniac.

"I don't understand!" I faltered.

"But the reward, you understand that?" said Mr. Doomstone, coaxingly.

"Yes, I understand about that."

"About the fine clo', and the pocketful of shillings—did I say sovereigns?—very goot, sovereigns, then; I'm a liberal man to them vat serve me well. No more vant, no more rags; always with a pellyful, and money to shpend, eh?"

"It would agree with me very well, no doubt."

"You shall have 'em, my tear. You are a lad of spirit."

"I am not wanting for a little pluck, if that's what you mean."

"Goot, goot!—very goot! we shall get at the 'short vay' I was speaking of after that, eh?"

"We shall if you show it me," I replied.

"Goot again! Vel', it ain't a mile off, my tear."

And here he again bent his black muzzle to my ear.

"It is here."

"Where?"

He unbuttoned his heavy pilot jacket, and showed me, protruding out of his inner pocket, the butt of a pistol.

"Loaded, my tear! loaded and capped," he whispered.

"Well!"

I could scarcely ejaculate the monosyllable, I was so frozen with horror.

"The shortest vay, my good lad! He trusts you! Very goot. He turns his face to the vall, and he goes to sleep! He *trusts* you, you know! Vy, bless my soul, you might bury the muzzle in his hair before you touched the trigger, and he would only think that you vas tucking him in to make him comfortable."

"What! shoot him—kill him!"

I am afraid, in my horror and amazement, I spoke dangerously loud.

"Hush, my tear! Think vat a little time it would take—not a minute—not a quarter of a minute; and then think on vat you vin! Now only a poy, and all your life till you grow up to be an old man, p'r'aps a shentleman, with as much money as you can shpend?"

It was on my tongue's tip to tell the cold-blooded villain that I would rather suffer death myself than be guilty of such an atrocity, but a sudden thought checked me.

The pistol, already loaded and capped, might be of use!

Those that the Golden Glazier owned had been taken by the Redpole when the treasure hole in the floor was rummaged.

Since it was my firm resolve to baulk Aaron Doomstone if it were possible, such a weapon would be invaluable.

"If you think that it will be best, why don't *you* do it?" I asked.

"I'll tell you vy, my tear. We are not goot friends. He could never be brought to turn his face to the wall and go to sleep while I was in the room, and it would never do to attack him face to face. I am too goot natured; I couldn't find the heart to do it!"

"Then give me the pistol."

"You vill do it?" and the unscrupulous villain quite gasped with delight.

"I'll do the best I can."

"Here, then. Hide it, hide it, my tear! Be very careful, or it may go off a little afore its time. Bear in mind, vait till his face is turned to the wall, and then make sure."

"And when will you come here again? —to-morrow?"

"To-morrow! Pless the lad! I vill vait. I shall not mind. I shall be on the stairs, so that, if my young friend finds his courage sinking, he vill only need to think how close by I am, and he vill be all right again."

As Aaron Doomstone uttered these words, he leered at me in a way that was not to be mistaken.

What he meant was this, "Don't attempt to play tricks, because, if you do, I shall be on the spot to settle scores with you."

But I felt a strange strength within me, such strength as only determination in a good cause can give.

"Don't fear for me," I replied. "You don't know what I have the pluck to do when I once set my mind on it."

And, with that, I took the pistol, and, concealing it in the waistband of my trousers, left Aaron Doomstone to wait in the dark while I stole upstairs.

Where a startling alteration in the aspect of affairs waited me.

## CHAPTER VIII.

### I INHERIT THE "GOLDEN GLAZIER'S" PRICELESS TALISMAN.

IN my eagerness and anxiety to escape from the hateful and perilous presence of Aaron Doomstone, I made my way up the stairs at a pace much more rapid than I had descended them.

At last I reached the door of the room in which I had left Samson Tuff, helpless and bedridden, and hastily turned the handle of the lock.

To my amazement I could not push the door open.

It would open just a little way, two inches or so, perhaps, but no further.

"It is me," I called out, thinking it possible that he might have taken a fancy by some means to barricade the door in my absence.

But nobody responded to my call.

Then I made a discovery.

It was by this time dark, and there was no candle burning in the room.

But the piled-up fire I had left in the grate had not yet burned out, and threw a ruddy glow on the floor.

By this light through the chink—I was able to push the door open—I saw a little scarlet stream, just within the door, and stealing out slowly towards the landing.

There could be no mistake as to the nature of the scarlet stream.

It was blood.

Whose blood I could only shudderingly conjecture.

Had it not been for Aaron Doomstone keeping watch on the stairs below, I make no doubt that the first glance at that ghastly evidence on the floor would have been the signal for my instant flight.

But it was better, or so it seemed to me, to face this new danger than to once again face that from which I had so recently escaped.

With a desperate effort I pushed at the door, and urging a dull dead weight before it, it slowly opened.

Then was the cause of my fright fully revealed to me.

Samson Tuff, *alias* the "Golden Glazier," prostrate on the ground, moveless, and with his face downwards!

No evidence of a struggle, or of any other person having entered the room since I left it.

It was plain that he had crawled out of bed thus far, and that the desperate exertion had caused the rupture of some internal blood-vessel.

Was he dead?

Hastily bolting the door, I struck a light and examined him.

He was still breathing, though faintly.

With prodigious exertion I contrived to drag him towards the bed, with the idea of somehow hauling him on to it.

But this my boyish strength would not permit, and the best I could do was to take the bolster and pillow, and make a rest for his head with it.

Then I bathed his face with some water, and after awhile he opened his eyes.

At his first knowledge of someone bending over him, he started violently, and raised his hands feebly as though to push me off.

"It's only Joe, mister!" I exclaimed; "it isn't nobody to hurt you."

I was trembling and crying, and hardly knew what I was saying.

"It's Joe Sterling," I continued, as he gazed bewildered at me; "I've done that job downstairs."

The mere mention of "downstairs" brought him to his senses instantly.

"It is him! the Lord be thanked, it is him!" he exclaimed, at the same time grasping my hand in his own. "I thought it was all over with you. Where is he, Harold?"

"It's Joe, I tell you," I replied—"Joe Sterling."

"Aye, aye, Joe. Poor Joe! where is he, I say?"

"Who?—the Jew?"

"Yes; I heard his voice, curse him, I heard his voice, and heard you cry out—and—and that is all I remember."

And as the Golden Glazier uttered these words in a failing voice, he passed his hand across his forehead mazily.

Now I could better understand how it was that the "Golden Glazier" came to be lying by the door.

As the reader may possibly recollect, it was when I had just finished the "trap," and Mr. Doomstone pounced on me, and seized on me from behind, that I cried out, and the Jew, too, uttered an exclamation that any one listening above might have heard.

It was at that moment that the sick man must have heard me.

Heard me, and, actuated by the sudden and mysterious interest he took in me, crawled from his bed to the room door.

With what result the reader has already been made aware.

"Yes," I replied to Samson Tuff's last question; "it was the Jew's voice that you heard; he's in the house still."

"In the house! Where?"

"Downstairs. Hush! or he'll hear us talking."

The Golden Glazier started, and gazed affrightedly towards the door.

"It is bolted top and bottom," I replied to his glance. "He can't get in very easily. Besides, he won't try; I'm in his confidence."

"Eh?"

"He has trusted me with a job."

"He—Aaron Doomstone trusted you? What job is it?"

"Murder!"

As I softly whispered the terrible word in his ear, the sick man opened his dreamy eyes, as if doubting whether he had heard me aright.

"Murder!" he repeated. "What? Who? I don't understand."

"I am to kill you! This is what I am to do it with; and I am to have lots of money, and be made a gentleman of for my trouble."

And as I spoke I reached from the table, where I had laid it, the pistol that Aaron Doomstone had entrusted me with.

A grim smile lit up Samson Tuff's pallid countenance.

"You are to be made a gentleman for killing me, eh?—*only* for killing me, Joe? Answer me that!"

"For shooting you, and finding for the Jew the secret that——"

The prostrate man interrupted me with a feeble laugh.

"If it was him instead of you, even if I could prevent his killing me, I ain't sure that I would prevent him," he remarked, with the old light of deadly hatred flickering in his eyes. "I'd let him do it for the sake of putting one more damning mark to his account to be settled at the Day o' Judgment. It wouldn't make much difference to me, my boy."

"Not to be shot? Why wouldn't it?" I asked, in wonder.

"'Cause I'm already dying," he replied, faintly. "I can feel it coming over me."

This was startling news for me.

By the alteration in his face I knew that he must be very ill, but it never came into my head that he was dying.

"If you don't mind being left just a little while, I'll cut off and fetch a doctor," I exclaimed, jumping up briskly.

But he held on tenaciously by my hand that he still held in his own.

"I'm past doctoring, my lad," said he, in a fading, quivering voice. "I'm past everything but dying, and—and the rest that comes after. Oh, Lord! it's that 'arterwards,' and the thoughts on it, that kept me such awful company while I've been lying here all alone!"

And real tears welled out of his sunken eyes, and rolled down his white face.

It was little consolation that a poor, little, ignorant wretch such as I was could give to a dying man.

"I shouldn't fret about that if I was you," said I; "'arterwards' will come all right if you're sorry—*very* sorry, mind you—for all the wickedness you've gone and done."

"I wish that I could believe that," he answered, shaking his head dolefully. "It's a'most too good to be true, though the parsons do preach it. Bein' sorry won't square all the wrong I've done even you."

"Me?"

"Aye. There's the miracle. I ain't a man; leastways, I *wasn't* a man to believe in miracles or Providence, or nothing wot I couldn't tackle and fight agin with my two hands. But I should be worse than the pig that roots in the gutter if my opinion wasn't altered now. Wot but Providence was it that sent you to me just at this time? And wot can Providence mean by it, 'cept that I might have a chance of setting right a deadly wrong, and making what amends I can?"

It was rather to himself than to me that he uttered these words, and that in a musing way, and in a voice that each moment grew fainter.

That he was dying I could not but be aware, and I could say nothing, but sat silent and trembling with fear.

"It was the little black cross that did it," he continued, flashing up a little. "'There might come a time,' I said to myself, 'when I might be glad to recognize him if he's in the land of the living,' and before I parted with you I put the mark on you."

A sudden thought thrilled through me.

"You are not my father?"

"No, no, not so bad as *that*," he replied, and with a strange expression on his countenance. "I've been a bad 'un all my life, the Lord help me! but I never sold my own flesh and blood. No, Harold, your father was a rich man. Was! *is*, for all I know, and I——Oh! God forgive me, the end is very close now."

It was a terrible time for him.

An awful time for me.

He seemed to suffer acutely for a few moments, and when he spoke again it was in short, fitful breaths.

"That is passed; but I can make you amends, boy. You shall be the Golden Glazier's heir. You shall inherit his gem, his rare treasure, his precious secret, that shall bring you a priceless fortune. Don't ask me who made it mine!" he gasped, shudderingly. "I bought it, and must pay the price. Take it, it is yours."

But before I could take it, it had to be produced.

This was the manner of its producing.

As, perhaps, the reader may bear in mind, on the occasion of Samson Tuff's first hinting to me of his possession of the precious talisman, and apparently in momentary dread for its safety, he clapped his hand to his mouth.

At the time I remarked on the oddness of the act, and wondered what it meant.

Now he again put up his hand to his mouth, and to my speechless amazement extracted therefrom a molar tooth.

There was a tiny golden spring attached to it, showing how it had been fixed between the others.

Was this the priceless treasure?

No; it was only the casket in which it reposed.

The tooth was screwed together in two parts, forming a sort of box.

The tiny box was opened and the treasure revealed.

A tiny blazing spark like a diamond.

Like a diamond, only, instead of being dazzling white, it was intensely red.

Ensconced in its little box, it gleamed like a chip of red-hot steel.

He had let it drop into my hand, and for several seconds my amazed eyes could do no other than gaze on its surpassing brilliance.

A sudden sound from the pillow withdrew my attention from my strange legacy to the giver of it.

The end was closer than even he anticipated.

He was at his last gasp, and without one other word of explanation so he died!

"HE HELD ME OVER THE YAWNING HOLE.'—(See No. 3.

# CHAPTER IX.

### IN WHICH I AM AGAIN DRIVEN TO DESPERATE STRAITS TO SAVE MY LIFE.

How long I sat there by the dead man's side, I cannot say.

Stunned, bewildered, and with a heart full of terror, I remained holding the charmed tooth in my hand, and gazing, unable to move, alternately from it to Samson Tuff's white face.

It was a sound without the silent room that aroused me.

A small sound, not louder than a mouse scratching against the wainscot might make, but it seemed to recall to my mind the existence of Aaron Doomstone.

I listened intently.

He was still downstairs.

I could hear him walking softly to and fro in the passage below.

What should I do?

I dare not venture down to him.

The mysterious treasure of which I had become the owner was that which the dastardly Jew was so eager to secure.

What was more likely than that he would behave as treacherously to me as to anyone else.

That he would, as soon as he had secured what he so hungrily coveted, proceed to take the "shortest way" with me, with a view of putting it for ever out of my power to betray him.

The "trap" in the parlour was still open.

I had already found out how small a chance there would be for me if he once got me in his tiger-like grip.

Then my bewildered eyes lighted on the pistol on the table.

If I knew how, I might at a pinch protect my life with that.

If I knew how!

I never in my life had fired off a pistol; how was it managed?

As already mentioned, the weapon was already loaded and capped.

I took it in my hand, my awkward fingers trembling violently.

With most disastrous results.

All of a sudden, and quite unexpected on my part, the hammer fell with a startling snap on the capped nipper.

There was a blinding flash and a loud report, and the little shaving-glass over the mantleshelf in which the dead man had been accustomed to shave was splintered into a thousand fragments.

Had the bullet struck me instead I could not have stood more appalled.

What the result would be I but too truly foresaw.

Almost before the black sulphurous smoke had cleared away I heard the sound of hasty footsteps ascending the stairs.

It was Aaron Doomstone!

Hurrying up to congratulate me on the neat and expeditious manner in which I had executed the little job of manslaying with which he had entrusted me.

Rousing instantly from my stupor I leapt to the door and convinced myself that the bolts top and bottom were shot well home into their sockets.

In bare time!

Next moment his hasty hand was laid on the door handle.

"It's all right, my tear," he exclaimed, giving the door an impatient shake, "it's your friend! Ah, ah! you're a smart poy! a poy of pisness!"

I was not smart at opening the door, however.

It was evident that the cunning villain thought that I had acted according to his devilish desires.

He had been anxiously waiting for the report of the pistol, and he had heard it.

How could he doubt that it had been discharged at the head of Samson Tuff?

Evidently he was in perplexity why the door was fast against him.

"Quick!" he exclaimed; "there ish no time to lose. Open the door and let me see your vorkmanship."

But I was altogether too frightened to return him any answer.

"Do you hear?" squealed Aaron Doomstone, giving the door an impatient shake. "Put down the pistol and unbolt the door, I say. Vy do you shtand there like as if you vas turned to an idiot?"

It was quite plain from this that he was spying through the keyhole, and could see me.

"You shan't come in here," I answered, desperately.

"Vat!"

It would be difficult, indeed, to describe the tone in which he uttered the word.

"Ishn't he dead?" he presently exclaimed.

"Yes, he's dead," I replied. "Poor fellow! he's dead enough; but you are quite mistaken if you think I killed him."

"Mistaken! He tells me that, with the plood of the man wetting my shoe soles. It ish *you* who are mistaken, my goot young friend, as you shall see, as you shall see."

And, with a terrible imprecation, he flung the full weight of his squat, heavy body against the door.

No wonder that my behaviour was so inexplicable to him.

He had heard the pistol shot, and there unmistakably was the blood welling out under the door to where he stood.

Why, since I had performed the most terrible part of the bargain, did I object to let him in so that it might be completed?

For a mighty good reason, as the reader is already aware.

As well as my life, I had to save the "priceless fortune" with which the penitent and dying robber had endowed me.

But how?

Here I was caged in the topmost room of a house five storeys in height.

It was night.

The only outlet besides the door was the narrow window.

The only outlook was the dark water of the river flowing sixty feet below.

And all the while I was casting about me, bewildered and panic stricken, Aaron Doomstone was not idle.

Finding his own strength insufficient, he had dragged up from the room below some ponderous weight, and, swearing hideous oaths, he kept ramming at the door with it.

But, as before mentioned, the bolts were massive, and held staunchly.

How long they would be able to resist an assault so vigorous it was impossible to say.

"——you! you tevil's imp! I vill cheat the hangman of his vork, ven I get you!" shrieked the infuriated Jew, through the keyhole. "I vill grill you on the fire!"

Suddenly it occurred to me what I had seen in the cupboard when Samson Tuff directed me to search there for the saw.

The coil of rope hanging against the wall!

Slender of make, but tough as iron wire, doubtless it had been made to assist such men as the Golden Glazier in the pursuit of their nefarious occupations.

Unhooking it from the wall, I rapidly told it out to see the length of it, and if it would reach from the window to the river.

Was it sixty feet long?

No; little more than half sixty.

Aaron Doomstone, still battering at the door, and peeping through the keyhole between whiles, saw what I was at.

"Ha, ha! You vill hang yourself, young murderer, eh?" he exclaimed. "You vill cheat me as well as the hangman! Make haste, my goot young friend, or I vill baulk you."

I answered him not a word.

I had enough else to do.

Mounting the table that stood under the window, I cautiously opened it and looked down.

It looked hopelessly, cruelly deep.

Smaller even than the stars overhead looked the twinkling lamps below whose light was reflected in the black water.

Moreover, my rope would reach little more than half the depth.

But I made one cheering discovery.

Before the windows of the second floor was a balcony, as was the ancient fashion with river-side private houses.

Was my rope long enough to reach this?

It was very doubtful, but it was my only chance and I resolved to risk it.

First, however, to secure the mysterious gift that had been bequeathed to me.

How? was the question.

I had no jacket, and the pockets of my trousers were fretted into holes long ago.

Stay, there was the dead man's money bag!

His money, likewise; but I did not want that. It was not the sort of money that I was inclined to.

All that I wanted was the bag.

Great, indeed, must have been Aaron Doomstone's amazement when, in my desperate haste, I took the bag by the corners and shook out its contents.

Sixty sovereigns, at least, ringing and spinning over the floor.

He paused in the midst of his hammering and swearing to listen to the delicious music.

But if his amazement was great to hear this pouring out and wasting of gold as though it were of no more account than water, what must it have been when, through the key-hole, he was made acquainted with my next operation?

When he saw me busily tying one end of the rope to a stout stanchion in the wall by the open window!

It was as though all of a sudden my real design had dawned on him.

He absolutely yelled in his fury, and dashed against the door as a newly-caught wild beast dashes against the iron bars of his cage.

He wasted no more of his breath in swearing.

Thud! thud! thud!

He had but one object; to beat the door in.

He would do it, too.

If the besieged door did not yield at the bolts it would at the hinges, was very certain.

I expedited my movements.

The precious bag I slung round my neck with a bit of string and tucked it in at the waistband of my trousers.

Suddenly I heard one of the bolts yield with a crash.

A moment's delay and I should be too late.

Leaping on to the table I cast the rope out into the darkness, and clutching at my end of it for dear life backed my legs and body out of the window.

Another moment and I was fairly launched.

It was an awfully close shave!

Barely was my head below the window-sill when I heard the remaining bolt go, and the door bang hard against the wall.

Heard Aaron Doomstone hurry to the window.

Felt him shake the rope where it was tied to the stanchion.

Felt something else that, as I was painfully and tediously descending hand under hand, thrilled me with horror.

He could not untie the rope, and he was cutting it!

He had descried the knife I had used, and left so foolishly lying on the table, and was severing the rope.

The parting of the strands vibrated through the rope's length, vibrated through my arms and through my whole body, chilling my blood and making me feel sick and giddy.

## CHAPTER X.

### THE DESERTED BOAT.

GRINNING in murderous spite as he hacked and sawed at the tough hempen rope from which I hung suspended, little did Aaron Doomstone dream that he was conferring on me not an injury but a benefit.

A boon that, beyond a doubt, was the salvation of my life.

Had he left me alone I should have been caught in a trap from which there was no escape.

My rope reached within five feet of the flooring of the balcony before mentioned, making it easy to reach.

But how was I to escape therefrom?

The river was twenty-five feet below, and the tide was out, so that of a surety had I essayed the leap I should have broken my limbs, or possibly dashed out my brains.

So there—on the balcony that is—I must have remained until the villainous Jew dwarf came down and captured me.

His deadly malice, however, saved me from both these disagreeable alternatives.

I might have been eight feet or so from my landing point when the rope was severed and suddenly snapped, and down I came on to the balcony floor a tremendous whack.

I fell on the flat of my back, however, and was not so much hurt but that I was aware of the danger of lying there a moment longer than I could help.

How was I safely to reach the shore of the river below?

How?

Why, Aaron Doomstone had considerately provided the means!

The rope that he had cut, and which I still held tight in my hands, was the exact thing.

To tie a knot over the balcony rail was but the work of half-a-dozen seconds, to scramble down it but as long again, and then I was free.

Free!

If my enemy chose to chase me now, he was welcome.

The hard necessity that had made me a "street prowler" had caused me to be intimately acquainted with the ins and outs of the river bank, and I could have led him a pretty dance amongst the stranded barges.

But he made no attempt to pursue me.

Plumping in the mud up to my knees, I scuttled off in the darkness to the lee of a coal-barge, and looked up at the window.

It made me shudder.

Looking down from the dizzy height was awful enough, but to look up was inexpressibly appalling.

The mists of night hung about the tall, desolate old house, and the light in the garret window shone hazily, as a solitary star in a fog-blurred sky.

It shifted hither and thither, the light.

Aaron Doomstone was searching for the treasure—picking up the gold, too, that lay scattered over the floor.

There could be no doubt of *that!*

But what he hungered after chiefly was the "precious bird" that had laid the late Samson Tuff his golden eggs.

That miraculous talisman, possessed of which, according to the Jew dwarf, a man would be empowered successfully to cry "open sesame" at the door of every treasure house in the country.

I knew the shape of the room in which the dead man was lying, and, watching the shifting light reflected on the garret window, could tell pretty well at what part of it Aaron Doomstone was occupied.

Now the candle was held high up, and moved slowly.

Aaron was examining the beading that ran round the room wall where the ceiling joined it.

Now the light sank down suddenly, and, for a long time disappeared, so that I thought that the Jew had left the room with it.

But he was busy on the floor.

Ripping up the carpet.

Plunging his knife in at chinks and crevices of the boards.

Tearing at mouse-holes till his horny fingers were pierced and set bleeding by the rough wood splinters.

Now the light again appeared for an instant, and then was lost.

Aaron was at the cupboard where I had found the rope.

Not there!

Then the light crossed the room towards the bed on which the dead robber lay, and there it remained for a quarter of an hour at least.

Aaron was overhauling the body.

When the dead man was discovered, he was lying in the middle of the room, half hidden under the upturned carpet, just as the ferocious villain had bundled him aside, so that he might with greater convenience get at the bed and the mattress, which he ripped open and emptied.

I knew that Aaron was emptying the bed, for a little cloud of white feathers came through the still open window, contrasting like snow-flakes with the darkness.

But, as the reader knows, he had no more chance of finding what he sought than he had of bringing the dead man back to life again.

It was about ten o'clock when I escaped from the window.

The chimes of the neighbouring churches had long since tolled the hour of eleven ere the candlelight slowly, lingeringly vanished from the room.

Aaron Doomstone had given over the hunt, finding how useless it was.

Good Lord! I would not have encountered that disappointed, furious dwarf, as he turned from that chamber of death, for all the bars and ingots of gold that cumber the cellars of the Bank of England.

And yet, goodness knows, I was poor enough.

It would have been difficult, indeed, to have discovered that bitter winter night, a boy of twelve in a plight more hopelessly deplorable than was mine.

Half naked, with my bare feet freezing in the river mud, ousted from my "lodgings," and without so much as a halfpenny to pay for new ones!

And with all this, the possessor of a priceless talisman—a key that, properly applied, would reveal to me boundless treasure!

It seemed too preposterous to be real.

Cowering under the stern of the grimy coal-barge, I stealthily withdrew my treasure from the bag, and, unscrewing the fantastic ivory box in which it reposed, wonderingly gazed on it.

The darkness seemed but to increase its brilliancy.

It glowed like a red hot diamond.

Trembling with apprehension lest I might loose it in the mud, I endeavoured to remove it altogether from the hollow tooth.

This, however, could not be done.

It was firmly set in the lower part of the tooth, that part to which the prongs are attached.

The prongs were of considerable length, so as to allow of firm handling between a strong finger and thumb.

That the strange, awful looking thing was designed to be so used there could exist no doubt.

But how?

On what occasion?

This was the puzzling, unfathomable mystery.

What should I do?

I could not stay where I was, or even near the spot.

Terror of Aaron Doomstone forbade that.

I had not forgotten his boast of being able to find me anywhere, either on the face of the earth or in the bowels of it, if I played him any trick.

He must, by this time, be strongly impressed with a suspicion of the fact that I had stolen off with what his greedy soul was so fixedly set on.

Without doubt he would lose no time in pursuing me.

And here it may occur to the proper minded reader—

"Then why, if you were the honest boy you profess to have been, why did you not adopt a course that must have suggested itself to you? Why did you not take to your heels, and make for the nearest police-station?"

Excellent advice, oh, worthy reader, sound and righteous to follow; but, you see, there were certain difficulties in my way.

In the first place being of that human tribe which it is part of the duty of constables to worry and molest, my faith in wearers of blue coats with metal buttons was not exactly perfect.

In the second place, I might, under existing circumstances, confide myself into the hands of the police, and in vain wish myself out of them again.

The business with which I had unhappily become involved was possessed of some ugly features.

There was a man's death to account for.

There was that suspicious-looking "trap" in the front parlour to be explained.

Truth is stronger than fiction, as the old saying is, and undoubtedly it was so in my case.

I might, with perfect truth and candour, relate how I came to be mixed up with so strange an affair; but what a cock-and-bull story it might appear to a listener of a sceptical turn of mind!

No; I would not trust the police—at least, at present.

I would go my ways as of old, and think about it; taking to give the waterside, and the vicinity of Rats' Castle in particular, 'a wide berth for some time to come.

But, as will very shortly appear, it seemed as though strange adventure had set in for me at full flood, and that my ways of old were for ever at an end.

Who can tell how any one of our apparently simple resolutions may influence us through the remainder of our lives?

As, for instance.

"It is no use thinking about what is to be done till the morning," said I, "where shall I stow away for the night?"

Not ashore.

Such was my mortal terror of Aaron Doomstone, that already I pictured him in council with his "agents," who would post themselves at every street corner between this and Ratcliffe and lurk there till they had effected my apprehension.

Suppose I crept aboard one of the coal barges?

There I should be sure to find shelter, and, maybe, a bit of tarpaulin or sail-cloth to protect me from the cold till daylight.

No sooner resolved on than put into execution.

But the first barge I mounted offered me no inducement to remain there.

It was one dismal surface of coals and frost, and the cabin door was pad-locked.

On to the next barge, with no better success, and so on to the next and the next.

The bargees had gone ashore to spend Christmas, and, as it was likely that they would not return for half a week or more, they had made all tight and secure before they left.

I can't tell how many barges I tried, for they lay in a long line, extending a hundred yards or so on to the river.

Hoping against hope, I extended my search until I arrived at the outside barge of all.

But all was bleak and inhospitable.

Not quite all!

Strangely enough, made fast to the stern of the last barge, there was a boat.

A commodious four-oared boat, and empty!

Empty, save for exactly the thing I stood most in need of.

At the bows of the deserted little craft was a large tarpaulin neatly folded.

I had no dishonest intention, and did not hesitate a moment.

"Here is a boat that is made fast here till morning," I said to myself, "and she'll be none the worse for having a boy in her to mind her, for which I shall charge nothing, but the loan of her tar-pauling as a counterpane."

And, with my teeth chattering with cold, it was not two minutes before I was curled up at the bows of the boat, with the heavy tarred canvas pulled securely over me.

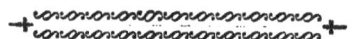

## CHAPTER XI.

### I AM TAKEN CAPTIVE BY RIVER PIRATES, AND MAKE THE ACQUAINTANCE OF HOPPY VIGORS.

IT was a strange bed, and stranger bed-clothing.

Nevertheless, I was so desperately tired that it seemed to me all that could be desired.

All through the preceding night, it should be borne in mind, I had had no rest, and now that I was stowed away in fancied security, it was but a very short time before my busy thought took that confused turn that denotes approaching sleep.

How long I slept, I cannot say.

I woke in a fright, and with a sudden start.

The boat was moving, and I could make out the sound of muffled oars plashing the water.

My repose must have been sound in-deed!

Quaking with fright, I listened in-tently, and presently made out the sound of men's whispered voices.

"That's the Tower yonder, isn't it?" one remarked.

"Aye, many a bold boy has swung there for flying at meaner game than ours. They don't hang a fellow in chains now, that's one comfort, eh, Billy?"

"I'd as lief hang in iron as hemp!" growled the man addressed, sullenly, "if it came to hanging; and I can tell you another thing, Tom Hornblade!"

"What's that?"

"I'd liefer have a cheerful-talking chum when I'm out on business than one who is always croaking and rattling chains in my ears."

"And I'd sooner you both held your peace, you chattering idiots," spoke a third voice at the further end of the boat. "Why don't you strike up be-tween you a roaring stave concerning where we are bound, and what for? D'ye want the wasps down on us?"

The last speaker, who evidently was

at the tiller, spoke in an authoritative voice, and the other two at once became silent.

But I could not lie still.

My limbs shook so that, but for the rippling of the water against the oar blades, they must have heard the stirring of the crisp tarpaulin.

Into what kind of a hornet's nest had I now dropped?

What was the nefarious business on which the three men in the boat were bound?

That it was nefarious I could have no doubt. Honest men went in no fear of the gallows or of " wasps " either.

My acquaintance with slang was, in those days, rather extensive, and I knew that " wasp " was a nickname for a river constable.

It was quite certain that at present the men had had no suspicion of my unwelcome presence on board their craft.

There was nothing for it but to remain quite quiet on the chance of being undiscovered, and by-and-by finding a chance of making my escape.

I cautiously looked out of a tiny crevice of my covering, and endeavoured to make out what the rowers were like.

But the night had grown darker than when I closed my eyes on it, and all that I could discern were the dusky figures of three men, two at the oars, and the remaining one at the further end, with the tiller ropes in his hands.

Silently down the black stream we glided for miles and miles, as it seemed to me, and as though the journey would never come to an end.

For the last half-an-hour not a word had been spoken, and then the man at the helm cautiously broke silence.

" Softly goes it, lads; there she lies. We'll be up with her in a dozen pulls."

" Aye, aye."

" No noise, remember. It is more than likely that Blacky is dead drunk with the bottle of rum the others bribed him with to say nothing to the captain of their stealing ashore for a spell of spreeing. But even if he should be awake and sober deal softly with him. Knock his thick skull in with a pistol butt if you are obliged to, but no shooting. d'ye mind ? "

" Aye, aye," was again the only answer of the other two men ; and by this time

I could feel, by the gentle grating of our boat, that she had reached the side of the craft to which her evil errand tended.

Evidently the men who manned her were ruffians to whom this kind of work was not strange.

Although, as may be easily imagined, the terrible fright that possessed me wrought my sense of hearing to its keenest, I could hear no sound either of their securing the boat to the ship's anchor chain, or of their somehow climbing on board.

All that I know is that I presently again peeped from my hiding, and, excepting myself, the boat was empty, under the overhanging stern of the big ship.

Now, had I been a man instead of a small and weak lad, was a chance for me.

I might untie the boat from her mooring, and when she had drifted away a bit I might raise my voice and endeavour to warn that unfortunate " Blacky," whoever he might be, of his impending danger.

I know, even as it was, that this was what I should have done; but the honest truth is, I was so benumbed with a sense of my own danger as to have no thought for that of other people.

Besides, it was just possible that my fevered imagination made more of the apparent danger than was justifiable.

Anyhow, I was in that frame of mind that prompted me to remain concealed where I was, and I did not stir.

But I listened with all the power of my two ears.

There was not a sound.

After the lapse of a minute, or perhaps rather more, the quick, sharp growl of a dog suddenly roused, met my ears.

In an instant, however, the growl changed to a brief cry of pain, and again all was still.

" If that was the ship's dog," I said, to myself, " ' Blacky ' must have heard it, if he has any sense left in him. There will be a row presently, I shouldn't wonder."

Nor was I mistaken—at least, as regards one part of my conjecture.

Blacky was roused.

Peeping out from my tarpaulin screen, I could make out a man—the ship's cook, in all probability—staggering towards the bulwarks, and struggling with another man, who was stifling the negro's cries by clasping his hands before his mouth.

Had the black cook been sober, his assailants would have found tough work with him.

He wore a light-coloured "guernsey," and I could see that he was a fellow of herculean build.

But three to one was odds against which he could not cope.

Presently I saw an arm raised and swiftly descend, and poor Blacky fell like a log to the deck.

Now, the business which the river pirates had undertaken was easy to their hands.

For some time, a quarter of an hour, perhaps, they disappeared, and then one of them lowered himself into the boat.

The other two appeared cautiously peering over the bulwarks.

"When you are ready," one of them whispered to the man below.

"Aye, aye!  Lower away."

"Steady, then.  Don't let it slip at the last moment."

"No fear.  Safe she is."

And, as the man spoke, a heavy weight, to which a rope was attached, bumped down into the boat.

The two men who had remained on board to look after the precious consignment, hastily joined their companion in the small boat, and then cast off, the rowers laying to the oars with a will.

Here was a new source of terror for me.

It was a sack of considerable bulk that had been stolen out of the ship.

What did the sack contain?

Safe "she" is, the man had said.

Was it a human creature, then?  A girl—a woman?

I was too young and ignorant to be aware that in nautical parlance everything that is strange and precious is alluded to as feminine.

My fears were presently allayed, however—to give place to worse.

"Shall we let it lie here?"

It was Tom Hornblade who spoke.

"Ay, it may as well.  Lug that tarpaulin this way; we may as well cover it over!"

I almost gasped for my breath as I heard the ominous words.

I was just at the point of emerging from my hiding-place, and imploring them to be merciful to a boy who would never, never reveal what he had been an unwilling witness of.

But the hair by which the sword of fate hung suspended over my head was not just yet to snap.

"No, never mind," whispered the ruffian in command, "haul it up to the bows and cover it over there; 'twill be snugger."

Now should I be discovered?

I could hear the fellow dragging the sack with the heavy bulky weight in it to my end of the boat.

I crouched down, making myself as compact as a hedgehog, and held in my breath.

The precaution saved me.

For the present, that is to say.

The man merely thrust the sack, as he thought, to the extremity of the boat, and pulled the tarpaulin over it, and returned to his seat at the oars.

At least I was now able to satisfy myself that the contents of the sack were not human.

It was pushed close against me; I could feel it.

There was metal in it.  One piece chinked against another as I laid my hand on it.

With the tide in their favour, the river pirates (for such I could no longer doubt them to be) propelled their boat through the water at a smart pace.

Now and then there would occur an interruption, but it was of brief duration.

"Ware wasp!" the leader, who was at the helm, would whisper.

Then the rowers would swiftly ship their muffled oars, and lay forward so that the boat concealed their bodies until the danger was passed.

"Pull with a will, lads, we shan't reach the 'Wreckers' before daylight else."

"Old Vigors will be up, I suppose?"

"Devil doubt him.  If we don't find a good breakfast ready, as well as the best his cellar can supply, I don't know the man."

Invigorated by these words of promise, the rowers bent their backs to their work with renewed exertion.

Presently I was startled to hear that part of the boat that was immediately beneath my head grate on the loose stones.

We had arrived at our destination.

Two of the men, leaping out of the boat, hawled her up on to the strand.

Now for it.

My term of respite had but a few brief moments to run.

And then——

The thrill of horror that set my whole frame tingling as I arrived at this dismal conclusion roused me from my stupor.

Might I not even yet escape?

It was still dark, and their amazement would be something in my favour.

Mustering all my courage for one desperate effort, I suddenly flung the tarpaulin off me, and, with a nimble spring, cleared the boat's side.

But, had the matter been planned by my enemies, I could not have been more unfortunate.

It is true that I cleared the boat, not to alight on the shore, however.

As ill luck would have it, at that very moment Tom Hornblade was stooping to adjust his water boots, and I plumped slap a-top of his broad back.

No one but a man of most uncomfortable conscience could have uttered a yell so uneartly.

It was such an overpowering fright for him that, had he been alone, I make no doubt that I might have got clean away.

But there were others besides Tom Hornblade to the bargain.

The leader of the gang had not yet left the boat, and had witnessed my unexpected exit from it.

He wasn't a fellow so easily scared.

Quick as thought he caught up an oar, and, just as I was regaining my legs after my tumble, he made a spiteful sweep with it.

The flat of the oar blade caught me between the shoulders, and I was bowled over on to my face, bleeding and half stunned.

They lost no time in securing me after that.

All three of them were down on me like hawks on a wounded pigeon.

I say all three of them, but there was a fourth. A lanky man, with a wooden leg, who carried a lantern.

"Who is he? What's he done? Don't hurt him," exclaimed the man with the lantern, compassionately.

But when he heard what the others had to say about me, he soon altered his tone.

"The sooner he is put to sleep again past waking, the better for us all," said the man with the lantern, savagely.

"That were easy enough, but for one thing," remarked the ruffian who had led the others in the boat.

"What's that?"

"Dead people tell tales, in spite of what old women say to the contrary."

But this cruel proposition did not appear to meet Billy's views.

"'Tain't lucky to kill kids," he replied, turning away. "Besides, it's growing too close to daylight, Hoppy Vigors."

"Then make this fast over his ugly head, and bring him along to the house," growled Mr. Vigors. "We shall be able to provide for him there, I'll be bound."

What was to be made fast over my head was a silk handkerchief, which the wooden-legged man withdrew from his pocket.

His advice was promptly acted on.

The handkerchief was made fast over my mouth, to prevent me calling out, while part of it was tied over my eyes, so that I could not see.

Then I was roughly caught up by one of the men.

Into a house (as I could tell by the unlatching of a door) and down a flight of steps.

Then another door was opened.

"What, dy'e mean to stow him with the 'swag' in the snuggery?" one of the fellows asked, with a half laugh.

"He can't be in a safer place," returned Mr. Vigors, with a brutal chuckle.

And, with that, I was bundled down on to the ground, and immediately afterwards heard the slamming to of a heavy door, and the grating of a key in its locks.

## CHAPTER XII.

### MR. DOOMSTONE AGAIN!—A TERRIBLE FOREWARNING.

ALTHOUGH my hands were free, it was some time before I could sufficiently recover from my terror to untie the handkerchief that was bound before my eyes, and look about me.

When I did so, I discovered that the place I was in was not by any means so dungeon-like as I had at first imagined.

By this time the morning had fairly broke, and by the light that found its way through a grating that guarded the dingy window, I could see tolerably well about me.

It was a spacious room or rather cellar, but boarded and perfectly dry ; as it had need to be, considering the quality of the goods it served as a storage for.

Ignorant as I then was of the nature of Mr. Vigor's business, it amazed me not a little that such a variety of articles, many of them evidently very costly, should be stowed in so unlikely and dingy a place.

Piled against the walls were parcels and rolls of silks and satins, besides many bundles and bales so well secured that it was impossible to guess their contents.

Here was a crate full of new boots and shoes.

There was a box, the broken lid of which revealed clocks of expensive workmanship, while close beside it lay a heap of great ivory tusks.

The last introduction was the bag or sack which the river pirates had brought away out of the ship.

But I had no heart to examine it, or, indeed, anything that shared with me the dingy apartment into which it was my hard lot to be cast.

I could think of nothing but the ominous words of the villainous woodenlegged man when he suggested, as an alternative to drowning me, like a dog in the river, that I should be carried into his house.

In my despair I wickedly lamented that I had baulked Aaron Doomstone when he was about to consign me to the muddy gulf beneath the parlour floor of Rats' Castle.

"I should have been out of my misery then," I sobbed, while bitter tears rolled down my cheeks. "What have I to live for ? "

From which doleful ejaculation it must be quite clear to the reader that I had quite forgotten the "fortune" that the Golden Glazier had left me, and which still hung in the bag which was slung by a strong piece of twine round my neck, and was hidden in the waistband of my ragged trousers.

Hour after hour passed, and no one came to me, but I felt neither cold nor thirst, nor hunger.

At last, towards the afternoon, a little trap in the ceiling was opened for an instant, and a hunch of bread thrown down.

But I neither saw nor heard who it was that had bestowed it on me.

I had no heart to eat the bread, but it at least convinced me that I was not to be "put out of the way" just at present, either through starvation or any other disagreeable process.

A few more weary hours and it was pitch dark.

Then I heard the noise of footsteps over head, and a tiny glimmer of light finding its way through the crevice of the rough ceiling, assured me that the apartment over head was, or was about to be, occupied.

This was some sort of company, anyhow !

If I could contrive to get nearer to the ceiling, I might even hear the voices of the speakers, if there were any in the room.

Full of this thought, I set about constructing a sort of platform of the bales and boxes before mentioned, and speedily made a heap, mounted a-top of which my head came within a foot of touching the beams.

Then I could make out the clinking of glass, and the muffled voices of men discussing together.

"DOWN I WENT."—(See No. 4).

Evidently the room over head was a drinking room, possibly the bar-parlour of the "Wreckers," of which water-side hostel worthy Mr. Vigors was the landlord.

But I could not recognise his voice.

Indeed, owing to the height of the ceiling from my head, and the thickness of the planking of which it was composed, it was impossible to hear anything but an indistinct and confused murmur.

"Perhaps I might hear something concerning myself if I could mount a little higher," I thought, and, after one or two failures (one of which caused my platform to tumble from under me with a most alarming noise), I managed to raise myself so high that, by craning my neck, I could lay my ear against the ceiling.

Then I could hear the voices with much more distinctness.

There were three speakers, seemingly, and, unless I was deceived, Mr. Vigors was one of them.

There could be no doubt that another was the leader of the river pirates who had attacked the black man and robbed the ship.

The third man's voice was strange to me.

As was their conversation.

Nothing about the excursion of last night; not a word respecting the unhappy little wretch who had been an unwelcome sharer of it.

Nothing but drinking and smoking, and loose, slangy talk, that to me was almost unintelligible.

"How goes the time, Vigors?" someone asked presently.

"Close on eight."

"He sent word that he would be here by half past seven, didn't he?"

"There's no occasion to be uneasy; it's too good a chance for him to neglect. No trouble; all clean for the melting-pot, without an ounce of dross in the whole weight of it."

It was the leader of the night before who uttered these words!

Could they be in allusion to the plunder in the sack that was lying within three yards of me?

It seemed so, and the expected man was to become the purchaser of the stolen plate.

Who was he?

Keenly cruel, the fates designed that the person in question should answer for himself.

"Here he is; who said he wouldn't come?" exclaimed Mr. Vigors, cheerily.

"My vord, shentlemen; my vord ish my pond!"

My ear at the moment was within a few inches of a narrow chink in the flooring, and, such was my sudden dismay, that it was brought into painful and violent collision therewith.

There could be no mistake.

The voice was that of Aaron Doomstone!

He was the individual whose "vord vas his pond." He had come to purchase the stolen silver!

"Well, it's a good haul this time, Aaron; as good as ready money," spoke Mr. Vigors.

"Not quite, my tear," chuckled the Jew; "if it vas as goot, no fear of your shelling it so sheep as you vill have to if I puy. Trade is pad, very pad. I shall have to porrow the monish to puy vith."

"You *have* borrowed it, you mean. You've got the money with you?"

"I never puy at night, my tear; my eyes are not goot."

This seemed to be relished as a joke by the company.

I didn't wonder at it when I recollect what bright piercing eyes the Jew's were.

"Well, come and look at it, and weigh it, and then you will know how much money to borrow by the morning," remarked Mr. Vigors, sneeringly.

"Is it here, in the house?" asked Aaron Doomstone, eagerly.

"Downstairs in the snuggery. Fifty pounds weight of it if an ounce. Come and look at it. Show a light, Vigors."

I had to clutch a beam to save myself from tumbling headlong from my platform.

But, from some private reasons, Mr. Doomstone obstinately objected to visit the snuggery that night.

Possibly he had money with him and knew his customers too well to trust them with him in secluded places.

"In the morning, my tear friends, in the morning," he replied, firmly; "I only vanted to know how much would likely to be required. Early to-morrow I vill pring my scales, an ve vill shettle the leetle pisness."

Nor could he be shaken from this de-termination.

Long and anxiously I listened to dis-cover whether they would inform him of the strange boy they found skulking in their boat.

Had they done so, I have no doubt that he would instantly have suspected who that boy was, and his resolve not to visit the snuggery that night would at once have been altered.

But it seemed that I was, for the time, completely forgotten; and after staying for an hour, and drinking sundry glasses of spirits at the expense of the others, Mr. Aaron Doomstone took his depar-ture, his last words being—

"I vill pe here pright and early in the morning, and then ve vill go down pelow and weigh the goots, and I vill pay for them."

## CHAPTER XIII.

### IN WHICH I DISCOVER THE MIRACULOUS VIRTUE OF THE RED TALISMAN.

With Aaron Doomstone's last words ring-ing in my ears, I still retained my perch close to the ceiling long after the hideous Jew dwarf had taken his departure, and Stumpy Vigors and his other customers had retired, and the parlour overhead was deserted and left in darkness.

The guilty criminal who hears sen-tence of death passed on him from the lips of the judge, could scarcely have felt more terror than did I.

"I will be here bright and early in the morning, and we will go below and weigh the goods!"

How could I doubt that he would keep his word?

From the few observations that had passed before Aaron Doomstone arrived as to the nature of the business to be done, it was quite clear, even to a lad so young as I was, that the advantage was all on the side of the Jew.

I already knew enough respecting him to convince me that the purchase of goods that had been stolen was not likely to press heavily on his con-science.

He would surely return in the morn-ing.

And then!

And then! That was the benumbing fear that kept me fixed like a statue of crouching despair, a-top of my crazy pedestal of stolen bales and boxes.

There I remained until the churches had chimed the end of the night, and two or three of the birth hours of morn-ing, until I was almost frozen with cold.

It seemed as though, unless I found something to distract my thoughts from the terrible peril that was overhanging me, I should die outright, or go crazy.

Suddenly I bethought me of my trea-sure.

Of the "priceless fortune" that, in his last moments, the "Golden Glazier," had bequeathed me.

Since yesterday it had hung neglected and uncared for, except that now and then, as I lay sprawled on the top of my platform, the prongs of the tooth the treasure was set in unpleasantly reminded me of its existence by digging against my unprotected ribs.

I slid down to the floor, and, all in the dark, took my "fortune" out of its bag, wondering could I get a peep at it.

I was not long kept in doubt.

Soon my benumbed fingers had con-trived to unscrew the little ivory box, and there it was, like the sudden kind-ling of a light.

London bred, and knowing only but through hearsay what the country and green lanes were like, I had never seen a glowworm.

Had I done so, the similarity must have struck me.

Ruddy red, instead of yellow, however, twinkling and quivering like a live thing.

Marvellous, mysterious little gem, yet what was its worth to me?

Even though it were worth a hundred times more gold than I had turned out of Samson Tuff's bag, it was impossible for me to realize it.

I might, supposing myself once again in possession of precious liberty, starve for lack of a pen'orth of bread, and own it all the time.

Stay though!

My precious liberty! Might I not regain it by parting with what was so useless to me?

What would be easier, when Aaron Doomstone made his appearance, than to make him understand, by some sign, that what he was so hungrily anxious after was mine, and might be his?

Already he must expect such to be the case.

My daring flight from the Golden Glazier's garret, his unsuccessful search in every nook and corner of the room, pointed most earnestly to that probability.

He would, without doubt, understand the least signal I made him, and act on it with his usual caution and cunning.

It should be done!

He should have it on the sole and simple condition that he got me out of the clutches of Mr. Vigors, and set me free.

I would, even if I had the chance, have nothing to do with Mr. Doomstone or his fine offers to make me a gentleman.

All that I wanted was liberty; freedom to run as fast as my legs would carry me and return to my old life of ragged roving.

This settled to my mind's satisfaction, I felt easier.

I began to take a more leisurely and calmly-curious interest in the tiny red sparkler that I still held in my hand.

What were its wonderful properties?

White diamonds, I knew, cut glass—would a red one?

Anything to pass away the dark dreary hours before Aaron Doomstone would come and release me.

As before mentioned, high up against the floor at the further end of the cellar was a little strip of window, protected by a row of stout iron bars.

What was on the other side of the little window, of course I could not tell.

I had noticed on the day previous that it was ground glass and apparently of some thickness; now a faint yellow light was reflected on it as thought at some long distance away there was a lamp, whose rays just reached it.

Without noise I removed the stacked-up boxes and bundles one at a time to that end of the cellar where the window was, and easily reached it.

Reached the bars, that is to say.

I might have contrived to squeeze my empty hand between them, and so have reached the glass, but I dare not hazard the safety of my treasure for a mere whim.

I was not much disappointed.

All that I desired was to pass the time.

It would have been easy enough to cut the glass, thick as it was, if the tiny red sparkler was a diamond.

All that was needful was to draw it smartly across the pane, like so!

And as I thought thus I drew my red gem across the face of the iron bar that was handiest to me.

With a result that was both at once curious and amazing.

It was not a dull, scratching sound that followed the application of the red gem to the face of the iron.

There was a spark as of real fire, and a quick, crisp sound like the sudden tearing of paper.

Plainly in the darkness, too, could I trace where the gem had scratched the bar.

The jagged mark displayed itself as distinctly as does a stroke on a dark wall made with a phosphorous match.

What did this mean?

Was the bar an iron one?

I scratched it and tapped it with my finger-nail; there could be no doubt of it.

I tried the experiment again; this time about a foot above the first scratch I had made.

Again the fire spark, again the sharp, cracking sound.

Again, also, the phosphorescent revelation of where the scratch had been made.

Before it could die out, for it did not in the first instance last more than a very few moments, I endeavoured to drag myself up a little closer, that I might more easily examine it.

To do so I clung hold of the bar itself between the scratched places.

It was cut through!

Fairly a foot of it came away in my hand, as though it had been previously severed and only temporarily replaced.

Was this latter the case?

Warm enough now with my amazing discovery, I shifted to the next bar, and first ascertaining, with all the strength I possessed, that it was fast and firm, submitted it to precisely the same operation as the other had undergone.

With exactly the same marvellous results.

The spark, the tearing noise twice repeated, and there was another length of iron bar in my hands—another gap in the grating.

I could scarcely hold my talisman in my hand, I shook so.

Was *this* its miraculous virtue?

Were iron bars impotent before it, tiny thing as it was, lying so snug in its ivory nest, and twinkling as I looked on it with awe?

Twinkling, like a living eye that winked in merriment at my breathless astonishment.

Then the memorable words that Aaron Doomstone had uttered respecting this same talisman flashed to my recollection.

The reader knows when; that time when I lay in the cupboard in Rats' Castle, and the Jew and his companion, the Redpole, were discoursing of the Golden Glazier's secret.

"We might cry 'Open Sesame' at every bank door in England; there is not a treasury or a repository for wealth in the kingdom that would not fly open at our bidding."

Those were the mysterious words that Aaron Doomstone had used.

Mysterious no longer, for here was the solution of the riddle.

Suddenly a heart-stirring idea flashed to my mind.

If my little twinkling talisman was superior to the resisting powers of iron, why not also those of wood and glass?

Through the open space that the two yielding bars had left, I could now reach the window easily.

If I could cut away through that I need not wait until the arrival of the treacherous Jew dwarf.

I might possibly make my escape at once, and that without the sacrifice of my wonderful iron-cutter.

My suddenly inspired hopes, however, were doomed to early death.

The red gem had no more effect on the window than though it had been a piece of common stone.

Leaping down from my perch I tried it on the woodwork of the door.

But with no better luck.

It had no power over either.

There were great iron hinges to the door, partly protruding towards the inner side, and when I tried my tiny red conjuror on these, it faithfully responded with those signs which so unerringly foretold that it had done its work.

But I could reach only a small part of the hinges, and could not get hold of them to snap them.

The thought of escape had seized me so strongly that I was bitterly loth to forego it.

Once more I mounted my mound of rolls and bales, and worked away at the bars till they were all removed, and the window was exposed.

But the glass could not be cut, and was too thick for me to break.

There was no help for me; I must await the coming of Aaron Doomstone, and abide my chance of escape as originally designed.

By the sacrifice of my strange treasure, that is to say.

I could not refrain from a deep sigh of regret as I arrived at this conclusion.

It was nothing to part with it while it appeared to me no more than a mere pretty piece of glass.

Now, however, that I had become acquainted with its miraculous power, the matter assumed a different complexion.

That necessity is the mother of invention, is a "saw" that has lost none of its edge through constant usage.

Did Aaron Doomstone really know the shape and nature of the Golden Glazier's gift to me?

Now that I came to think of it, it seemed more likely than not that he was completely ignorant on that score.

It was hardly likely, had he known that it was a red diamond enclosed in a false tooth, that he would have hunted so long in the dead Golden Glazier's mattress, in the cupboard, under the floor-boards for it.

Besides, had he known, he probably would have informed me when I was pretending to be in his confidence, in order that I might the easier discover it.

These rapidly occurring ideas encouraged me.

If I were lucky, I might after all out-wit my enemies, old and cunning as they were!

But it was no use attempting what I designed till morning.

I must first be able to see about me.

So I lay down with a roll of rich silk for a pillow, and awaited with feverish anxiety for day dawn.

It came at last.

Then I set about the execution of the bold idea I had conceived some hours before.

Half-an-hour sufficed for its completion.

Satisfied as I was, however, I had no time for rest and self-congratulation.

Hardly was my task completed than I heard a sound of footsteps over head, announcing that Mr. Stumpy Vigors was up and stirring.

A quarter-of-an-hour afterwards, I heard a knock at the street door.

"Goot morning, my friend. I keep my vord, you see!"

It was Aaron Doomstone!

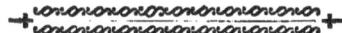

## CHAPTER XIV.

### IN WHICH I PLAY A DESPERATELY BOLD GAME, AND WIN.

DROWNING men catch at straws.

I was not a drowning man, but only a boy in immediate danger of being quietly knocked on the head.

Nevertheless, the "straw" that I had caught at, and which, in my extremity, "the mother of invention" had so kindly suggested to me, filled me with such confidence, that the sound of the Jew dwarf's voice caused me no apprehension.

And this, although I knew that, according to last night's arrangement, I should shortly be confronted with him.

He stayed above some time, however, awaiting the arrival of the two men who were in his company last night.

As soon as the last-mentioned worthies came, there was a move towards the steps that led down to the "snuggery."

It was not yet so light but that they deemed it necessary to bring a candle with them. I saw its light shining under the chinks of the door as they approached.

I took my seat on a box just by the door, summoning all my courage.

Presently the great key was turned in its socket, and Mr. Vigors appeared, holding the candle above his head.

Aaron Doomstone caught sight of me at the same moment.

Or, rather, he saw something living and moving there, and he started back with an exclamation of surprise.

"Don't be alarmed, Aaron, it isn't old Nick!" grinned Mr. Vigors; "it's only one of his cubs that's put here for safety just now."

"Got pless me, Mr. Vigors, I did not know as you vas in the shlave trade," returned the Jew, pleasantly, his confidence returning. "I did not know that you stole children to sell aproad. Vat would you take for this von?"

"He isn't for sale," returned the wooden-legged man, with an oath. "He's bespoke."

"How?"

"Never mind how; he's booked, I tell you; but if you wish pertickler to know what——"

"Tevil and—— Vat's this?"

This from Aaron Doomstone, who, while Mr. Vigors was speaking, had caught sight of my face.

"Hulloa! made another discovery?"

"Vat's this, I say?" continued Aaron, fiercely, and at the same time pouncing on me; "vat does it mean? Do you know who he ish? Do you know?"

And all the while the hideous Jew was making sure and surer still of his grip on me, as though resolved never, never to let me go.

"Ask these fellows what it means, they can tell you better than I can," returned Mr. Vigors, sulkily; "and p'raps you'll be good enough, Mr. Doomstone, to bear in mind that you are not on Salisbury Plain before you yell out in that way again."

The Jew still held me, looking at me with his eyes fixed with the deadliest malice, when I made a sign to him with my lips.

He understood it instantly, as I could see, but had no belief in it.

I withdrew the bag just a little way above the waistband of my trousers, so that he might get a glimpse of it.

But at that instant something occurred that did more towards convincing him than if I had talked for half-an-hour.

Mr. Vigors had made a discovery.

Holding the candle high up, he saw that the iron bars in which he confided so much as protectors to his snuggery, were one and all removed, and lying here and there on the ground.

His rage and dismay rendered him almost inarticulate, and he advanced towards me with one of the broken bars in his hand, raised as though he would brain me with it.

"Is this *your* work, you devil's imp?" he presently ejaculated.

But by this time I had found a fast friend in Aaron Doomstone.

He saw the stout iron snapped as short as a tobacco pipe might be, and he no longer doubted.

He at once interposed.

"*His* work! That's goot. Vy, it vould peat a grown Samson, let alone a shild such as he ish to do it. No, no; you must look somevere else for the bar breaker, my tear."

Luckily for me, Tom Hornblade and the other man joined in the laugh the Jew raised as to the possibility of a boy of twelve snapping half-inch iron bars.

"Whether it's him or not, I'll know something about him before I'm many hours older!" exclaimed the furious Mr. Vigors.

"My goot friend, you need not vait as many minutes," spoke Mr. Doomstone, in his oiliest tones. "I can tell you all apout the little villain."

"You?"

"Ask him, my tear. He ish von of my poys."

"When did you lose him?" Mr. Vigors asked, incredulously.

"Five days since," Aaron Doomstone returned, giving my shoulder a pinch, as a hint that I was not to contradict anything he might say. "He robbed me, and ran away."

"That I never did," I answered, indignantly; "it was you who——"

"Ah! he knows me, you see," exclaimed Aaron, triumphantly, while he prudently clapped one of his great hands over my mouth, lest I should say any more.

"Come along, you ungrateful rascal; you shall not run away again for von vile. Excuse me, shentlemen, I vill just take him round to my place, and pe pack in ten minutes."

But Mr. Vigors plucked him aside.

"He knows all about——"

The remainder of the sentence was lost in a whisper.

"No fear for that. My score against him is as deep as yours," returned Aaron Doomstone. "Only let *me* deal with him. As a favour I ask it."

And he asked the "favour" with a depth of malice in his tone that quite satisfied Mr. Vigors and his friends that I should be well looked after.

Still keeping a tight grip on my arm, Aaron Doomstone conducted me up the stone steps, and so through the public-house, and into the waterside alley it opened on.

Almost before we were out of the hearing of Mr. Vigors, who accompanied us to the door, enjoining the Jew not to be long, Aaron accosted me.

"It ish in the pag, eh? it *ish* in the pag?"

I nodded my head, and made for taking the string from my neck.

"Not here—not now; they would suspect," he hastily exclaimed. "Vait till we get to a quiet spot; vait till we get home."

"I'm not going home with you," I boldly answered.

"Vat, not going home vere all the goot things vat I promised you are?"

"What, the grilling and that, you mean, I suppose? No, I shan't go home with you. I'm afraid to."

"Vat do you vant, then? Vat shall I give you?"

And his voice trembled so I could scarcely make out what he said.

"Nothing at all," I replied. "I will give you what's in the bag, and you leave me to go where I choose; that's all I ask."

It was impossible for him to haggle over a bargain that leant so liberally on his own side.

By this time we had turned out of the lane in which the "Wreckers" was situated, and emerged on the river shore.

"Give it me, then!" exclaimed Mr. Doomstone, making a snatch at the string to which the bag was attached; "give it me, and go your way."

But he was not so eager as to let me go before he assured himself that the bag contained the mysterious talisman.

Tearing it open, while with his body he penned me in a corner of the dank river wall, he pounced on what it contained and brought it to light.

But it wasn't a false tooth.

It was nothing approaching it either in make or shape.

It wasn't bone or ivory at all.

Yet it was the queerest and most fantastic little affair imaginable.

An impostor, a bare-faced cheat!

Even at this distance of time it almost makes me catch my breath as I think on the desperately daring trick I was practising on the hawk-eyed Jew.

## CHAPTER XV.

### DIAMOND CUT DIAMOND.

It was evident that Aaron Doomstone not in the least suspected the barefaced cheat that was being put on him.

It is not fit, however, that the reader should any longer be kept in the dark as to the way in which, vulgarly speaking, the changes had been rung on him.

As already stated, when the idea came into my head, it was still dark, and I was compelled to wait till daylight before I commenced operations.

My first business was to discover something that might pass muster on sight with the keen-witted Jew for the genuine article.

It must be something small.

Something quaint and odd, if possible.

Certainly it must be nothing of common-place appearance.

Where should I find what I wanted?

As already hinted, Stumpy Vigor's cellar was a repository for all manner of stolen valuables, but there was nothing to suit my peculiar purpose.

As far as a cursory search revealed, that is to say.

There was the sack I had not yet looked into.

The sack that was brought from aboard the ship by the river pirates, I mean.

It was made of some light, tough leather, secured at the mouth with a running string of a kind of whipcord.

It was "neck or nothing" with me, and I untied the fastening, and the contents of the leather sack were revealed to me.

Seemingly the thieves had not ex-aggerated its value.

Every article was of sterling silver.

Bran new and glistening as when it left the maker's hands.

Platters, and plates, and cups, and vases, evidently it was a magnificent present consigned to some far-away individual, but doomed never to reach its destination.

But the various goblets and dishes were nothing to me.

I had taken them nearly out, so that they made quite a splendid heap upon the dirty floor.

At last I hit on something that might suit my purpose.

It was a sort of centre piece of silver, elaborately chased.

A kind of bowl, upheld on either side by figures of soldiers of the ancient school.

In his right hand each silver warrior grasped a spear, the head of which was steel, inlaid with gold.

A short, sharp, little head terminating in a gold knob, where it joined the haft.

To break one of these tiny spear-heads from its holding was but the work of an instant.

As luck would have it, it broke short off just under the tiny gold ball, so that there was no raggedness about it at all.

The next step was to replace the silver goods and secure the sack as I had found it.

Now where should I bestow my "priceless treasure," my clever red gem in its tooth-box?

It would never do to trust it in either of my doubtful pockets.

The bag that had contained the Golden Glazier's hoard of savings I required for another purpose.

There was only one resource.

Ragged as were my old trousers they were still sound at the bottom seam.

This must do as a hiding for lack of a better.

Unpicking a few stiches, I inserted in at the slit the cunning false grinder that Samson Tuff had so long worn, and with a pin made the place secure.

Then I took the fantastic, strange-looking little spear-head and placed it in Samson Tuff's money-bag, and tucked it in at my waistband as it had been all along.

It was this that Aaron Doomstone gazed on so lovingly as it lay on the palm of his hand and we both stood in a corner by the reeking river wall.

"So this is the vonder, the miracle, the tiny leetle shentleman vat nibble his way through hard iron as easy as a rabbit eat up a carrot stalk! Ah! my little shiner! ve shall pe goot friends, posom friends, ve vill never, never part!"

And the deluded villain hugged the innocent little spear-head to his heart and pressed it against his hideous stubby mouth.

"I must be going, I don't want to stay here any longer," I remarked.

My voice seemed to rouse Aaron Doomstone from his rapture.

With a sudden start he thrust his treasure in the bag again and concealed it in the inner depths of his waistcoat, and then confronted me fiercely.

"Look you, my tear!" he exclaimed, fixing me with his terrible sharp eyes, "you vish to go, to have your liperty, eh?"

"That's all I ask for."

"It is pefore you, take it; put listen to me, my goot lad—ven you go away, far away, you understand, don't come pack again!"

"I don't intend."

"But I mean *never* come pack," continued Aaron, glaring on me with his yellow fangs set close together; "as long as you live never come within miles of this, and never say so much as von vord of vat you knows, if you do, I'll kill you!"

"I'll give you leave the next time you catch me," I replied, already a dozen yards away from him.

And off I ran with Simon Tuff's tooth bobbing against my ankle and spurring me on.

Once I turned my head, and, lo! Aaron Doomstone had returned to the dingy and secluded corner of the river wall, and with his back to the light was once more gloating over his wonderful little spear-head.

---

## CHAPTER XVI.

### IN WHICH I MAKE THE ACQUAINTANCE OF AN ARCH IMPOSTOR, AND LEARN FROM HIM THE STORY OF HIS FATHER'S BASE AND CRUEL IMPRISONMENT.

I TURNED no more to look after the deluded Aaron Doomstone, gloating over the talisman he supposed to be so precious.

Steadily running, I skirted the river shore until I reached London Bridge and crossed it, and soon found myself in a locality the slums and hiding places of which were familiar to me.

But I was a restless and wretched boy.

I dare not seek my old companions lest any of them should be bought over by Aaron Doomstone to betray me.

I was penniless, hungry, half naked, with all the time the weight of the "priceless fortune" bequeathed me by Samson Tuff cumbering my conscience.

What should I do with it?

To be sure my late experience had given me an insight into its peculiar, its terrible value, but that did not tend to make my mind easy.

It haunted me—that fiery red little conjuror!

I was afraid of it.

A dozen times in the course of an hour I would cautiously feel if it was still safe, with a beating heart lest it might not be, and then a sickening terror to find that it was.

How I obtained a few mouthfuls of food that day it would not be easy to tell.

At night I sought the dark Adelphi arches.

Not to sleep, however.

I squatted in a corner on a bit of straw, with my legs tucked under me, and my tormenting prize tight grasped through the hem of my trousers.

I could almost fancy that it burnt my hand.

If I closed my eyes, in an instant, like a tiny, blazing star it appeared to me—a burning star that grew bigger and bigger, till it became of the size of the dead face of Samson Tuff, just as it looked when, as I slid out of the window, I caught a last glimpse of it.

Then it would change into two fiery stars, and they would blink and twinkle till they wrought themselves into the shape and form of Aaron Doomstone's eyes, and they were set in Aaron's hideous face, and attached to it grew his great shoulders, and his long arms and hairy hands ready to grasp me.

To escape such horrors, long ere it was daylight, I was out into the highway, and so began another hungry, wearisome day.

Come the afternoon, I found myself in the neighbourhood of London Bridge again, and down on the river shore, with a sort of desperate fascination to go and have a peep at Rats' Castle again.

All at once I began to suspect that I was followed.

Not by Aaron Doomstone, however.

It was not a man who was apparently dogging my footsteps.

It was a boy.

A long-legged, pale-faced boy, thin and haggard looking.

He was somewhat older than I was, if I might judge from his appearance.

To be sure, it was nothing uncommon to meet boys on the shore of the river.

Scores of them pick up a living there everyday.

But this was an uncommon boy.

When I first perceived him he was lurking in the lee of a stranded coal-barge.

From what quarter he had come I could not say, but he looked hot and flushed, as though he had been running.

I don't suppose that I should have noticed him at all, only that his dress was too sound and decent for that of the professional mudlarks.

Besides, I thought for the moment that as I passed him, he uttered some sound as though to attract my attention; but I passed on without heeding him.

I speedily discovered, however, that he was keeping me in sight.

He was a shy pursuer.

When I slackened my pace, he slackened his; when I turned my head to see whereabouts he was, he, too, would turn his head in a contrary direction.

But all the while he was never more than fifty yards behind me.

This was alarming.

There was no use in my escaping from Aaron Doomstone if I allowed myself to be followed and my hiding-place known.

For what other purpose could the boy be following me?

Filled with this dread, I grew desperate.

He was a bigger boy than me, older and taller.

But in self-defence I had fought and licked many a boy as big as he was.

When I reached the London Bridge arch I made a halt, and faced about.

He stood still, and I beckoned him to come on.

He came, slowly and shyly, and so evidently afraid of me that I grew quite bold.

Brutal, too, as I am sorry to relate! or so I thought at the time.

Now that he was close to me, he looked so awfully pale and thin that I felt quite a sturdy giant beside him.

"Take that!" said I.

And as I uttered the ferocious words, I dealt him a blow on the face that set the blood trickling from his nose.

"Take that for following me," said I, dancing about him with my fists still doubled, as he staggered and leant bewildered against the wet buttress of the bridge; "if you want some more, there's plenty to be had at the same shop."

"I was not—not following you," he began, scarcely able to speak, his breath was so short.

"Not following me! you're a liar as well as a sneak then! Come on, and I'll bung your precious eyes up!"

"I mean that I was not following you

for any harm," continued the pale boy, feebly warding off my fists.

"But why were you following me at all?  Who set you on me?"

"No one."

"No one!  D'ye mean to tell me that you don't know that villainous old Jew, Aaron Doomstone?"

"Yes, I know him—that is, I mean I have seen him, often."

"And the man at the public-house—the man with the wooden leg, d'ye know him?"

"Oh, yes; I know him," answered the pale boy, sorrowfully, as the tears welled up into his eyes.  "I know him better than the other."

"Then what do you mean by saying that you wasn't set on to watch me?"

"I wasn't.  I don't know what made me come after you."

"Gammon."

"I don't, indeed.  I suppose it was because I thought that you was a poor miserable boy like myself.  I—I thought that we might be friends, if you didn't mind!"

There was something in his tone that took all the "bully" out of me.

He looked so wistful toward me with the blood I had so barbarously caused to flow staining his white face, that I instantly felt my own countenance reddening with shame.

My guilty fists relaxed their clenching, and, observing this, he timidly held out one hand.

But I was not quite convinced yet.

"Who told you that I was miserable?" I asked.  "How could you know it?"

"I heard you say it."

"When?" I asked, in amazement.

"The night before last."

"The night before last!—*you* heard me the night before last?  Ha, ha! now I know that it's gammon.  You're mistaken, my friend.  There must be some other chap so very like me that you can't tell the difference.  Good afternoon!"

And quite convinced that the pale boy was labouring under a delusion, I was moving off.

"No, no—I am not mistaken, I am not indeed!" he exclaimed, laying his hand on my naked arm.  "I did hear you when I say; my bed is on the floor just over where you were shut in."

"What; at the public-house that the wooden-legged man keeps?"

"Yes!  I heard you crying, and saying that you were a poor, lonesome boy, who had nothing to live for."

He was quite right.

As he repeated the words, I distinctly recollected having used them, little dreaming that they were overheard.

I grew each moment more and more perplexed.

"You knew that I was in the cellar, then?"

"I did not see you brought in, but I heard them talking about you.  I heard them whisper of the way in which you was to be put out of the way," continued the pale boy, shuddering, "but I couldn't help you."

"You could have helped me by going out and telling a policeman."

"But I dare not.  You don't know them as well as I do.  It was I who threw that lump of bread down to you."

After this avowal, I could no longer entertain a doubt as to the pale boy's friendly intentions.

I took the hand that he had been shyly edging forward, hoping that I should presently give it the shake of friendship.

"I'm precious sorry that I gave you that crack on the nose; you can give me one back for it, if it'll make you feel any better."

"Oh, it didn't hurt much; it's all right now, we've shook hands and are friends."

The young hypocrite!

"We'll say good-bye then, eh?" said I.  "I'm rather in a hurry you see.  I was running away when I stopped to see why you were following me.  You won't tell your father or anyone which way you saw me going?"

"My father!"

"Ah, the wooden-legged man.  He's your father, isn't he?"

"What! the cruel wretch who keeps the public-house!  Heaven forbid!" returned the pale boy heartily, and with an upward glance as though thanking his stars for the blessing.

"But you live there you say, and you sleep there?"

"Yes; and I work there and drudge there, and am served worse than a dog there; but Stumpy Vigors, as they call him, is no relative of mine."

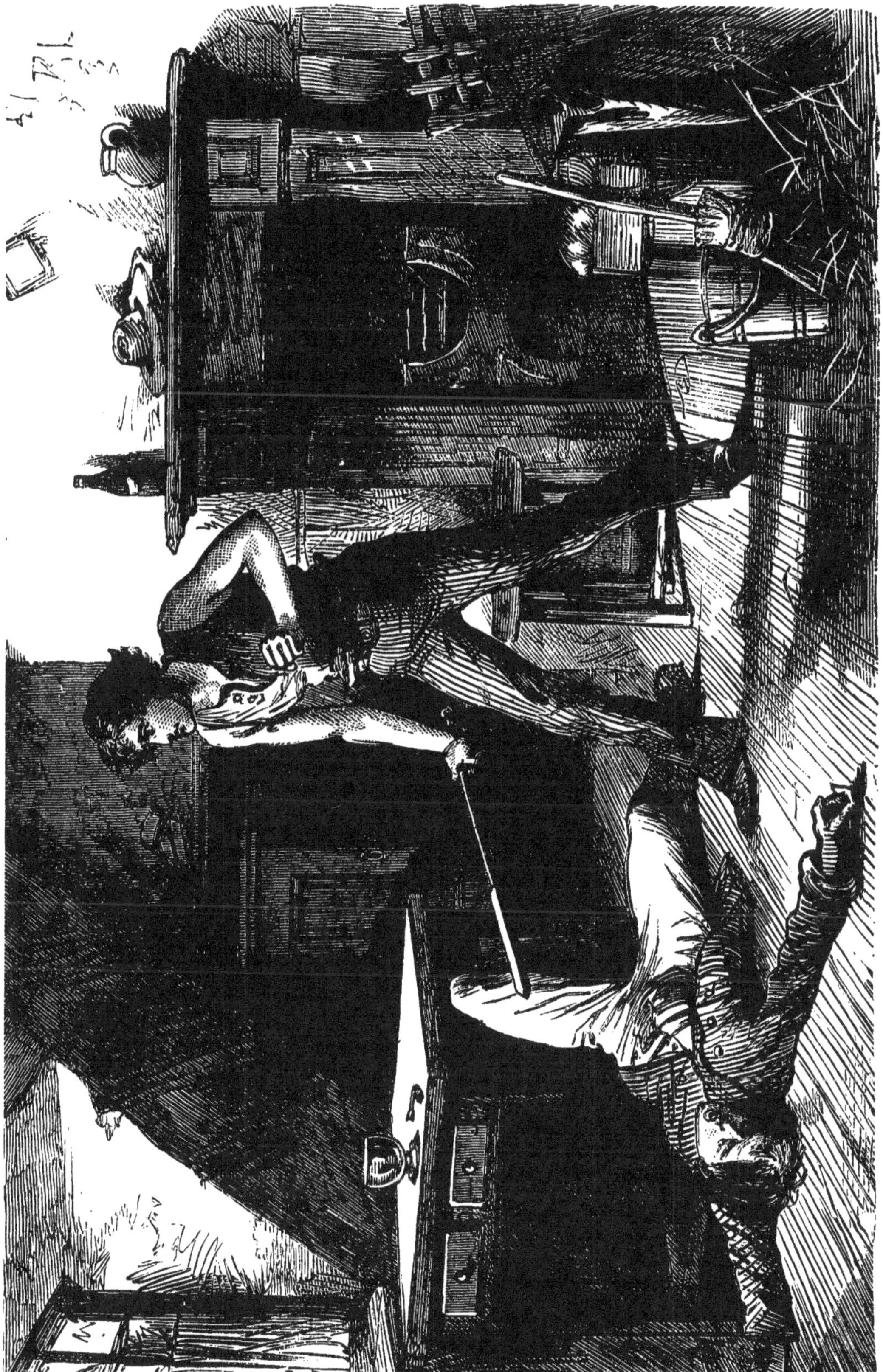

"I WAS HALF MAD WITH RAGE AND DISAPPOINTMENT."—(See Next Week).

"He's your master, you mean—you've got a place there?"

"Yes; he's my master," returned the pale boy, abruptly, as though he was thinking of something else.

"Then, if I were you, I'd get another situation," said I; "a 'pectable-looking chap like you might get a place anywhere. You ain't obliged to live along with them, and bad characters, you know, without you like. P'r'aps you didn't know that they were thieves and bad characters?"

The absent look had not left his face all the while I was giving him the above recorded good advice, and I don't think that he heard a word I was saying.

In the most deliberate manner, he proceeded to unbutton and divest himself of his decent jacket.

I thought that he had altered his mind, and, on reflection, had arrived at the conclusion that he would feel the better for repaying me that punch on the nose I had lent him.

But I under estimated his generosity.

"I mightn't see you any more," said he, "I wish you would take this, it won't be much too large for you."

But half naked and shivering as I was, I had a little pride left in me.

"Get out! don't you come cocking it over me with your presents of jackets; you ain't so well off as to have one to spare, I'll wager. You put it on again, I'm more used to roughing it than you are."

"I'm warm enough without it; see, I've got a flannel on as well as a shirt," he returned, persuasively; "besides, I want you to do something for me."

"So I will, anything I can; didn't you give me that lump of bread?"

"I want you to keep a secret."

And as he whispered the words in my ear, he looked with scared eyes this way and that, as though afraid for his life that he might be overheard.

"It's a queer sort of secret that won't keep without a jacket is buttoned on over it," said I; "let's hear it."

But his sad, grave face at once checked my jocularity.

"If I don't tell somebody," said he, still whispering and wringing his hands in strange agitation, "it will kill me. I have kept it till it has grown too burning hot for me to hold; but it was for

his sake! because they told me that they would kill him, if I dared so much as open my mouth."

Since the pale boy so obstinately insisted on it, I had by this time put on his jacket, and as he wore a coloured flannel and a waistcoat, he did not look very conspicuous without it. We turned out from the bridge arch on the river shore, and strolled towards Southwark.

That was only by chance, however.

So amazed was I at the startling change that had suddenly taken place in the pale boy's language and demeanour, that I forgot all about the way we were going.

"I don't know if you rightly understand what you are talking about," said I. "I don't, at all events. Who is it that is going to be killed if you so much as open your mouth? If I knew anybody whose life depended on me opening my mouth, I think that I should keep it shut."

"But I can't any longer. I have kept it shut for four months and more, and I must tell someone, though it's only a helpless boy like yourself, who cannot help me. It is my father they threaten to kill."

"Who threatens to kill him—the wooden-legged man?"

"He and his companions at that dreadful place where you was brought to yesterday. They have had him shut up there months and months, before the winter began. I don't know why."

And then, as we paced round the Borough Market, the pale boy, who gave me to understand that his name was Guy Foster, told me a strange story indeed.

How that his father was a diamond merchant one time of Scotland, but now of St. Petersburg, in Russia.

How that he was agent for many great firms in London and elsewhere, and at the end of the last summer having important business to execute (the exact nature of which Guy did not understand) he had resolved to take ship himself, bringing his precious goods with him.

How that he had been persuaded to bring young Guy with him.

How, on the very first day of their visiting London they were, by some base pretext, induced to enter a house somewhere in the neighbourhood of the waterside tavern Mr. Vigors was landlord of, and how after being then drugged and detained till night, they were privately conveyed to the "Wreckers."

Finally, how that ever since he had been there incarcerated in a strong room, with a fetter and a chain on his leg which was bolted to a staple in the wall.

"I was allowed to be with him at first," said Guy (who, although as I have already stated, was bigger and taller than I was, he turned out to be no older), "but after a few days they took me away from him, and I only see him just now and then through a little panel in the door. My poor father!"

And at this poor Guy gave way to such a sudden outburst of grief that I was afraid the market beadle would want to know what was the matter.

I believe that his tears went a long way towards convincing me that he was speaking the truth; otherwise, I might have thought that Master Foster's wonderful story had no better foundation than some romance he had been reading.

"Well," said I, "since you know where your father is, and that he has no business there, why don't you try and get him out?"

"Because, as I before told you," said he, the tears still streaming down his face, "they swear horrible oaths that if I dare say a word they will cut his throat the moment they know of it."

"I wonder that they chance it though," said I. "I wonder that they let you go free, while they keep him so safe."

"They have a reason for that, too," replied Guy, dolefully.

"What reason?"

"They made him believe that they are making a thief of me," he whispered, his white face suddenly glowing with indignation; "they carry up to him and show him all manner of goods, and tell him that I stole them, and what a clever thief they were making of me; and all to make him do something I know not what, but rather than do which he says he will let them kill him."

"But when they let you go up now and then just to see him, why don't you tell him that you are not a thief if——"

"If what?" Guy asked, quickly.

"Well, if you *can* look at him and say so, that's what I mean."

"Aye, that I can!" returned Guy,

determinedly. "I can do no more than look at him, for they will not let me speak, and I try to look as honest as I can, despite all their lies to the contrary. I hope and trust that he is able to read my looks."

"But what are you going to do?" I asked.

"Trust in you not to breathe a word of what I have told you," returned the simple fellow. "If it should come to their ears, I have already told you what will happen. We must wait patiently, and hope for the best. What else can I do?"

I did not know.

As the reader knows, even had I been able, I was in no condition to burden myself with the difficulties of others.

Was I not fleeing for my life, as it were?

Was it not highly probable that Aaron Doomstone would shortly discover (even if he had not already) the barefaced cheat that had been put on him?

Would he not, as soon as his eyes were opened to the unpleasant fact, at once set about finding me out?

Had he not, on a certain memorable occasion, warned me that on the sea or on shore, or in the bowels of the earth even, I was not secure against his vengeance, if I failed in obtaining him what he wanted.

What he wanted! And all the time that inestimable gem was nestled in the bottom seam of my ragged muddy, corduroys.

I felt it there as we both stood against one of the market pillars and I was chafing one naked foot over the other to rub a little warmth into it.

Was it possible that it might be made to help Guy's father out of the perilous predicament in which he was placed.

It seemed as though some good fairy had whispered the suggestion.

"At what part of the house is the room in which your father is confined?" I asked Guy.

"In the front part," he replied; "in the top room but one."

This was not promising.

Had it been at the back, which looked on the river there might have been a chance.

"You may see the window of the room from the street," Guy continued; "there are iron bars across and across it ; " and he sighed dismally at the recollection.

"And how is the door of the room fastened ? "

" By a bar and chain."

" Does anyone sleep on the same floor ? "

" No one ; the man Vigors sleeps in the room over, and the potman in the room beneath."

" Is the door of the room you sleep in locked of nights."

" Always."

More and more unpromising.

Had Guy been able to leave his room of a night I might have entrusted him with the precious talisman ; but, under the circumstances, that would have been useless.

" Ah, I see ; you are thinking of my poor father's escape. There are none at all, I assure you," Guy remarked, shaking his head, hopelessly, " the place is like the inside of a prison."

But Guy was mistaken.

My thoughts were of a more selfish character.

This man so wrongfully detained was, according to his son's account, rich.

If he was grateful, likewise, what might not I gain if I were only able to release him ?

The risk would be great.

Greater than any I had as yet encountered.

But think of the gain !

Think of the splendid stroke of business it would be to achieve that fortune honorably and honestly, by means of the questionable means the Golden Glazier had bequeathed me !

" Well, I will be getting back," sighed poor Guy, interpreting my silence to mean that I wished the interview at an end. " Good-bye, Joe Sterling, and if you ever say your prayers———"

" Stop a bit," said I, " we won't say good-bye just yet ; come into this quiet lane, I have a few more questions to ask you."

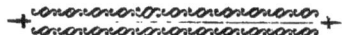

## CHAPTER XVII.

### I ARRANGE A TREMENDOUS PLOT WITH THAT ARCH-HYPOCRITE, GUY FOSTER.

HALF-an-hour afterwards we emerged from the secluded and quiet market avenue, and shook hands, promising to meet again.

Never were two lads so trusting and reliant on the honesty and good faith of each other !

The generosity and simple confidence of Master Guy Foster was quite touching.

He insisted on my keeping his jacket.

" But you'll get into trouble for parting with it," I suggested.

" Can I get into deeper trouble than I am at present ? " he replied, with a look of angelic resignation. " Let them flog me—let them kill me. What does it matter, so long as my conscience is clear ? "

The crushing sense of my own wickedness made me feel quite miserable in the presence of such a perfect little martyr.

He gave me something besides his jacket.

A beautiful four-bladed pen-knife, with a buckhorn handle—a present from his father, the captive diamond merchant!

" I have no money," said the generous lad, " but take this—sell it for as much as you can get for it, and buy yourself something to eat. It is many hours between now and ten o'clock to-night."

That was the hour at which we were to meet !

And where does the reader imagine ?

At the " Wreckers " of all places in the world.

Without revealing to Guy Foster the miraculous means at my disposal (although by his strange and puzzling questions he sorely tempted me to make a clean breast of it), I pledged myself to assist him in releasing from imprisonment his unhappy parent !

The tears of gratitude that streamed down Guy's face when I made him this promise were copious enough to have saturated a large-sized pocket-handkerchief.

" Have no fear as to your reward, dear

Joe," said he, embracing me affectionately, "you shall be his son, and we will be brothers, and in far away St. Petersburg you shall partake of the sweets of our happy home!"

I had no idea of where St. Petersburg was, but it was very nice to hear him talk so. If the undertaking before me had been ten times as perilous, I believe that I should have set about it without flinching.

It was to be put into practice that very evening, which was Sunday evening.

There could not be a more convenient time, Guy Foster explained.

On Sunday night business was always slack at the "Wreckers," and Mr. Vigors in consequence chose that time to walk abroad and visit his friends.

Guy was to assist me all he could.

Between nine and ten o'clock I was to be there, and he would be at the door of the "Wreckers," as though looking out for his amusement.

Then I was to slip in while he screened me.

I was to crawl on my hands and knees so as to escape the observation of the man in charge of the bar, and make for a flight of stairs at the further end.

These stairs, as my confiding young friend informed me, led to the top of the house, on the top floor but one of which, and in the front room, his wretched father was a chained captive!

Adjoining this room was a small chamber used for stowing away useless lumber, and seldom entered.

That I might not mistake the door of this little room, Guy good-naturedly promised to put a chalk mark on it.

The room once gained, there I was to remain until I saw a chance of putting my scheme into execution.

"How you will accomplish it I can't even guess," Guy remarked, insinuatingly; "I think that I am nearly as strong as you, and I couldn't break a link of the chain with which the door is made fast if I tried for a week."

"You leave that to me!" I replied, proudly; "I'll manage it."

"It must be a very, very sharp file that you use!"

Poor, simple Guy.

"Yes, a sharper file than *you* are," I replied, with a grin of confidence.

"Ah! they use that sort of file in the diamond trade," returned Guy, innocently. "I've heard my father speak of it. Where do you keep it? You've got no pockets."

"Don't you be inquisitive," said I; "wait till we get to St. Petersburg, and to the happy home you were speaking of, and then you shall know all about it."

And at that, as I have already stated, we shook hands and parted, agreeing to meet again between nine and ten that night.

And up to this point, no more than the reader, had I a suspicion that Master Guy Foster was any other than he appeared.

Had I followed him, my eye would have been open to his villany.

Scarcely had a hundred yards parted us, when there emerged from the shade where he had been hiding, a gentleman it had been my misfortune to meet before —the Redpole!

## CHAPTER XVIII.

### I FALL HEADLONG INTO THE PITFALL THAT GUY FOSTER HAD DUG FOR ME.

THE reader recollects the "Redpole."

He was the dissatisfied thief, who, at Aaron Doomstone's instigation, had gagged and robbed the Golden Glazier as he lay sick a-bed.

But with my innocent young friend's interview with that redoubtable robber, and what precautions the latter took to keep me in sight through the remainder of that day, need not be here discussed.

My first move after my young friend left me was to dispose of the four-bladed knife he had given me and buy some food, for, as may be well imagined, I was by this time not a little hungry.

It was Sunday, but, to the initiated, it is no more difficult to "trade" on that day than any other.

I sold the knife in Kent Street for fourpence, and immediately proceeded to invest it in hot tea and bread and butter at the first coffee-shop I came to.

Then I gave my attention to the safety of the miraculous little instrument that was to play such an important part in the release of the incarcerated diamond merchant.

I found it quite safe, except that it was grimed with mud, which had quite filled up the prongs of the artifical tooth in which the red gem was set.

The dirt had worked into the screw part that connected the top with the bottom of the strange little ivory box.

It was a snug and secluded part of the coffee-room where I was sitting, and I tried to unscrew the top.

It resisted all my efforts, the grit held it so firmly.

With the point of the knife that was brought to cut my bread I endeavoured to ease it a little.

Then followed a catastrophe that made me gasp for breath!

The lower part of the box, that in which the red gem was set, was split in two, and the tiny twinkling talisman fell out loose in my hand.

Here was a pretty predicament!

Sheer across and across again the little box was split, not in two pieces, but in three, without a chance of mending it.

How could I secure it?

How was I to keep so small a thing safe from being lost?

I was so long engaged in pondering the momentous question (keeping the red gem close concealed in my mouth the while) that twice the coffee-shop waitress looked into my box to see if I had gone to sleep, I think.

At last an idea occurred to me.

At the very last moment, too.

Indeed, had it not been the very last moment—the moment, that is to say, when, in dispair, I was buttoning my jacket all ready to take my departure— I should not have made the discovery.

Buttoning up the jacket did it.

It was somewhat too small about the body for me, and to fasten it required tight pulling.

The buttons of the jacket were brass buttons, half round and hollow.

Tugging at the top button, striving to make it slip into its proper button-hole, the upper part of the button was dissevered from the shank part.

"That's a pity, now!" said I to myself, and at once tried to set the top of the button on again.

It was very accomodating! A little click, and there was the shank part and the top part of the button joined as neatly as if it had never been broken.

Then came the idea—most precious and life-saving for me, as by great good luck it afterwards proved.

Here was a safe and handy little box in which to bestow my red gem.

A most handy receptacle, because it would be quite close at hand the moment it was wanted.

As easy done as said. In another moment my "priceless fortune" wrapped in a morsel of paper, was safely ensconced in the hollow of the button.

Soon after the churches had chimed eight o'clock I turned my face towards Millbank and to the "Wreckers."

It was something after nine when I arrived at the dirty little thoroughfare in which the hostel in question was situated.

It was a turning out of a more frequented thoroughfare, and halting at the mouth of it, I could see the lurid light of the red lamp that overhung the tavern door; but my friend Guy Foster was not yet in sight.

I was not sorry for this, since it afforded me a little respite.

To confess the truth, the closer I got to my job, the less I liked it, and would have been glad of an excuse for shirking it.

Once, twice, thrice I walked past the entrance of the narrow lane, but as the lamp-light showed me, the door of the "Wreckers" remained closed, and my young friend was not to be seen.

Perhaps he was prevented!

Perhaps he had got beaten so awfully for parting with his jacket, that he had not left strength enough to get as far as the door!

"I will walk past three times more," said I, "and then if I can't see him, I will be off."

But the very next time I looked down the lane, there he was.

Not standing in the doorway, but out in the road, looking this way and that.

It was a moonlight night, and presently he spied me, and eagerly beckoned me to come on.

This gave me courage.

There can't be much danger, I thought, if he is at liberty to come out and signal as openly as that!

And then I thought of the unhappy diamond merchant's terrible sufferings, and how, that if I were only lucky enough to relieve him of them, my fortune would be made, and quickly scudded down the lane.

Master Foster advanced a few steps from the public-house door, and welcomed me with a beaming face.

"I was afraid that you would not come," he whispered, as he squeezed both my hands. "Come along! we are more lucky even than we could hope for. There is nobody at home but myself and the old woman who cleans the pots, and she's down stairs in the kitchen."

And affectionately hitching his finger and thumb to a button of my jacket — to *the very* button, I declare — he hurried me in at the portals of the ogre's den.

"There is nobody here you see!" he whispered, encouragingly. "There are the stairs! you recollect the room I told you about? But I may as well come with you and show you. Hurry up, quick!"

I hurried up as he desired, resolving as I went, since the opportunity was so fair, to make short work of the hapless diamond merchant's locks and bars.

"Here's the little lumber room," exclaimed Master Foster, when we reached the third landing, "here's the door and the chalk mark I told you that I would put on it. In with you, and be hanged to you, you thunderin' young greenhorn. Hurrah! Hold him tight, Stumpy! and fork over the ten bob if you think I've earned it!"

For the moment I was stunned, bewildered and aghast, as though I had fallen over a precipice, and had not yet reached the bottom on which I should be dashed to pieces.

"Hold him tight, Stumpy!" screamed the traitorous villain who had betrayed me, and in an instant the door of the room was slammed behind me, and a man's horny fingers encircled my throat!

---

## CHAPTER XIX.

### IN WHICH I SEE THE TINY SPEAR-HEAD MADE RED-HOT TO BLIND ME.

SOMEONE lit a lamp, and then was revealed to my appalled gaze the terrible trap into which I had fallen.

It was Mr. Vigors who held me by the throat, pressing his broad thumb against my windpipe, so that I could not cry out.

As for that villainous imposter, Guy Foster, his malicious glee at witnessing my terror and dismay was such that he could hardly keep his legs; he screamed with laughter, as, mocking the contortions of my visage, he held on by the mantle-shelf.

"Don't detain him, Vigors," he cried, between his burst of merriment, "he has got an engagement! Don't you know, Stumpy, that all the while you are keeping him here that a unfortunit' diamond merchant is chaind to the wall in the next room? Ho, ho! ha, ha! isn't it good? Bust me, if I wouldn't be the ten bob out of pocket rather than lose the pretty pictur'!"

"Hush, you fool, he'll be coming up in a minute, and wondering what you're laughing about; *he* ain't laughing, I'll warrant."

"But how can I help it, Stumpy?" rejoined my innocent young friend, breaking out afresh, "you haven't been all through it like I have!"

And then, as though suddenly remembering a certain part of the performance that had not pleased him so well as the rest, his jocularity suddenly disappeared before a scowl, and while the wooden-legged man still held me fast pinned, he darted at me with his fists clenched.

"D'ye recollect how you served me when I first met you, young milksop?" he exclaimed. "D'ye remember the punch in the face you gave me, and which, 'cos of my dooty, I couldn't give you back, though I itched to do it? D'ye recollect it. Now—now—now, do you?"

And at each "now" he sent his bony

knuckles with all his force at my eyes, nose and mouth.

The coward!

"That's my jacket, Stump," he exclaimed, as he wiped his stained knuckles on his shirt-sleeve. "I only lent it to him, don't you know. Old Doomstone will be sure to claim it as his, if he finds it on young Greenhorn's back!"

And in a jiffy he had off the jacket he had so kindly lent me, and slipped his arms through the sleeves of it.

But I had no power to resent either this or any other of the atrocities he practised on me.

Even the painful punishment he had inflicted on my unlucky visage was forgotten at mention of that terrible name—Aaron Doomstone!

And, verifying the old saying respecting the appearance of certain persons as soon as they are spoken of, at that very instant the door was flung open, and there stood the hideous Jew dwarf!

Yes, there he stood, with his great head scarcely higher than the door-lock, but more to be feared than a dozen men of the Vigors' breed.

As the reader is already aware, more than once I had seen Aaron Doomstone furious.

That time, for instance, when he caught me in the act of making a trap for him, and held me over the gulf of mud; and again, when, as I was slipping away from him down the rope; he gazed on me from the garret window.

On both occasions he had looked terrible, but almost amiable compared with what was now his expression of countenance.

Before, fury had flushed his sallow face and made the whites, or rather the yellows, of his raven-like eyes bloodshot.

Now, his passion was fierce—it burnt with a white heat.

His face was all white—lips, cheeks, everything—excepting his stubby head, and his beady black eyes so cruelly twinkling.

He did not rave and swear at me—he did not say a word.

With no more emotion than the quivering of his thick white lips denoted, he came into the room, shutting the door and turning the key in the lock.

Then he pounced on me and plucked me out of Mr. Vigors's hand, and in an instant had me down on the flat of my back as a butcher tumbles over a lamb he is about to stick with his knife.

But Aaron Doomstone's designs were not against my life, but against my old corduroy trousers.

He snatched at the pockets, first on the left side then on the right, and tore them away.

Finding them empty, with a gasp of rage that is indescribable, he threw the rags away.

But he had not concluded his investigation yet.

Without waiting to undo a single button, he clawed the poor old trousers off me, tearing them to ribbons, and turning them inside out, while he held me down, straddling his bandy legs over me.

But what he wanted he could not find, and he vented his disappointment in a growl like that of an angry dog.

As an angry dog or a mad dog might, he tore at the muddy bottom seams with his teeth and laid them open.

But again he was doomed to disappointment.

The wonderful talisman was not there?

Where was it, then?

Unless his villainous young spy, Guy Foster, had deceived him—which was not likely—there could be no doubt that I had brought it with me.

How else could I have hoped to make my way into the captive's room and sever his chains?

Evidently Aaron Doomstone was at a loss as to what should be his next move, and he sat crouching beside me, gnawing his nails, which were all muddy from his savage assault on the legs of my old trousers.

Presently, however, he started up suddenly and turned on me.

With a cry of exultation, as though he had just hit on what he never should have forgotten.

With one hand he seized my hair and flung my head back.

With the other hand he forced open my mouth, and thrust his dirty, hairy fingers into my mouth.

Under my tongue, between my cheeks and gums—not the least part of my mouth's interior escaped him.

Not there!

With a howl of rage he flung my naked

body from him, glaring on me, and panting as though he had just been running a mile.

Then another idea occurred to him.

"Who saw him come in?" he demanded.

"I did," the treacherous Guy replied with a grin, "I spotted him at the further end of the lane, and it was a regular lark to see——"

"Silence, you chattering idiot," Aaron fiercely interrupted, "vat did he wear when you saw him, when he came in?"

"What he has got on now," replied Guy, surlily.

"Nothing else—no cap? Where's his cap?"

And he gazed eagerly round the room.

"He didn't have no cap, Aaron," Mr. Vigors interposed, "he had only them old trousers that you pulled to bits, and the jacket."

"What jacket?"

"This jacket," said Guy. "Hi! d'ye mind what you're up to, so I tell yer! It's my jacket; I only lent it to him!"

Nor was it without reason that the conscienceless young rascal raised this outcry.

Had the garment been the lawful property of the Jew dwarf, and he had detected my innocent young friend in the act of stealing it, he could not have pounced on him with greater ferocity.

"You thief!" he exclaimed, "you daylight robber! would you, too, attempt to play tricks on me?"

And in an instant he had the collar of the jacket tight in his grasp.

But Master Foster was too wary for him.

The art of slipping out of a jacket the moment the hand of an enemy was laid on it was quite familiar with him.

No sooner did Aaron Doomstone grasp the collar, than with a dexterous wriggle the boy's arms were out of it, and it was left empty in his assailant's hands.

But the Jew had no intention of assaulting him.

He had got all he wanted—the jacket!

Quick as thought he dived his hand into the left pocket.

Into the right.

Empty, both of them!

Into the inner pocket at the breast.

Empty—save for one thing.

A perplexing and mysterious thing, the contemplation of which amazed Aaron Doomstone not a little.

What he had discovered in the jacket's inner pocket was the shattered remains of the tooth.

The little ivory box in which the precious talisman had so long and so snugly been deposited.

Over and over again he turned the queer-looking fragments in his hand, with his shaggy eyebrows knitted wonderingly together.

Suddenly, however, the truth seemed to flash to his mind.

This was the key to the Golden Glazier's secret!

No wonder that he had kept it so well!

Despite his fierce rage, Aaron Doomstone could not refrain from a grin of admiration for his departed friend's cunning.

"This is vere it vonce vas," he exclaimed, turning to me threateningly. "Vat have you done with it. Speak—quickly!"

It would have been easy enough to have told him, and it was a great wonder that, in my fright, I did not do so.

Master Guy Foster was at present its custodian.

After ransacking every pocket of the jacket, Aaron Doomstone had flung it down, and its owner had picked it up and put it on.

But what might I hope to gain by telling him?

Was it likely that he would treat me more mercifully?

Not in the least likely. Half dead with fright—as I was—I still had left strength sufficient to tell me that, unless through a miracle, I should never leave that room alive.

"Vill you speak, young devil's imp!" exclaimed Aaron, enraged beyond description at my sullen silence.

But I still remained dumb, as much through terror as resolution.

Grinding his teeth savagely, Mr. Doomstone reflected for a few moments, and then whispered to Stumpy Vigors, who, with a shrug of his shoulders, seemed to assent to the other's proposition.

"You may go down stairs, Guy," said he, addressing my treacherous young friend, who all this while had been looking on with as much amusement as though what he was witnessing was a stage play.

"What's up, then?" observed the boy, with a look of disappointment.

"Ask no questions---be off."

"Oh, hang it; you know you might let a feller see the end of the game. I ain't like a milksop; I shan't split, tain't likely!"

And the young ruffian gave himself the airs of a well-seasoned and trustworthy villain; but it was of no use, and, to his great disgust, he was pushed out of the room, the door of which was made fast.

"Now, we shall see!" exclaimed Aaron Doomstone, with a look of devilry in his eyes that made me shiver. "Do you know vat they do to little pirds as vill not sing as petter as they can? Do you know that, my tear?"

I was so frightened that I had now no voice to answer him even if I had the inclination.

"You don't know, my goot poy; then I vill tell you—they plind 'em!"

The involuntary start of horror I gave caused the hideous dwarf a grin of satisfaction.

"They bind fine needles to the end of a bit of stick, and they make them hot, and they purn away their sight."

Horrible as this may seem, I knew it to be true.

Amongst the ruffianly community of "bird fanciers" who train tiny feathered songsters for singing matches, it is not at all uncommon for the revolting device mentioned by Aaron Doomstone to be resorted to.

It "sobers 'em down," and gives force of expression to their song, the bird-blinding monsters say. No doubt of it. When the great day of reckoning comes, it will appear with how much force of expression the poor blinded birds appealed for vengeance on their torturers.

But what had the villainous custom of the bird-fanciers to do with Mr. Doomstone's designs against me.

That I was not long in discovering.

With diabolical coolness he produced from his pocket the tiny little spear with the gold knob.

The reader recollects it—the little instrument with which I so cleverly cheated the Jew dwarf into believing that he was the possessor of the Golden Glazier's legacy.

The last time that I beheld it in his hands, I could scarcely forbear laughing at how neatly I had fooled him.

But I didn't laugh now!

"Ve vill not treat you cruel as they treat the little pirds, my tear," he remarked, with a diabolical chuckle, "to make them sing, they poke out poth their eyes at once, put ve vill only put out one of your peepers, only one, if you sing out sharp and at once; if you don't, ve shall vant t'other one to-morrow!"

Now I saw the terrible fate that was in store for me!

There was a window in the room, and, reckless of how high it was, indifferent to the fact that I was stark naked, and with but one idea—to escape the dreadful torture of having my eye thrust out—I suddenly sprang up and made a desperate jump, flinging myself with all my force against the window, that was only protected by a dirty Holland blind.

But my tormentors were two quick for me.

True I succeeded in smashing the window, and utterly demolishing four or five panes of glass, and shattering the frame.

But all I gained by the daring attempt was to cut both my elbows and bruise my forehead.

In an instant, both Vigors and the Jew had hold on me, and I was hauled back and flung on the floor.

Then the man with the wooden leg withdrew from his pocket a stout cord, and bound my arms to my sides, and with a rag of my dilapidated trousers made an off-hand gag for my mouth.

Then with fiendish deliberation, and with his great hand shaking all the while with fury, Aaron Doomstone held the tiny steal spear in a pair of pinchers in the flame of the candle.

"Better knock him on the head at once, Aaron," suggested the more humane Stumpy Vigors; "infernal work this!"

"My tear, we would knock his head all to pieces with much pleasure, if we could knock the secret out of it," returned the dwarf, with a devilish grin; "put since we can't do that, we must try vat coaxing vill do?"

And he ejected a spirt of spittle from

his ugly lips, to try if the little spear was yet hot enough.

And I have no doubt in the world but that it was his full intent to perpetrate his horrible design.

But it was not to be.

After all, I had not bruised my head and cut my elbows in vain.

Both Vigors and the villainous Jew looked startled as they heard hasty steps ascending the stairs.

Then came a hasty knock at the door.

"It's the poy, curse him; drive him down, Vigors; we don't vant him here!" exclaimed Doomstone.

"D'ye hear?"

This from my young friend who had his mouth at the keyhole.

"What is it?"

"Stow your game, whatever it is. Trap downstairs! Wants to know what the smashing of winders means."

With a growl of impatience and an imprecation on the whole fraternity of "traps," Aaron Doomstone continued to busy himself at the candle flame.

Mr. Vigors, however, was in a terrible state of alarm.

"Cut it, Aaron—you *must*, I tell you! It's hot enough for me already, as you know. This is the second time this week they've been here."

"I von't detain you a half-minute, my goot friend," replied the dwarf, and he withdrew the little steel spear from the candle flame red-hot.

"No, I tell you!" exclaimed Stumpy Vigors, not sorry, I am willing to believe, that the diabolical sport was interrupted. "Take him away to your own house, and do as you like with him. I won't share the risk. I can't afford it."

With a growl of rage Aaron Doomstone flung down the terrible little implement that had so nearly cost me an eye.

"And this is vat you call friendship, ish it?" he snarled; "very goot! I vill have him at my own house, and then there vill pe no interruption; p'r'aps you can lend me something to make the slippery little devil safe till the morning."

"He's safe enough, isn't he?"

"Vat, tied vith a bit of string! No, my goot friend, he ish not safe enough. A pair of handcuffs would pe the thing!"

"You're easily served, then, if that's all you want," returned Mr. Vigors, and hastily quitting the room he speedily returned with a pair of small, stout handcuffs, with which, after the cord that bound me had been cut, were made fast about my wrists.

"Where's the poy?" asked Aaron Doomstone.

"He's outside. Here, Guy?"

And my young friend entered, and cast a keen and curious glance about the room to see what had happened during his absence.

"Vill you earn a pound, my tear?" the Jew dwarf asked him; "ready money paid down on the nail?"

"Ah, or thirty shillin's either," returned the young fellow, waggishly; "I'm not particular to a bob or so. What's the job?"

"Mind him," said Aaron, at the same time giving me a malicious kick as I lay on the ground; "stay up here with him, and never once take your eyes off him, d'ye hear? Mind him till the morning."

"Well, it isn't a hard job, but it isn't a warm one," returned Master Guy Foster, glancing with a shrug of his shoulders at the shatterred windows; "can't I have a bit of fire?"

"How can you with the chimbley blocked up," remarked Mr. Vigors.

"Well, then, let's have a drop of something warm and some bacca," replied the accomplished young rascal (he was older than me by two years, as I afterwards found); "throw in a taste of hot rum and some bacca, and I'll say done."

And this being agreed to, with a meaning wag of his head and a shake of his fist, Aaron Doomstone hastily took his departure with the landlord of the "Wreckers."

"'STAND WHERE YOU ARE!' SAID HE, IN A HARSH VOICE."—(See next week.)

# CHAPTER XX.

### IN WHICH I GNAW A PRECIOUS BUTTON OFF GUY FOSTER'S JACKET.

A FEW minutes afterwards, Mr. Vigors returned to the chamber in which I lay a handcuffed prisoner, and brought my precocious companion a steaming glass of rum-and-water and a short pipe and some tobacco.

To my great amazement, too, he brought in, flung over his shoulder, an old pair of trousers many sizes too large for me, but none the less acceptable on that account.

"Poke your legs into these, you miserable young beggar," said he, at the same time assisting me to do so. "You're half dead now, and the cold will finish you quite by the morning, if you lay here naked all night."

Then he retired, locking the door behind him.

As for my young gaoler, he proceeded to make himself comfortable.

There was a kind of drugget on the floor, and this he took up and rolled himself in it, and squatted in a corner on the ground, and then proceeded to the deliberate enjoyment of his grog and pipe.

Not to the silent enjoyment of those luxuries, however.

Evidently he had made up his mind that some prime sport was to be got in the way of jeering and "chaffing" me.

In this, however, he was mistaken.

Stupefied by the fast succeeding perils I had of late undergone, I lay completely indifferent to his brutal jocosity and his taunts.

Finding these unavailing to rouse me, he proceeded to acts of petty barbarity, and as I lay helpless kicked and pinched me, and pulled my hair, and blew his vile tobacco smoke into my eyes.

At last, wearied and disgusted with his efforts, he gave me a final kick, and having finished his glass, coiled himself in his drugget, and composed himself to sleep.

He knew that I was safe enough!

The door was locked. He was stronger than I was; moreover, my hands were manacled with the handcuffs, that galled my wrists terribly.

In a few minutes the short pipe dropped out of his mouth, and the fumes of the grog overcoming his brain, he began to snore.

As for me, it would be superfluous to say that I could not sleep.

I lay awake, tearless with terror, and with but one thought—what would become of me when, to-morrow morning, Aaron Doomstone caused me to be carried to his own house?

Would he repent of his horrible intent to blind me?

As I thought of that dreadful little spear glowing with heat, my eyes winced beneath their lids, and, cold as the night was, beads of perspiration stood on my forehead.

Meanwhile, the night was advancing—twelve, one o'clock chimed from the churches, and Master Guy Foster was still snoring most unmelodiously.

Yes, there was the little villain warm and snug enough, for, besides the drugget about his shoulders, he was fully dressed even to his cap.

He was fully dressed, and wore the jacket the warmth of which I knew.

The jacket, in the topmost button of which lay concealed the cause of all the terrible anguish I had endured.

The Golden Glazier's most unprofitable legacy!

"Of what use is it to me?" I sighed. "Of what use was it ever? I wish from the bottom of my heart that I had never seen nor heard of it!"

And so I lay moaning and lamenting, while my young gaoler was comfortably snoring, when, all on a sudden, there came into my head a bold idea.

Would it be possible to escape if I had my little red twinkler?

True, my hands were bound—but!

And that I thought it over for a little while, with all my pulses throbbing at a pretty rate.

What was the risk?

Just nothing at all.

There could be no doubt as to what would be my fate if I was compelled to remain where I was.

It was impossible to increase my peril.

I would chance it !

The corner in which Master Guy Foster was lying was so close to me that his feet touched my body almost.

The tallow candle was nearly burnt out and was terribly in need of snuffing; nevertheless, there was light enough from it to enable me to see the position in which my companion was lying.

His jacket was buttoned tight under his chin, and his arms were folded over his breast.

This was unfortunate !

As before mentioned, the hollow button in which my jewel lay so snug was the top button, and his arm covered it completely.

Nothing could be done until this condition of affairs was altered.

The floor was strewn with the shreds Aaron Doomstone had made in tearing up my old trousers ; and, taking a longish strip of rag between my bound hands, I softly shuffled closer to the sleeper.

Never, before or since, in all my life did I ever listen to sweeter music than was his snoring !

Stooping over him, I allowed the end of the rag to dangle over his face and just tickle his nose.

At first he only snored louder under the infliction, and did not alter his position in the least.

I tried again, with my heart in my mouth, as the reader may be sure.

Better luck this time !

With a noise between a snore and a growl, he flung up an arm—the arm that had been covering the precious button—made a feeble attempt to scratch the irritated organ, and then, to my great joy, let the arm drop by his side !

As the reader will remember at a certain stage of these proceedings my tormentors had tied a strip of rag about my mouth as a gag.

This, however, was easily removed.

It was necessary to remove it, as will presently appear.

I waited a little while to make sure that my enemy had relapsed into his former condition of profound slumber, and then I commenced operations.

## CHAPTER XXI.

### I AM COMPELLED TO ADMINISTER A SEDATIVE DOSE TO MASTER GUY FOSTER.

I WANTED that precious little jewel out of its shell, and the only way I had of accomplishing the feat was by means of my teeth !

Noiselessly shifting and shifting, until my mouth was just over the button, I closed my mouth on it.

My first idea had been to bite it short off at the threads that attached it to the jacket.

But the shank was sunk into the stuff, and I could not get at the stitches.

There was nothing left for it but to endeavour to crack the shell of brass with my teeth.

And this—for my young jaws had been used to rough work—would not have been so difficult a job had the button been detached and I had it all to myself.

As it was, however, it was a very different matter.

I dare not pull it forward so as to get it between my back grinders and take a good grip at it.

I was compelled to nibble it with my front teeth.

But, thanks to the potency of Mr. Vigors's rum, Guy never abated a jot of his snoring.

At last, to my inexpressible satisfaction, though my unlucky front teeth ached dreadfully, and were all set a bleeding, the top of the button was released from the bottom.

There lay my red twinkler, safe and sound, in the hollow beneath.

I spat on the button top, and, dipping my tongue's tip down onto the gem, fished it out triumphantly.

Still Master Guy Foster snored most musically.

Now to release my hands of their iron fastening !

Holding the red gem between my teeth, I drew it across the links that connected the wrist-bands, all the time in fear lest, after all, I was mistaken in its peculiar virtue.

No!

Again the crisp, crackling sound, and the faint flame such as accompanies the striking of a lucifer match (I could almost imagine that I felt the heat of it on my lips), and when I gave the links a twist my hands were free!

What next?

Might I escape by the door?

Would my miraculous talisman help me there?

No; not a chance of it.

With no more noise than a cat would make, I examined the fastenings by the candle light.

I could see through the chinks the heavy bolt shot into its socket; but it was impossible to reach it with my invincible iron-cutter without danger of losing it.

Then I turned to the window.

Large enough was the aperture I had made in my previous frantic endeavour to escape, to admit of the passage of a man's body, let alone one of the diminutive size of mine.

But I dare not make my exit that way.

Had there been a water-pipe or any other means of descent visible, I am sure that I should have taken my chance.

But I could see nothing.

When I held the curtains aside and looked out, it was like facing a solid black wall.

Again I was at a standstill.

My "good fortune," as I thought it, was all a mockery then.

I was no nigher liberty than when my cunning little talisman lay snug in the button of the snorer's jacket!

Stay! there was the chimney.

Yes; but had I not heard Stumpy Vigors declare that it was blocked up?

In what way was it blocked up?

I turned from the window, resolved on satisfying myself.

And then I made a terrible discovery!

My villainous young friend was awake!

When I drew the window curtain aside, I had stood, I dare say, as long as half a minute looking out, and all the while the keen night wind was blowing in on him.

There he was, sitting bolt upright in his drugget, rubbing his sleepy eyes, and growling and swearing horribly at being disturbed.

At present he had not seen me,—he was evidently under the impression that I was lying down where he had last seen me.

A slight noise I made, however, startled him to sudden wakefulness, and then he discovered his error.

Never shall I forget his look of blank amazement and terror, as he saw me with my hands free!

He recovered his self-possession quickly, however, and, snatching up the poker that lay in the fender by his side, he scrambled out of his bedclothes and made at me.

It was an awful moment, and I can only account for what immediately followed, on the supposition that, goaded by disappointment and desperation, I was not far from mad.

With a savage growl he raised the poker, and in another instant it would have descended on my unlucky head.

But I was too quick for him.

The iron bands of the fractured handcuffs were still about my wrists, and springing at him, I struck him with all my might across the face with the one with which my right wrist was encircled.

So sudden, severe, and unexpected was the blow, that he staggered back, catching at the table for support.

This was an advantage not to be lost.

Before he could recover, I followed the first blow with a second, the iron ring this time cutting a terrible gash over his temple, and down he tumbled to the ground without a word or a groan even.

Was I afraid that I had killed him?

Not in the least, I am ashamed to say.

A boy, young as was I, friendless and ignorant, I was not even aware of how hideous a crime murder was.

To be sure, I was aware that it was a hanging matter; but to my benighted mind that was only a convenient way the law had of "squaring" the affair.

Besides this, as before stated, I was half mad with rage and disappointment, and with this, truth, though a shameful one, must not be shirked.

I took up the poker that had slipped from his hand and dealt him a crack over the head with it, that assuredly would have broken it had it not been of extraordinary thickness.

Now for the chimney!

Had it been "blocked" with bars of iron I should not have been daunted.

My tiny crimson conjurer was safe in my mouth, and by this time I had full faith in it.

But the obstacle was of no such a formidable nature.

It was only a sack of shavings that was stuffed into the aperture, and though it was a hard tug I managed to haul it down.

Now for the ascent!

And was there nothing I could wear over my naked shoulders?

Still madly bold, wickedly desperate, I at once resolved to strip my prostrate enemy of his jacket.

It was not theft; he had given it me once!

Stunned and insensible, had he been a Guy by nature as well as name, he could not have submitted to the operation more passively.

I took the jacket and I took his cap, callous young villain that I was, and, buttoning the one up to my chin and pulling the other well over my ears, I stepped up on to the hobs of the fireplace, and was speedily half way into the chimney's sooty throttle.

Not so very sooty either.

Evidently there had not been a fire in the grate below for a very long time, and the chimney pot was off; which I daresay was the reason why the sack of shavings had been employed.

It was not a very high climb—not more than twelve or fifteen feet—and then I enjoyed the blessed sensation of the air of liberty blowing on my grimy face.

---

## CHAPTER XXII.

### I AM LOCKED UP IN THE CAGE AT GREAT SNORLEY—I FALL IN WITH STRANGE COMPANY.

I WAS doomed, however, to discover that sweet as is the breath of liberty, like many other good things it is possible to have too much of it.

If anyone doubts my assertion, let him try it for himself on a strange and lofty housetop at between three and four o'clock on a winter's morning.

It was fortunate, indeed, that I had despoiled my fallen enemy of his raiment, otherwise I should have stood an uncommon good chance of being frozen to death.

As it was, my situation was by no means an enviable one.

It was still so pitch dark that it was at the risk of breaking my neck that I moved forward this way or that; yet, for my life's sake, I dare not remain in the immediate vicinity of Mr. Vigors's chimney.

Supposing that I had not killed Guy Foster, he might at any moment recover and give the alarm, when vigorous search would certainly be the immediate result.

So I made my way, slowly clambering up the ridges and sliding down into the furrows, always making quite sure of the safety of my foremost foot before the other followed it, until I had put twenty houses at least between myself and my enemies.

Then, discovering a snug crevice between two chimney stacks, I crept in there to wait for the dawn of daylight.

With the very earliest glimpse of it I was astir again.

I had no plans.

My only thought was to escape down into the street, and to put a long distance between the "Wreckers" and myself as soon as possible.

And in this my lucky star once more showed itself in the ascendant, though its rising startled me as much as the evilest of omens could.

I was still crouched between the chimney stacks, when all of a sudden my amazed ears were saluted by a gruff voice exclaiming—

"Look alive, Teddy. Let's make short work of it. It's precious little we shall get by the job anyhow."

Had I been at the summit of the stack instead of at its foot, I do believe I should, in my fright, have slid down the first convenient chimney-pot, even though I had alighted on somebody's breakfast kettle.

It was fortunate that I remained quiet.

Had I been on the parapet instead of in the middle of a centre gutter, I think that I must have tumbled headlong down into the street with fright.

What was it that the men were to make short work of?

What but me?

Judge, then, of the sensation of relief I experienced when I saw rise from the front of the house immediately before me the unmistakable visage of an honest Irish bricklayer's labourer with a hod of mortar on his shoulder!

He landed on the roof, and his mate quickly followed, bearing a load of slate.

Hastily concealing myself behind a chimney stack, I waited a little until they both crossed the ridge of the roof, and were out of sight.

Then I crept hastily forward, and, to my inexpressible joy, found that it was exactly as I had hoped.

The bricklayers had ascended by means of a ladder.

Before you could count ten I had hold of it, and disregarding the stepping rails, clapped my legs about the sides of it, and slid swiftly down to the ground.

Free again!

Such was the involuntary exclamation that I almost cried aloud, as, five minutes afterwards, I halted, panting and breathless, at a street corner, fully half-a-mile from the place from which I had so miraculously made my escape.

But instantly came the reflection— "Free to do what?"

Free to be collared by the first policeman who happened to notice me.

How could I hope to avoid such a fate?

A jacket I had, and a serviceable cap, but my lower extremities were as bare as when I was born.

Bare, that is to say, excepting the coating of soot they had contracted in my ascent of the chimney, while my hands and face were hideously besmeared with the same sort of dirt.

But it seemed as though a lucky day had set in for me after the many dismally unfortunate ones I had of late endured.

"Clo'! ole clo'!"

An early bird of the Hebrew species was already abroad, and presently, turning the corner, he faced me.

"Clo'! any old clo'!" I'll puy your preeches, sir," he remarked to me facetiously; and then, evidently struck by my strange appearance, he exclaimed, more seriously—

"Hallo! vat ish this? Vat lunatic asylum have you escaped from, eh?"

It is wonderful how readily the father of lies steps forward to the aid of his apt little pupils!

"No lunatic asylum at all," said I. "I'm running away from—from my master, who whops me so I can't stay with him any longer."

"Running avay in sich a hurry that you hadn't time to put on your trousers, eh? Vat vas your master, eh, my lad?"

"A sweep," I answered, bodly.

"To be sure; I might ha' known that by the look of you," returned the "old clo'" man, completely thrown off his guard. "Poor leetle poy!"

And then, his dominant desire for doing "pisness" surmounting his sympathy, he continued.

"I shay, do you vant a pair of trousers? I've got a pair in my pag as vill shoot you as though they vas made to measure. Not much vorn, they ain't, and you shall have 'em for a shillin'."

There was a chance if I only had a shilling.

"I haven't got any money," said I; "I wish I had."

It was a street that was not much frequented we were in, and, as yet, it was so early that there were very few people about.

The "old clo'" man seemed resolved to do business somehow.

He clapped down his bag and felt the texture of the jacket I was wearing.

As before mentioned it was a very excellent jacket—the produce of some robbery in all probability—and, grimed with soot as it was, my friend at once saw that it was a garment out of which something might be made.

"Vill you svhop?" he asked.

"Will I what?"

"Will you svhop and shange? I've got a whole shoot as vill——"

I understood him well enough now.

"All right!" said I, interrupting him. "I'll change fast enough, if *you're* agreeable. Where's the things you are speaking of?"

Young as I was, the immense advantage of exchanging Master Guy Foster's clothes for others that were not known was too apparent for me to overlook it.

The "shoot" that the "ole clo'" man produced from his bag was neither new nor fashionable.

From its appearance, I should say that it had been once the property of a plasterer's boy of decidedly untidy habits and, moreover, it was at least three sizes too big for me.

It was a complete suit, however—jacket, vest, and trousers.

"Will you give 'em to me for my jacket?" I eagerly asked.

"Yes—for the jacket and cap I mean," replied the hungry Israelite.

"But—but I want 'em now," said I. "How shall I——"

"Nothing ish more eashy," replied the ready-witted ole clo' man. "Shtep into this doorvay, and I vill hold my pag pefore you. There you are, ash private ash though you vas a shentleman in his ped-room!"

In two minutes the metamorphosis was accomplished; the Jew stuffed my, or rather Guy Foster's, jacket and cap into his bag, and, fully rigged, excepting as regards cap and bouts, as a plasterer's boy, I ran off at a rate that must have caused him astonishment.

As to where I was running I neither knew nor cared.

My only idea was to escape the clutches of Aaron Doomstone.

And it may occur to the right-minded reader that this might have been accomplished in the easiest way in the world.

I might have made for the nearest police-station and confessed all.

I had done no great harm, after all, and the police would protect me.

But the reader forgets about Guy Foster.

I could not forget him.

Ever since I had quitted, by means of the chimney, the room in which I had been a fettered prisoner, I had been haunted with dismal fears as to the fate of my gaoler.

Had I killed him?

He looked awfully still and ghastly when I took a last peep at him.

If I went to a police-station and con-

fessed all, my murderous attack on Guy Foster must, of course, be included.

No, I dare not face the police.

I dare not stay in London.

It was many hours since I had eaten anything, but my situation was too desperate for me to think much of that.

I would make for the country. What part mattered not.

Once fairly away from London, I would seek work in the fields, or at some farm, and never again return to the scenes of my many perils.

With this firm resolution I set forward at a steady pace, and never once slackened it until I was fairly out of London, and on the Kentish country road.

Then, quite worn out and exhausted, I came to a halt.

There was nothing for me but to beg a bit of bread and a drink of water.

I, the Golden Glazier's heir, the possessor of a "fortune" to rob me of which the wealthy Jew thief, Aaron Doomstone, would sacrifice his eyes almost, was fainting for a mouthful of food!

Many a time since have I thought with a smile of the peculiarity of the situation, but I did not smile then.

I derived no comfort from my mysterious treasure.

Ever since I had bitten it out of the button as Guy Foster lay asleep, I had carried it in my mouth, and there it still was, an inconvenience to my tongue, and an impediment to my free breathing.

I had no use for it.

It had been the prime cause of all that I had suffered, and, only that it seemed such a childish thing to do, I believe that I should have spat it out and left it on the road.

I am quite sure that if it would have proved as grateful to my palate as a morsel of bread, I should have swallowed it.

Well, I begged a bit of bread.

It was the first time in my life that I had been subjected to such humiliation, but I am sorry to say that it was not the last.

It will not be worth the reader's while to come tramping with me through the many, many days following that first day, or to discuss with me the sorry meals I did odd jobs for, or failing that, that I begged for.

I very much doubt if the reader

would care to sleep as I slept during that miserable time—under haystacks, in out-houses, cattle sheds, anywhere.

It was a desperate attempt to better my lodging that led to a break in the dreary monotony of my vagabond existence.

Hitherto I had carefully avoided an enclosed place to sleep in.

My terror of Aaron Doomstone was so great that I dare not risk it.

The lee of a hay-rick was not so comfortable as the interior of a barn; but the barn had a door to it, and supposing that one fine night I should wake up to discover that the hideous Jew dwarf had found that door, and had entered in at it, closing it behind him.

But it was now nearly three weeks since I had set eyes on my arch enemy, and I began to grow less afraid of him.

One bitter cold evening, therefore, having somehow picked up a meal in the picturesque village of Great Snorley, I availed myself of the open door of a barn, at the extremity of the said village, and finding some loose hay there, and a few sacks, I curled up in a corner, and composed myself for a sounder and warmer night's rest than I had enjoyed since the happy time of the parlour cupboard in Rats' Castle.

But, alas! I had yet to discover that tramps, and trespassers, and vagabonds of every degree were hated as the vilest vermin in Great Snorley, and treated with as little ceremony.

I had been watched to my roost, it seemed.

Anyhow, I had barely completed my first hour's enjoyment of it when a lantern light flashed in my sleepy eyes, and I was dragged by the legs out of my warm nest.

My first thoughts, of course, were of Mr. Doomstone, but it was a much more impatient a personage than the stunted Jew fence of Lambeth.

It was the beadle of Great Snorley.

"Come out, you skunk! Come out o' this, you trampin' villain! Ah! it's no use you're strugglin'; I'm a match for you, you big, hulkin', rick-burnin' ruffian! Out you come."

As he truly observed, it was no use my struggling; nor was there much danger in his boast that he was a match for me, considering that he was close on

six feet high, and stout in proportion, and I was such a tremendously big fellow that his waistcoat would have made me an entire suit.

Straightway he lugged me to the road-side "lock-up," which was about a quarter of a mile distant, and opening the door by means of a massive key, thrust me in and banged to the door again.

He pushed me into the place with such force, that I was sent staggering back almost to the further end of it, and was then only brought up by coming into collision with a previous occupant of the watch-house, who was crouched on the ground.

I speedily discovered that it was a man.

"Confound you! curse you! you blundering fool! I'd wring your neck, if I only had the use of my hands."

The place was in utter darkness, so that, as I need not mention, it caused me a pretty fright to hear this.

To be sure I had stumbled against him roughly, and caught him by the hair with both my hands to save myself from falling.

"I beg your pardon, sir," said I, retreating to the other end of the cage. "I didn't mean to do it; the man pushed me so hard."

"Hang him! Rot him! He pushed me hard too. He pushed *her* hard, and she so sick and weak! Pushed her down in the mud, the beast! He did, sir, as true as you are a living man. But I spoilt the gold lace on his coat. Curse 'em all. I would have strangled him, had they not been so quick at slipping the handcuffs over my wrists."

I could make him no answer—I was so much afraid of him.

He ground his teeth in rage as he spoke, and was evidently half mad with drink or excitement.

Who was " she " that he spoke of?

Was she his wife? Was she, as well as he, crouching over there in the impenetrable darkness?

But my wondering speculations on this score were speedily set at rest.

"Hu-sh! what is it, my darling?"

It was the man who spoke, and curious indeed was the sudden change in his voice. A moment ago so harsh and furious, now so gentle and woman-like.

"I am just a little thirsty—only just a little."

It was not a woman's voice, but that of a child. A mild voice, full of sweet patience.

"Aye, so you are, my darling, both hungry and thirsty; and they shut us up here with less compassion than though we were prowling dogs. Perhaps they place a pitcher of water in these places. Man, do you know if there is any water here ?"

This was to me.

My entry had been so sudden that he had no opportunity of seeing how little I was.

"I am not a man, sir," I answered. "I am only a boy. I don't know if they place water to drink in watch-houses, for I was never in one before. But I will feel about."

And I did; but there was no pitcher or water vessel of any kind.

"Never mind," spoke the little girl, in a voice that betokened how parched and dry her mouth was. "I am not *very* thirsty. I can wait."

But now that she spoke again it seemed to me that there was something strange in her tone. I don't know how to describe in what way it was strange, but she didn't speak as though the man with her was her father, or her brother, or any near relative.

I longed for a look at the strange pair; but, though I strained my sight till the effort became painful, I was unable to penetrate the black darkness.

Presently the man spoke again.

"You are a boy, I think you said ?"

"Yes, sir."

"How old a boy ?"

I told him as well as I was able.

"What have they brought you here for ?"

I told him that, too.

"I see," said he; "you are a poor, houseless wanderer as we are, eh, Sissy ? Tell him that we are the same as he is, my darling. He speaks like an honest boy."

"Yes, indeed, we are wanderers," spoke the little girl.

And again her tones were so strange and sad, that I longed more and more for a sight of her.

"Come and sit with us, boy," said the strange man. "Don't blunder again, stupid !" he exclaimed, as I felt my way across the cage to the corner where I knew they were. "My little girl is on this side of me; sit you down on the other side."

I was afraid to refuse him, and did exactly as he told me.

"What's your name, boy ?" he presently inquired.

"Joe, sir."

"And my name is Blott; and this is Sissy. Now we understand each other, eh ?"

It was evident that he expected me to make some answer, so I said "Yes," though so far from understanding each other, I grew more perplexed each moment.

"You are a boy who has travelled about a great deal ?" he presently remarked, giving me a nudge with his elbow.

"No, not very much," I began.

"Don't deny it ! " he exclaimed, nudging me again, and by the tone of his voice, giving me to understand that I had best not contradict him; "you may trust us. We want you to trust us, because we want your opinion, eh, Sissy ? "

"Yes, we want you to trust us," said Sissy, in her sad voice.

"You have travelled about a great deal," continued the man in the dark, "and you have seen those placards stuck about the walls? Of course you *have* seen those placards on the walls! You couldn't have missed 'em ! "

And this time he nudged me once, twice, thrice, as though to warn me to take mighty good care how I contradicted him this time.

"I've seen a good many placards on the wall, sir," I replied. "Which one was—was yours, sir ? "

"Ours ! Do you hear that, Sissy ? He knows, you see, that there *is* a placard out about us."

And he nudged me approvingly.

"To be sure, my boy; how should you know which placard alludes to us ? But you'll recollect it when I describe it. Do you understand ? You will recollect when I describe it ! "

And once again his elbow gave me a significant hint.

"Yes, I understand, sir."

"To be sure you do ! Well, the placard I mean is one that offers ever so much money—a thousand pounds, I think — for somebody's apprehension. Now, *don't* tell me that you don't remember seeing that."

If I told the truth, I should undoubtedly have told him that I did not remember seeing it; but, under the peculiar circumstances, I hesitated to make any reply at all.

"A thousand pounds reward," continued the mysterious man in the dark, "for the capture of a little girl with flaxen hair and dark blue eyes. For her capture, dead or alive!"

"I can't say," I began.

But he interrupted me with a dig of his elbow so ferocious, that I was almost compelled to utter a cry of pain.

"A little girl with dark blue eyes and flaxen, curly hair, I tell you," he repeated, "in company with a ragged man—a tall man with a bushy head. Now, perhaps, you recollect?"

What did it all mean?

I had seen no such placard.

I did not believe that anything so monstrous was in existence; but it was quite certain that the man, whoever he was, was terribly anxious that I should father the lies he was uttering.

But how did I know the harm I should do as regards the child that was with him, and whom he evidently wished to impose on?

I was just on the point of telling him that I had neither seen nor heard anything of the placard, when I felt a little soft hand feeling for mine, and when it found it, it pressed it meaningly.

At least, so it seemed to me.

It seemed, by the urgent pressure of its slender little fingers, to say, "Humour him; don't thwart him. It will be better for me if you let him have his way."

"You remember it now?" he repeated, savagely.

"Oh, yes, I remember it now."

I had done right, the little hand pressed mine thankfully.

"Very good, very good indeed," returned the mysterious fellow in satisfied tones; "dead or alive. You distinctly remember that the placard says 'dead or alive?'"

"Oh, yes; I recollect that quite as well as the other part."

"I knew that you would. Now I want your opinion. What should you think of a man who would rescue that little girl from the hands of the bloodthirsty wretches who would as soon give a thousand pounds for her dead as alive?"

"I should say that he was the right sort. I should think——"

"Stop a minute. What would be your opinion of a man who had sworn to protect that little girl with his life—to fight to his last gasp for her? To kill her rather than that they should take her from him?"

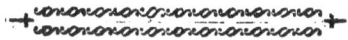

## CHAPTER XXIII.

### I AM, THOUGHTLESSLY, THE MEANS OF ARMING MAD BLOTT WITH A TERRIBLE WEAPON.

As Mr. Blott proceeded he became more and more excited.

I could not see him, but I could feel him rising gradually from his recumbent position until he was on his knees.

"Yes," he repeated, loud enough for the midnight traveller on the road to have heard, "to kill her rather than they should lay a finger on her; what is your opinion of such a man?"

The little hand that rested on mine trembled very much.

Nevertheless it again pressed mine, enjoining me still to humour her strange companion.

"I should say that he was a very brave sort of man," said I; "but I shouldn't kill her if I was him."

"He would not kill her," he returned, his fierce voice suddenly subsiding, and becoming soft and gentle. "I am only speaking of what he might in the last extremity be driven to. Unless they drove him to it, he would not hurt one hair of her darling head."

And I could feel and hear that he

stooped over the little girl and kissed her.

"And now," said he, presently recovering himself, "since I have heard your opinion, and since Sissy, too, has heard it, I think we had best try and get a little sleep."

Of all the strange company it ever was my lot to fall in with, surely this was the strangest.

Had I been older and more experienced, I daresay that I should have been able at once to have found a clue to the mystery; but, as it was, I could only lay wide awake, as the reader may be sure, puzzling my brain as to what it all meant.

It was like a page out of one of those story books with the coloured pictures that my old chums of the "dark arches" used to buy, and read out to us till our hair stood on end.

It was certain, too, that the "tall man with the bushy beard," who would fight for the little girl to the last, and even go to the length of killing her rather than she should fall into the hands of her enemies, was no other than the strange personage whose voice I had heard but whose face I had not as yet seen.

Who was the tall man with the bushy beard who bore the odd name of Blott?

Who was the child Sissy?

How had they come together? Where had they come from? Where were they going to?

All in the dark, and while my companions were fast asleep, as I thought, over and over again I turned those various questions in my mind, and in the end was exactly as wise as when I began.

I was mistaken, however, when I imagined that my companions were both asleep.

One of them, at least, was awake.

It was the man.

"Good heavens! I never thought of that till now," he muttered, half afraid, and as though some frightful conviction had suddenly dawned on him. "They won't let us go in the morning. They will send me to prison. I shall lose her."

The bare idea was so agonising that he started up on to his feet, and I could dimly make out his tall figure, with the hands fettered at the wrists.

"Cursed fool that I was to strike the wretch!" he exclaimed. "I should have borne with his brutal usage; I should have licked the boot that kicked me rather than raised his anger against us. And I have been lying here like a foolish calf awaiting slaughter! Up, Siss; we must be off. We must break away out of this infernal place. Ah! Bones against bolts. We'll see which is strongest."

And as he spoke these words, in a voice that might have been heard five hundred yards away, in a frenzy he flung his whole weight against the cage door.

It was of heavy, solid oak, with a massive square iron lock, the bolt of which was as thick almost as a man's wrist.

The little girl rose in terror.

"He'll kill himself!" she exclaimed, laying a hand on his arm. "Dear, good Davy, for my sake, desist."

But Davy would not desist.

"Bones against bolts!" he cried, and again and again his tall, sinewy body went crash against the door.

Presently, however, he recoiled from an effort more desperate than the rest, and sank to the ground, groaning in rage and pain, while the little girl stood over him, weeping piteously, and wringing her hands.

Through all my tramping and hard faring, I had taken good care of my tiny red conjuror.

Snugly pinned in a bit of rag in the corner of the soundest pocket my clothes could boast of, there it was still.

I had never tested its marvellous power since the memorable night when I escaped from my prison in Stumpy Vigors's house. I had found no occasion to use it.

At least I might relieve this poor fellow of his handcuffs.

It was a delicate task to handle my tiny iron cutter in the pitch dark, and with my fingers benumbed with cold.

I managed it, however.

Stooping over the prostrate man, I applied it to the connecting links of his iron wristlets, and immediately there followed the crackling and the spark.

He did not see it, for his eyes were closed, but Sissy did, and uttered a little shriek, at which he started, and in doing so the iron links were severed, and his hands were free.

"'WHAT HAS DETAINED YOU?' HE ASKED, SUSPICIOUSLY."—(See Next Week).

With a cry of exultation he leapt to his feet.

He never for an instant suspected that his liberty was owing to any agency of mine; his own strength had accomplished it, he thought.

"Hurrah! Now who will say that bones are no match against bolts?" he exclaimed, with a laugh of mad defiance. "Now let them come and attempt to rob me of my darling!"

And highly elated with his supposed victory of bone and muscle over iron and blacksmithry, he once more flung his weight against the door, and shook it with his now free hands, until it creaked on its hinges.

But it would not yield.

The smith who wrought that lock seemed to have borne in mind that it was for the safe keeping of sturdy vagabonds chiefly, and to have measured out his materials accordingly.

It made me feel quite proud of my tiny talisman when I heard the great fellow wasting his gigantic strength against the stubborn bolt, and reflected with what ease I could overcome the difficulty.

I still held it between my finger and thumb, and, as before mentioned, the door-post had shrunk with time and weather so far from the door, that a finger and thumb no larger than mine might be inserted in the interstice.

Unperceived in the darkness, I applied my charm to the iron, and with the invariable result.

"Once again!" cried David Blott; "hurrah! Once again, and this time it yields!"

And he was right, though it was little enough that he had to do with the achievement.

The door opened outwardly, and as he sprang back, and then bounded forward again to challenge the oaken panels with his broad shoulders, there was heard a loud and sudden crash, and a great gust of chill night wind came blowing in upon us.

Upon Sissy and myself, that is.

The man who called himself David Blott had disappeared.

The force with which he had burst the door open carried him headlong with it, and it was several seconds ere he appeared, panting for breath, and with his face all grazed and bloody (for by this time it was growing towards grey of morning, and I could dimly make out his figure), but laughing loud and in a delirium of joy at his success.

"Ha, ha, ha!" he almost shrieked, "they thought that they had pulled my strength down. They thought, with their infernal blistering and torture, that they had spoilt my claim to my old nickname —Bull Blott! They will alter their opinion when they hear of this—when they see *this!*"

And as he spoke, he released from the box of the lock the fragment of the bolt that still remained there.

A most substantial fragment.

An almost square block of iron, an inch and a half through every way.

He flung away the broken bolt with a gesture of contempt, and then turned to Sissy, who, all this time, had been crouching on the ground with her little face so white with terror, that it showed almost like a light in the dark.

"Come along, my darling!" he exclaimed, catching her by the hand; "we must be off. We must run for our lives, Sissy. Yes, for our lives. Come along."

And he hurried her out of the cage, and as she passed me, she plucked me by the jacket as though she wished me to come too.

Nothing loth—indeed, curious to hear something more about the strangely-matched pair, I made for doing so.

But the man stopped abruptly, and put me back with his hand.

"No spies!" he exclaimed, sternly. "Be content that I have broken your prison for you. Yonder is your road."

And, as he spoke, he pointed the way that was contrary to that to which he was turning his steps.

But Sissy spoke up for me.

"Oh, pray let him come too, Cousin Davy," said she, in imploring accents. "He is homeless, and—and—— Oh, pray let him come with us!"

"No, no, he does not wish to come," the man replied. "He has his own way to go—we have ours. You *have* your own way to go, haven't you, boy?"

But Sissy shook her head at me meaningly.

"All ways are the same to me, sir," I answered. "If there was a way by which

I could do a good turn for anyone, I'd rather take it than any other."

"Oh, pray let him come; only for a little time then," pleaded Sissy.

The man drew me towards him, and, in the uncertain light, peered into my face with his wide-open, staring eyes.

"I can't well see you," said he, "or I would tell you quickly enough if you might be trusted. Since she wishes it, you may keep by us till daylight, till I can see you and make out the sort of boy you are. Step out—step out. Catch hold of her other hand, and help her to run as fast as I run."

But this she could do but for a very little time.

The strange man took such prodigious steps, that before we had run a hundred yards her feet dragged the ground, and she would have fallen, had not his strong arm upheld her.

Then he took her in his arms.

I could see how big she was now; as big as ordinary girls of eight or nine are; but he made no more of her weight than if she had been a mere baby.

And the worst of it was, that being burdened with her had but little effect on his speed.

At a steady run, with a long step, he cleared the ground at so great a pace that I speedily found myself lagging behind and puffing and blowing.

I believe that I should have given up in despair, had it not been for Sissy beckoning and encouraging me over the man's shoulder.

So we continued until at least three miles from our starting point, and well out of the inhospitable village of Great Snorley.

Then he slackened his pace, and waited till I came up with him.

It was daylight now, and for the first time I was enabled to contemplate the shape and make of my strange comrades.

It was the little girl that chiefly interested me.

As before mentioned, she was a child of about eight or nine years old, and, shorn as it was of natural advantages, I think I never beheld a more winning face.

By "shorn of its natural advantages," I mean that the "golden curls" that had been mentioned were missing.

It was evident that they had been clipped close off by an unpractised hand.

Her clothes, too, although of the shabbiest, failed to make *her* look shabby.

It was plain at a glance that they were not *her* clothes—her proper clothes, that is to say.

The delicate white arms that appeared under the coarse and dirty serge sleeves of her frock matched but ill with it, and the common ungainly straw bonnet perched on her little head seemed much more like a joke than the stern reality of poverty.

It is less easy to describe the man.

He must have been at least six feet in height, and, from his build, should have been possessed of prodigious strength.

He looked like a man who had lain ill, however.

His face, which, as regards the lower part, was covered with a bushy beard, was sickly pale, and his eyes were sunken under his massy eyebrows.

But they were not dull eyes.

They glowed in their cavernous hollows like those of an animal of prey.

As I stood still before him, they were turned on me with an expression that caused me to feel anything but comfortable.

Nor were my alarms dissipated when Sissy, perceiving my dismay, made with her pale lips a short, single word there was no mistaking—

"Mad!"

That was the word, and it at once furnished an explanation of his strange behaviour.

It did not account for his possession of the helpless little girl, however.

Worse still, it provided no assurance of her safety. Exactly the reverse.

"Stand where you are, and let me look at you," said he, in a harsh, sharp voice,

I obeyed readily enough.

It was the toss up of a halfpenny, as the saying is, whether I stayed in such strange company, or run away.

But then I did not know the peril that poor, helpless little Siss stood in.

The madman's inspection of me appeared to satisfy him.

"Yes, you are right, my darling," said he, addressing Sissy. "He is honest. He may remain with us. Now I think of it, we may make him useful, He shall be our messenger—our servant; he shall be our watchman against spies. What do you say to that, Joe?"

Anything to humour him.

"I'm agreeable," said I, cheerfully.

"Very well; then the sooner we see about getting some breakfast the better. We must push on, though, 'till we find some sort of shelter."

I was glad to hear him mention about breakfast.

It wasn't as though he had spoken of it speculatively, and as a happy event that a turn of luck might bring about.

He spoke of it as something that he had the means of insuring, and my legs, as well as my heart, went the lighter at the prospect.

A mile or so further and we spied, about a hundred yards off the main road, a sort of rudely-built hut, that at one time evidently served as the abode of some brickmakers; but the clay of the surrounding fields had been long ago used up, and the rough-and-ready little domicile had lost its tenants, and fallen into dilapidation.

It was good enough for our purpose, however.

It had a roof and a hole that represented a fire-place and a chimney, and there were several fine dry bricks about that at a pinch might be made to serve as a tolerable substitute for stools.

But where was the breakfast to come from?

Mr. Blott speedily settled this all-important question.

Instead of a coat, he wore a sort of frock or blouse of dark stuff, and, raising it as high as his waist, he disclosed, buckled round his body, a wide belt of coarse canvas.

From this he took a handful of gold and silver coin.

"We are rich for tramps and beggars, eh, Joe?" he exclaimed with a mad grin that exposed his great white teeth. "It is a rare trade, my boy, properly followed. Prove yourself a faithful servant, and perhaps we may put you in the right way, eh, Sissy?"

He then gave me money enough, and orders to go and buy in the next village some bread and some cooked meat if I could, and a quart of milk in a bottle.

"And look you," said he; "here are five shillings. If you can find a shop where they are sold, buy a pair of boots for yourself."

This was an act of thoughtfulness and generosity that immediately made me feel ashamed of the bad opinion I had all along entertained for the mysterious madman.

"I am very much obliged to you, sir," said I. "I hope that I shall know how to remember it in any way that I can serve you."

"Then we may soon cry quits," said he, eagerly. "Come outside for a moment."

He spoke these words in a low tone, but Sissy heard them, and looked towards us in dismay.

She seemed to know what he designed, and behind his back shook her head imploringly to me, though with what meaning I had not the least idea.

"I have another little errand you can execute in the village," said he, when we were outside the hut.

"Yes, sir."

"It appears to be a largish village, and I daresay besides a shoemaker's you will find an ironmonger's there."

"Yes, sir."

"I wish you to buy me a hammer. There are times when I find a hammer very useful. I generally carry one. I had one when that scoundrelly beadle took me into custody thinking we were beggars and vagabonds, curse him! but they took it away from me. Now you must buy me another."

"I'll try, sir. Is it a little hammer that you want?"

"No, no," he replied, with a shy half look towards the hut as though he thought it not unlikely that Sissy might be listening; "a large hammer is what I want; a heavy hammer with a good long handle."

It was an odd thing for a man who had no trade to follow to require.

"If you could tell me what you want it for, sir, I might be better able to judge of the sort of hammer that will suit you," I ventured to remark.

"I use it for cracking nuts," he replied, quite seriously, but with a strange expression twinkling in his mad eyes. "Now go, and ask no more questions."

Where was the use of asking questions of such a man?

After all, it was no business of mine what he wanted a hammer for.

It could scarcely be concerning that that Sissy had shaken her head.

Perhaps she simply meant that I mustn't refuse to buy him anything he ordered.

Anyhow, I went into the village as directed, and, by good luck, found a store where shoes were sold as well as an ironmonger's, and returned to my new master with a good pair of stout boots on my feet and the materials for breakfast, and the implement he was so anxious for.

It pleased him mightily.

"We only keep one sort of hammer with a long handle," said the ironmonger, "it is the kind that stonebreakers' use; this is it."

A long handle indeed!

Three feet long at least, and with an iron head as large as a turkey's egg, and shaped like it.

Mr. Blott was as pleased with it as is a child with a new toy.

"Now if they come we are ready for 'em, eh, Sissy! Ha, ha! I would not give much for the skull that came within swing of this pretty nut-cracker."

## CHAPTER XXIV.

### I AM TEMPTED TO TURN TRAITOR—THE STRANGE MEN AT THE INN.

AND he swung the hammer round his head and laughed so loud and savage that I was glad to shrink into a corner out of his way.

As for Sissy she was white as paper, and trembling so that she could not keep a limb still.

"You should not, oh, you should not!" she whispered to me tearfully. "You don't know how terrible he can be!"

It was plain enough to me now.

I had been guilty of a dreadful blunder.

It was for no harmless or useful purpose that the desperate madman wanted the hammer, but as an offensive weapon to be used against those whom he regarded as his enemies.

Woe betide the unlucky wretch who ventured within reach of that egg-shaped weight of iron swung in mad Blott's strong arm!

Presently he grew calmer, and assisted me in collecting a stock of old wood with which to make a fire, and we had breakfast, Sissy all the time keeping close to me, and Blott lying down before the fire.

He had not closed his eyes through all the previous night, and I don't know how many nights before; and the heat made him drowsy. It was in vain that he resisted the temptation to sleep.

"Keep a sharp look-out, watchman," said he, to me. "If you see anyone coming this way, no matter who, wake me instantly."

And in a few minutes he was soundly asleep, with the hammer handle fast grasped in his hand, however.

This was the opportunity for which I had been longing.

"Who is he?"

I asked the question of the little girl in a low whisper, but, instead of replying, she laid a finger on her lips, and shook her head.

It was plain that she doubted whether the madman's sleep was genuine.

Possibly she had had experience of his cunning.

After a little while I remarked—

"I am going outside to find some wood for the fire; "will you come and help me?"

And to this she nodded assent, and we both crept out together, while Davy Blott lay snoring on the ground.

"Now tell me who he is," I said. "You are afraid of him, I can see. Who is he, and why do you stay with him?"

We were standing within a dozen yards or so of the hut door when I asked Sissy the question, but she motioned me to come away still further.

"Yes," said she, "I am afraid of him. He is not unkind to me, poor Davy! but I am afraid of him. He talks so strangely and looks so. And now he has that dreadful hammer!"

And she wrung her hands piteously, while the tears rolled down her cheeks.

"But who is he?" I asked; "you have not told me that."

"He is Cousin Davy. Mamma used to call him so. Poor mamma!"

"Where is mamma, then?"

"Dead. They put her in the ground the day before Cousin Davy brought me away."

And I could feel my own eyes growing moist as I gazed on the poor, forlorn little creature, with no better protector than the great rough madman.

"Yes," said I, "he brought you away; when?"

"In the night," she replied.

"In the night?"

"Hush! If you speak so loud you will wake him. Yes; he came into my room the night after the day when they buried poor mamma, and he brought these clothes with him, and he made me put them on, and he tied a handkerchief round my mouth, so that I might not make any noise, and he carried me away from papa's house by the back garden way. Oh, dear! That is many, many days ago, but he has kept me so close with him that I have not been able to tell anyone."

And she sobbed and cried as she laid her fair little face against the breast of my dirty jacket as though her heart would break.

But I was too amazed at the wonderful story she was telling me to offer her consolation or sympathy.

I was very young; but I had prowled London streets long enough to know what "gammon" meant.

But there was no gammon in this case.

Innocence and artlessness spoke as well from her eyes and gestures, as from her trembling lips, and though it was hard, indeed, to understand, to disbelieve was impossible.

"But how do you know that he is mad? Who told you?"

"No one that I recollect told me so," she replied; "but everybody knows that he is. Not always terrible like you have seen him. Sometimes he would be so mild and good that his keeper had no trouble with him, and would let him move about the house, and go out by himself as though he was quite well."

"He lived at your father's house, then, Sissy?"

"Always; as long as I can remember."

"You didn't want to remain with him?"

"Oh, no, no. It will break papa's heart to lose me, and he will die as poor mamma did!"

And again she broke into a paroxysm of grief.

"But he shall not lose you, Sissy," said I, feeling at the moment as valiant as Jack the Giant-Killer, "you shall go back to your father. I will take you if you like. Come, let us start away at once while he is asleep."

But Sissy shook her head despairingly.

"I don't know the way," said she; "it is miles and miles off. It must be, for we have been always walking and hurrying and running."

"But you know the name of the place where your home is?"

But before she could answer, we were interrupted.

His mad dreams had roused Davy Blott from the profound sleep he was in when we left him, and we heard his great voice shouting Sissy's name in accents of fright and alarm.

It was lucky for us that it was so.

If he had crept out of the hut quietly, he could have seen at once that some sort of confidence was already established between us, and I make no doubt that I should have received my discharge there and then.

Hearing his voice, however, we instantly separated, and, when rushing to the door with his formidable hammer in his hand, he discovered us busily engaged in searching for bits of old wood.

Nor did it fret me much that his passion took a turn that cost me a stinging box on the ear.

"You impudent villain! you saucy beggar!" he exclaimed, darting at me, and cuffing me left and right; "how dare you ask her to soil her hands to save your own vile paws? Do you know who she is, sir? Do you know?"

I was smarting under the undeserved chastisement, and it was at my tongue's tip to tell him what I did know, and to warn him that I did not intend to remain silent under the said knowledge.

A look from Sissy, however, restrained me.

"How should I know?" I replied, grumblingly; "if she's a tramp like I am it won't hurt her to pick up a few sticks; but I don't want her to help me if you don't like it. I don't want to stay with you any longer if you are going to turn disagreeable."

My blunt and apparently reckless reply seemed to quite disarm him of any suspicions he might previously have entertained.

He laughed, as though his mind was relieved, and flinging me a shilling out of his money belt, bade me be quick with the wood, and retreated with Sissy into the hut again.

Now what was to be done?

Imperfect as was the outline of the story that the little girl had confided to me, there could be no doubt that she was in imminent danger.

However mad and absurd the man's claim to her custody, there could be no question that he was fiercely resolute to maintain it.

After what I had seen and heard, I could have no doubt that, if driven to extremes, he would carry out the deadly purpose he had assumed, and kill Sissy, rather than be parted from her.

But to what extent dare I interfere?

Suppose, instead of returning to the hut, I ran off and gave information of what I knew?

This might be only hastening the peril I would avoid.

It would be better to wait a little.

To bide my time through that day, at least, and seek an opportunity for further questioning Sissy as to her home and its whereabouts.

But it seemed as though the said opportunity was not to occur.

Brief as had been the madman's slumber, it satisfied him for the present, and after a few hours' rest he made ready for moving on again.

In this he was baulked, however.

The clouds had loomed black and heavy through the fore part of the day, and now the rain began to descend with that steadiness that denotes a long continuance.

This did not tend to make our lodging the more comfortable.

What little wood there was to be picked up under the hedges and in the deserted brickfield was wet, and the rain beat down into our open chimney, half blinding and suffocating us.

Sissy was shivering with cold.

Mad Blott was not unmindful of her comfort.

He had taken off the heavy blouse he wore, and wrapped round her; but still her teeth chattered, and her trembling limbs denoted how much she suffered.

"This will never do," said Mr. Blott, after awhile; "my darling will take cold. Good heavens! if she should fall sick, and we with such a long, long way to go."

And desperately casting about him for wood to make a fire to warm his poor little captive, he discovered the window frame, from which every pane of glass had long been shattered, and with a few strokes of his hammer, reduced it to splinters of a size fit for burning.

But this slender supply was soon exhausted, and the rain still came pelting down, and the wind blew keen and chill.

"We will have some wine!" exclaimed Mad Blott. "Go into the village, boy, to the best tavern you can find, and buy a bottle of the best. Say that it is for a sick child, and perhaps that may move the tavern-keeper to treat you fairly."

And he gave me a half-sovereign, and off I set to the village, distant about half-a-mile.

It was growing late in the afternoon now, and the rain was still pouring down.

There was not much chance that the madman would shift from his quarters to-night.

Unless he was compelled.

Should I have a hand in compelling him?

Now was my chance.

It seemed that I ought to do so, but still there was a sort of treachery in it that was not at all to my mind.

Mad though he was, he had acted kindly by me.

Were it not for him, my naked toes, instead of the stout boots in which they were encased, would be splashing in the muddy road.

He had provided me with a meal—he had given me a shilling.

Ought I, under these circumstances, betray him—to consign him to hopeless, endless imprisonment?

Had I been left to myself to make up my mind, I think it not at all unlikely that I should have bought the bottle of port wine and carried it back without saying a word concerning the strange man who had sent me for it.

But it was differently ordered.

The chief tavern of the village was one

of considerable size, and owned a public parlour, in which, as I could see through the open door that faced the bar, a jolly fire was blazing.

I was wet through to the skin nearly, and after I had bought what I had been sent for, I took the liberty of stepping into the parlour for a bit of a warm.

There was company there.

Two bluff-looking men, in rough overcoats, buttoned up to the chin, and the landlord.

They had evidently been sitting there some time, for tobacco ash strewed the table at which they were sitting, and the big rummers before them were nearly empty.

"How's the weather, boy?" one of the strangers inquired, addressing me.

"Still raining hard," I replied.

"Means to keep it up, too, through the rest of this blessed day," remarked the second stranger, raising the red stuff curtain that screened the window of the snug parlour, and looking out. "What do you say to another jorum, Mr. Leathers?"

"Well, if I thought that it would be consistent with my duty as head constable," returned the man addressed, wagging his head doubtfully, "I shouldn't so much mind."

"Your duty! Why, it's part of it," remarked the other, with a laugh, and a wink at the landlord; "it's the first law of nature, man. Look after yourself first, and your neighbour afterwards."

"That's all very well; but if it isn't your neighbour, but an enemy—an enemy of the law, I mean—that you're to look after, I'm not sure but that a man in my position should make some little self-sacrifice. However, you as a valet and a confidential servant of a highly-respectable family, should know as well as any man what is good for me, and so I think I will indulge in just another glass, Mr. Quail, and then we'll move."

"We might as well stay where we are till morning for that matter," remarked Mr. Quail. "It isn't likely that he'd drag the poor little mite about in such wretched weather as this; he's snug in hiding somewhere, you may depend."

I pricked up my ears at this.

I was just on the point of slipping off.

That one of the big, bluff-looking strangers was a constable, was quite enough for me.

The sooner I took myself out of his arm's reach the better.

This last observation, however, about a certain somebody who "would not drag about a poor little mite through such wretched weather," and who, moreover, was adjudged to be in snug hiding somewhere, resolved me to stay just a few moments longer.

"I will stand this with your permission, gentlemen," the landlord observed, as he brought in two steaming glasses of rum and water; "it is not often that one is honoured with the chief constable's company."

His motive for so splendid an act of generosity was soon made manifest, however.

There had been a story begun, or, at least, hinted at by his guests, and he was curious to hear it to the end.

"Well," he remarked, insinuatingly, as the barmaid brought him in a third "jorum" matching in heat and magnitude those already provided for his guests. "Well, gentleman, I make no doubt that romances of the sort you were just now speaking of are common enough with professional persons like yourself, but it certainly beats anything I ever heard before!"

"Not so common as you might suppose, my friend," replied Mr. Quail, mysteriously.

"He hasn't heard the strangest part of it, or he wouldn't think it very common," said Mr. Leathers, sipping his grog with a relish.

The landlord fidgetted his chair nearer to those of his guests.

"Really now! Well, if it wouldn't be regarded as too great a liberty——"

"Oh! not at all," returned Mr. Quail, magnanimously. "Of course it is well not to tell tales out of school, but amongst men of honour—men of the world, you know, eh?"

"As you say, sir, it is altogether a different thing," responded the landlord, promptly, and edging in his chair still a little closer.

"Well, the strangest part of the affair," continued Mr. Quail, lowering his voice, but still not sufficiently so for it to escape my listening ears, "the strangest part of the affair is that this is not the first child he is suspected of smuggling away."

"Good heavens! what a monster."

"Mind you, I don't state it as a fact," said Mr. Quail, cautiously. "Anyhow, I speak of the child vanished."

"And has never since been heard of?" asked the landlord, with horror.

"Has never since been heard of," responded Mr. Quail, puffing out a mouthful of tobacco smoke with a sigh.

"That's eight or nine years ago, if I understand rightly, put in Mr. Leathers, the chief constable.

"Nine years come the fourteenth of next October, sir."

"Was that, too, a little girl, may I ask?" said the landlord.

"That, sir, was a boy. Ah! he'd a been a big chap by this time—big as that young lout warming himself by the fire there."

"You see it is a queer story from first to last," continued Mr. Quail, warming with the rum and water. "Holding the position in the family that I do, of course I am mum, but one can't shut his ears to rumour. My lady, the Lord be good to her, is dead now, so it is all as one to her; but it is said that this one should have been her husband."

"Which one?" asked both the landlord and Mr. Leathers in a breath.

"The one we are after; Davy Blott, as he has taken it into his mad head to call himself."

I gave a start so sudden and violent that my knee came in contact with the tongs that rested on the side of the fireplace, and down they came with a clatter.

"You'd better be off, my lad; we don't want that row here," said the landlord, angrily. "You must be warm enough by this time. Cut away. Your bottle is on the counter."

But Mr. Leathers was my friend.

"Let him stay a little longer," said he, compassionately. "Phew! hark at the rain how it bangs against the windows. Well, as you were saying, Mr. Quail?"

"Yes, it was the mad one that should have married her—so the gossip goes. They are cousins, you know."

"What! the man you are after and the widower—the father of the child he went off with?" said the landlord.

"Exactly."

"But how could he have married her if he was mad?"

Mr. Quail screwed his lips together and looked wise.

"I say, you know," said he, "you are drawing me out rayther further than I ought to go. But there, it'll all be in the papers soon, I shouldn't wonder. Well, then, they *do* say that he wasn't mad at all in those times, but that he was only just a little—well, what shall I call it?—soft, you know, and that it was his handsome, strong-willed cousin coming in and carrying the lady away slap out of his arms, in a manner of speaking, that turned him quite——"

And Mr. Quail tapped his forehead significantly with his forefinger.

"He was never raving mad, then?" inquired the landlord.

"Bless you, no! mild as a lamb. To be sure, he's always had a keeper, but a nice gentleman's life he's always had of it. Davy wanted no looking after; a child might lead him. Fact, a child *did* lead him, oftener than anybody else. The youngster he has gone off with, I mean."

"When was it that he broke out into the mad fit that ended in his going off, then?" the landlord asked.

"When our lady died," replied Mr. Quail; "he began to grow fierce and restless from the time that he heard she was dying, and to speak of our governor in language that I shouldn't like to repeat in polite company."

"Accused him of killing her, didn't he?" spoke Mr. Leathers.

Mr. Quail puffed at his pipe, and nodded.

"And of doing away with the boy—the one that was taken away nine years before?"

"Pooh! where's the use of listening to mad people. They say anything," returned Mr. Quail, complacently. "It is trying enough at times to listen to people who have credit for being sane. You'd hardly think, now, that in our parts there are folks who believe that Mr. Harold—that is my master, you understand—did have a hand in putting that boy out of the way, and further, that he wouldn't be at all sorry to see his little daughter, Sissy, put under the turf so that he might become sole master of the estate!"

"Preposterous?" remarked Mr. Leathers.

"One of the most ridiculous stories I ever heard of," chimed in the landlord.

But I neither chimed in nor did anything else at present.

My bewilderment was too complete.

I could now have no doubt that Davy Blott, "as he called himself," the man who at that very moment was lurking in the brickmaker's ruined hut, was the man that chief constable Leathers and Mr. Quail were anxious to lay hands on.

It was equally certain that the poor little girl "Sissy," towards whom I felt such a strange attraction, was Sissy the daughter of "Mr. Harold," the cousin of the madman!

"I suppose, now, if the truth was known that this Mr. Harold would not be a penny the richer for the death of his wife and her two children?" presently observed the landlord.

"Well, I don't know as to that," returned Mr. Quail. "He would be the richer undoubtedly, because the estate, as far as I understand, was so willed by his wife's father; but I don't pay any attention to such idle talk."

"It isn't likely that he would offer five hundred pounds reward for the recovery of the fugitives if he would rather that they were never found," remarked Mr. Leathers. "I doubt if more than one of 'em ever will be found."

"You don't mean that, sir? And which one, pray?" asked the landlord, in a startled voice.

"The man—this Davy Blott," replied the chief constable.

"And what do you think will become of the little girl, sir?"

"I think that he'll kill her, if he has not done so already," responded Mr. Leathers, with professional coolness. "These quiet mad people are devilishly desperate and cruel when they are roused. He'll do it out of sheer love for her, sir, I shouldn't wonder. I've known lots of such cases."

I felt my lips growing white, and a sensation as though all the blood in my body was retreating to my heart.

Why, this was but an echoing of the madman's own words!

"Rather than she shall fall into the hands of her enemies I will kill her."

There was something terrible in the thought that even at that moment, left alone with her in that deserted hut, he might be tempted to the perpetration of his mad threat.

I was so overcome by the dreadful thought that I lost my presence of mind.

Turning from the fire-place, I hurriedly approached the table at which the men were sitting.

"No, no; he surely will not kill her," I cried. "Do you—do you think he could do such a horrid thing?"

As the newspapers say, the sensation produced on the three men may be more easily imagined than described.

They had been speaking in a very low tone of voice, and had no reason for supposing that I had heard a word of their conversation.

Mr. Leathers was the first to break the alarming silence that followed my appeal.

"Why, what the d——l does the boy mean?" he exclaimed.

"I don't know what he means, but I'll very soon show him what comes of his prying into the affairs of his betters."

And, jumping up, the irate landlord had both my ears between his broad fingers and thumbs in a twinkling.

But the shrewd Mr. Quail was more moderate.

Possibly, he saw more in my terror than was to be accounted for by my idle listening to a tale in which I had no concern.

"Nay, don't hurt him," he exclaimed, disengaging me from the landlord's cruel grip. "D'ye hear, lad, this gentleman —and since you have been listening, you must have heard who he is—has asked you what you meant by interrupting him as you did?"

"I mean just this, sir," I replied, summoning all my courage, "that it I thought there was the least chance of what you was just speaking of happening, I'd——"

And here I paused.

"You would what? Come, tell us what you would do?"

"I'd tell you where they are hiding," said I, boldly.

The landlord stared with his heavy mouth ajar.

Mr. Leathers screwed his mouth to the shape of the letter O, and emitted a low whistle.

"Dashed if I didn't think so, exclaimed Mr. Quail, jumping up briskly. "You know something of these runaways, eh? P'r'aps you'll be good enough to describe 'em."

I was in for it now.

I couldn't have backed out had I tried.

In a few brief sentences I described both man and child in a manner that convinced even the suspicious Mr. Leathers.

"And you know where they are, you say?" said he.

"I know where I left them not an hour since," I replied.

"But how do you know that they have not decamped since then?"

"Because he is waiting for what he sent me for."

"For a bottle of the best old port!" exclaimed the landlord, in amazement.

"That's right. Bought and paid for, and now standing on the counter. Told me it was for a sick lady as was staying at a house at t'other end of the village."

This was true.

I was wise enough to know that a boy that looked like an out-o'-work plasterer's boy was not a likely customer to require the best port wine for his own consumption, and had invented the fib to account for my requiring it.

Mr. Leathers's mouth resumed its ordinary shape, and then relaxed to a grin.

He whispered with Mr. Quail, who nodded approval.

"Pray," said he, turning severely to me, "do you happen to know anything of an interesting youth who escaped with this man out of the lock-up at Old Snorley?"

"Yes," said I, without hesitation; "I know him very well. It was I."

"Now, then, you can tell us," continued Mr. Leathers, with much eagerness in his manner, "who it was that helped him break the great bolt of the cage lock?"

I could have better told him *what* it was.

My tiny red conjuror!

The reader must suppose, because I have not mentioned it of late, that it is either lost or forgotten.

My new boots, or one of them, at least, had been converted into a receptacle for keeping it safe.

I had cut out a little plug in the inner sole just where my heel set, and stuck it in, and replaced the plug as neatly as I could.

Not so neatly, however, but that it caused the leather to project a little, as I could feel at that moment.

But it wasn't likely that I was going to make confession to the sort of man I at once discovered Mr. Leathers to be.

"He broke it himself, sir," I answered.

"What! from the inside!" exclaimed the chief constable, incredulously.

"From the inside. He flung all his weight against the door, and shook it, and the bolt came in two."

"And d'ye mean to tell me that he burst his handcuffs without help?" asked Mr. Leathers, looking rather uncomfortable.

"He gave them a twist, like so, and his hands were free," I replied, enjoying the big man's perplexity.

"Good Lord; he must be a regular Samson!" said he. "I'm not a chicken" (judging from his big limbs and the great breadth of chest, he certainly was not), "but I'd rather be excused from tackling such a fellow single-handed."

Then, after whispering aside with Mr. Quail for a few seconds, he again turned to me.

"Look here, my lad, do you know the penalty for prison breaking?" said he.

"I didn't break it; it was him," I answered.

"Aye, aye! but you helped him, no doubt. A great strong fellow like you would be able to give him most valuable assistance. Well, the penalty for prison breaking is transportation beyond the seas!"

I was not such a hardened ruffian but that the opening up of a prospect so terrible brought the tears into my eyes.

"But if you behave well in this matter, and help us all you can, I don't say but that when it is all over I'll let you go scot free!"

I earnestly expressed my gratitude to Mr. Leathers for his generosity, and at once promised to do all that I could.

Perhaps had I been a little older I should have seen at what it was the cunning gentleman was driving.

He was afraid that I should stand in the way of himself and Mr. Quail touching the reward of five hundred pounds.

"Now," said he, "just you sit down here, and in as few words as possible tell us all you know."

And, having no other object in view than the rescue of poor little Sissy out of the madman's hands, I did as he requested, hiding nothing, not even "Bull Blott's" possession of the hammer, mention of which made Mr. Leathers whistle and scratch his head.

"HE HAD BARELY CLEARED THE THRESHOLD WHEN HE FELL."

## CHAPTER XXV.

I CONSPIRE WITH "MAD BLOTT'S" ENEMIES FOR HIS DISARMING AND CAPTURE.

IN less than half-an-hour our conference was at an end, and it was arranged how Davy Blott was to be trapped and taken.

I must confess that I felt heartily ashamed of the part that I agreed to play in the performance.

The landlord was politely requested to leave the room while the two men discussed the matter with me, and at the same time seemed a hint to Mr. Leathers that the less he said about the business just at present the better it might be for him.

"We don't want any other fingers in the pie excepting our own," said the worthy head constable, as the landlord closed the door on himself; "it may be a tough job; but if we can manage it, it will pay for shin-plaister."

"Yes," rejoined Mr. Quail, "it certainly would be more pleasant if it wasn't for that hammer. By George! you know, fancy a weapon like that swinging in a pair of arms such as he has."

"I don't fancy anything of the kind," returned Mr. Leathers, knowingly; "it won't happen, so there's no use in fancying it."

"I should feel easier in my mind if I was of the same opinion," remarked Mr. Quail.

I said nothing, but I certainly thought as Mr Quail thought.

"Ah, you see, you haven't had the experience that I have," said the head constable, with a smile of conscious superiority.

"Unless your experience has rendered your skull hammer proof, I don't see how it will help you in this case," returned his companion.

"We shall see."

And Mr. Leathers, with his eyes twinkling confidently, rang the bell.

"Bring me the bottle of wine that our young friend here ordered," said he.

"Thank you. Now bring me a corkscrew and a sound cork similiar to the one with which the bottle is corked."

This too was brought, and Mr. Leathers placed bottle, cork, and corkscrew in the capacious pocket of his heavy overcoat, and put his hat on.

"Excuse me just for ten minutes, I shan't be longer," said he.

And he left the room.

Not a word passed between Mr. Quail and myself during his absence, and within the time specified he was back again.

"There you are, my lad," said he to me, handing me the bottle of wine apparently in the same condition as when he had taken it away; "now make haste back to your master as fast as you can."

"Yes, sir. What else?"

"Nothing else."

"But I thought you said, sir, that I was to—to help you, and that you would help me if I did?"

"Exactly; and I meant what I said. All the help I want you to give me is to hold your tongue, and say nothing about having met me or anyone else. D'ye understand?"

"Yes, sir; I understand what you say."

"You are not to say a word, mind, or act in any way that may make him suspicious of his danger."

All at once a clue to Mr. Leathers's strange behaviour flashed to my mind.

"Supposing that he asks me to have some of the wine, sir," said I, "shall I drink it?"

The head constable regarded me with a look of sudden surprise, and then broke into a laugh.

"By George!" he exclaimed; "you are a keener young customer than I took you to be! Well, since you ask the question, you had best *not* drink, if he asks you. You must know that this is wine of a very strong kind—a very heady kind, and it isn't good for boys to drink."

"Or girls, sir?"

"Oh, hang it, you know, you had better take my staff and warrant, and do the job all by yourself, if you are going on like this," rejoined Mr. Leathers, with a mixture of anger and amusement in his expressive countenance. "Well, it is *not* good for girls either, and girls had best avoid it."

"Thank you, sir; I think that I understand all about it, now," said I, and at once took my departure.

And surely it was not difficult to understand!

Something had been mixed with the wine to make Davy Blott's capture all the easier.

As I remarked before, I felt ashamed of the part I was taking.

I had made a dirty, treacherous bargain.

Through my instrumentality the man who had given me a meal and a pair of boots was to be delivered into the hands of his enemies, bound hand and foot, as it were.

Still there was Sissy.

He himself had said that he would kill her rather than part with her, and I already knew enough of the desperate maniac to believe that he would, if driven to extremes, keep his word!

And comforting myself in this way, I hurried along, and in a little while reached the hut in the brickfield.

Mr. Blott was at the door.

"You have been a very, very long time. What detained you?" he asked, suspiciously.

There was no help for it but to tell a lie.

"I thought that I saw someone watching me, and I went a long way about to make sure," I replied.

"And were your suspicions correct?" he asked, eagerly.

"No; it was nothing after all. He turned another way."

"I am glad of that," said he, with a great sigh of relief. "She is ill, Joe. Her shivering is worse, and her dear little head is burning hot. We shall have to stay here some time, I am afraid; that is, if they will let us. It would kill her to carry her out as she is."

Poor kind madman!

He had now taken off his waistcoat as well as his blouse, in order to make up some sort of a bed for sick Sissy in the corner.

"Here is the wine, sir," said I, for, in his anxiety about the little girl, he seemed to forget all about it.

"Aye, to be sure," he returned, eagerly taking it from my hand. "She shall have some; it may do her good."

Now here was a pretty predicament!

That the wine had been tampered with I had not the least doubt.

Probably it was dosed strong enough with some drug to stupify the brain of a man strong and powerful as this one.

What its effect might be on a child so young and delicate as Sissy was terrible to think of.

As he had said, the little girl was very ill, and, knowing what I now knew of her story, I pitied her more and more, and felt as though there was nothing so desperate but I would undertake it to save her.

We, of course, had no corkscrew, but Mr. Blott quickly got over that difficulty by neatly chipping off the neck of the bottle by tapping it against the iron head of his hammer.

"Ah! it smells good," he exclaimed, applying his nostrils to it. "This will put life into my darling; but we must find something for her to drink out of."

And, while he cast about him, I took the opportunity of making signs to Sissy.

I pointed towards the bottle he carried in his hand, and shook my head emphatically.

But she was too ill and indifferent to understand. She only smiled, and held out one of her hands to me.

I stooped down as if to press it, and, with a rapid glance towards Mad Blott, brought my lips close to her ear.

"You musn't——"

But, unluckily, he turned round on the instant.

"She must drink it out of the bottle," said he; "we must pour a little into her mouth. And my hand shakes so that I am afraid that I shall cut her with the jagged glass! Look you, Joe, your hand is steady; you pour a little of it into her mouth. Just a little, Sissy, darling! it will do you good."

It was growing towards evening by this time, and nearly dark within the hut.

I took the wine bottle as he directed, and stooped down to her as she lay on her rough couch; but I dare not even whisper to her, for he had stooped down too, and his face was as close to hers as was mine.

It was a terrible moment.

Bad enough would it be to witness him administer to her what, in all probability, would act as deadly poison, but a thousand times worse that she should take it from my hand!

She should not! If he killed me she should not taste a drop of the drugged wine.

"A rat!" I exclaimed. "D'ye see it? there it runs!"

And, springing forward, I dashed the bottle against the wall, so that every drop of its contents were spilled.

I had to be mighty quick to escape his infuriated grasp as he started forward to catch me.

"You clumsy brute!" he cried; "you thick-headed, blundering blockhead! you shall suffer for that!"

And, gnashing the teeth in his mad head, he made at me again, while poor Sissy, terrified out of her life almost, sat screaming in alarm.

It was no great trouble for me to elude him, and to dart out of the hut into the field.

He followed me a few yards, but Sissy's screaming recalled him, and I was safe from further pursuit.

Safe so far, indeed; but what had I gained by my clever manœuvre?

I dare not return to the hut!

Worse still, maybe I had rescued poor Sissy from the frying-pan presently to plunge her into the fire, as the vulgar saying is.

There was no drugged wine for Mr. Blott!

Making sure that he had partaken of it, the men who reckoned on his easy arrest would presently arrive—with what result who could tell?

What ought I to do?

It was still raining fast, and night was rapidly drawing on.

Should I run back to the village and tell what had happened?

If I did so, perhaps while I was gone Mr. Blott would come out to look for me, and, not finding me, would guess my treachery, and, ill as she was, hurry away with the little girl.

No, I dare not leave the neighbourhood of the hut.

I waited and waited till it was quite dark.

Then, with cautious steps, I crept up over the soddened grass, and listened outside the hut.

At first I could hear nothing, but pre-sently I could make out a soft sound of "Hus-s-sh!" just such as a nurse makes when she is soothing a baby.

It was mad Davy, with Sissy in his arms, lulling her to sleep.

Without the least noise I made my way to the front of the hut so as get a peep in at the open doorway if I could.

The wind was blowing in fierce gusts, and rattling the loose tiles with which the ruined shed was roofed, so that even had I moved with less caution, I don't think that he would have heard me.

I stooped close to the earth and peeped in.

But I might as well have attempted to look through a wall, all within was so dark.

But I could hear the mad nurse still "hus-s-sh-ing," and the rustle of his clothes as he softly rocked his huge baby to and fro.

I have said that all within the hut was pitch dark.

This was not quite so, however.

Within six feet of the doorway, on the ground, was a something long and white, that was dimly distinguishable.

It was the hammer, with its long, white handle!

If I could only get this!

It was impossible, though I tried very hard to reach it by laying quite flat on the wet earth and thrust my arm in.

True, engaged as he was, I might have made a sudden dash into the hut and secured the murderous weapon before he had time to hinder.

But that would be at once to betray my treacherous designs, and how he would then act it was impossible for me to say.

And in the midst of my trouble and perplexity it seemed that a gust of wind brought to my ears the sound of softly approaching footsteps!

I listened intently with my ear to the ground.

There could be no doubt of it!

The head constable and his friend were coming, making sure, no doubt, that the work they had cut out was already half done.

I could plainly hear their heavy, stealthy steps on the soddened grass, but mad Blott heard nothing.

His whole soul was engrossed in his tender occupation, and I could still distinctly hear his rocking to and fro and his constant " hu-s-sh, hu-s-sh ! "

The approaching men were so close now that when the wind blew sharp I could even make out their whispering voices.

## CHAPTER XXVI.

### " THE HAMMER AGAINST THE PISTOL "—THE FIGHT--MAD BLOTT'S DEFEAT.

BETWEEN the two fires, as it were—for I had a right to conclude that after miscarrying in my instructions, Mr. Leathers, no less than the madman, would regard me as his enemy—I was in such a state of bewilderment and confusion that I knew not what to do.

Suddenly it came into my head to climb up on to the roof of the ruined shed.

I recollected the broad, unguarded chimney within, and I had a vague idea that by its means I might be able yet to help poor Sissy.

It was by no means a difficult ascent.

Projecting bricks extended from the basement to the summit of the side wall, and I was on the roof before ten might be counted.

There I made a discovery.

There was a hole in the tiles large enough to admit of the passage of a man's body, and this rather puzzled me, because I well remembered that there was no hole in the roof visible from that part of the shed where Sissy and Davy Blott found shelter.

A little examination, however, explained the puzzle.

A few feet of the shed had been divided from the main part of it, forming a sort of ante-room, and used, in all probability, in prosperous times, as a bed-room by a member of the brick-maker's family.

How it communicated with the larger shed, however, I, at present, was quite unaware, or whether the madman knew of its existence.

My examination, however, was brought to a sudden termination by hearing whispered voices immediately under the wall.

" It is all quiet enough," one remarked. " It would be amusing if they have all three been having a pull at the bottle."

" Not so amusing, my friend. It would possibly be the death of the youngsters if they drank a couple of glasses of it."

I had no difficulty in making out Mr. Leathers to be the first speaker, Mr. Quail the last.

" Well, one of 'em might swig at it to his heart's content for all it would trouble us; of course, it is different with the little girl," whispered Mr. Leathers.

" Rather ! I can hear no sound ; no sound at all," rejoined his companion. " It will be a nice sell if that young villain gave him warning, and they are off."

" It isn't likely, I should think. At all events, I shall go in and see," returned the doughty head constable.

" And serve you right if you get a broken head for your pains," I maliciously thought to myself.

I hadn't forgotten the charitable remark he had uttered concerning me not a minute since.

It must have been just at this moment that mad Blott became aware of the whisperers, for Sissy uttered a sudden cry, denoting that her nurse had disturbed her.

" That's the child ! " exclaimed Mr. Quail, with energy. " I could swear to her voice among five hundred. Quick ! come along ! "

And, with no further affectation of stealth or secrecy, both men ran round to the front of the hut, in hopes of finding the madman asleep and insensible.

But they were dead out in their calculations.

" In the name of the law——."

I heard the authoritative voice of Mr. Leathers utter these words, and then there instantly followed a terrible crash and an exclamation of pain and amazement.

It was fortunate for Mr. Head Constable that he had brought his bull's-eye lantern with him.

Mad, faithful Blott was on the alert.

Knowing that the enemy was at hand he had sprung to the doorway, with his long hammer poised ready for a blow.

As Mr. Leathers appeared, he flashed the light into the almost black darkness so suddenly that Blott was for the instant dazzled, and swung the hammer higher than he had intended.

Consequently, instead of descending on Mr. Leathers's head, as inevitably it would have done, it caught the row of bricks that fringed the doorway overhead, and sent them flying in the faces of the constable and his friend, causing their temporary retreat.

"That infernal boy has deceived us," I heard Mr. Leathers exclaim in a savage tone; and then, raising his voice, he exclaimed—

"It will be better for you not to resist the law, my man. If you like to come quietly with us, well and good; if not, I have only to call out, and a dozen of my fellows will be down on you in no time."

"The Lord forbid!" replied Mad Blott. "I shouldn't like to have so many lives to answer for. Take warning. Whoever attempts to enter this doorway will lose his life. I've sworn it."

"And we are sworn to do our duty," exclaimed Mr. Quail. "You know me. You had best give in and let us have the little girl; you had indeed."

But if Mr. Quail hoped to appease the man with the hammer with this sort of blandishment, he must have felt disappointed.

"Hang you! I know you very well," Blott roared out, furiously. "You are at the bottom of this, curse you! Have at you first, traitor!"

And he sprang out into the darkness, and made a dash with his long hammer at the spot from where the voice proceeded.

Whether he succeeded in inflicting a blow on Mr. Quail's bulky person I cannot say. I only know that the first attempt was not followed up by a second.

The madman's attention was otherwise engaged.

Taking advantage of his confederate's drawing the madman out of the shed, Mr. Leathers resolved on a bold, though, as it transpired, a decidedly rash step.

Holding his lantern above his head, he made a dash into the hut, and caught up the child in his arms.

He might as well have attempted to rob a jungle tigress of her cub.

Sissy uttered a cry, and Blott sprang to her rescue in an instant.

I could hear a smash of broken glass, which was Mr. Leathers's bull's-eye lantern dashed to splinters against the wall, and, quickly following, came a smothered, choking cry of—

"Help! He's throttling me!"

Then a heavy thud of a man's body striking the earth!

With the strength of three ordinary men, mad Blott had taken the burly head constable neck and crupper, and fairly pitched him out at the doorway.

Then, quick as thought, he proceeded to an act, that occasioned me no small amazement.

Davy Blott knew of that slip of the shed that was parted off from the rest!

He must have discovered it while I was away buying the wine.

Quick as thought he thrust open the door that led from the shed to the little space, and pushed Sissy in, and pulled to the door again with a heavy slam.

"Now come on!" I heard him roar. "It was only for fear that in the dark my darling might be hit that I let you off so easily. Come on, and we'll see which is hardest, your villainous skull or my good hammer!"

Mr. Leathers, by this time, had scrambled up from the ground.

"Look you, David Hawk, or Blott, or whatever you choose to call yourself," he exclaimed, in a passionate voice, "I hold a warrant for your arrest on a charge of child stealing, and I'm not a man to be cowed by bluster. I hold a warrant, and I mean to execute it. I'll give you half a minute to reflect on it. Then I'm coming in. I'm coming in with a loaded pistol, and if you again molest me, I'll shoot you."

But Mr. Blott was too mad to heed the head constable's threatening.

"Hurrah!" he cried, flourishing his formidable weapon round his head as he stood guard before the door of the little place wherein Sissy was stowed. "The hammer against the pistol! Come on if you dare! Ha, ha! were you ten times as strong and a hundred times as cunning, you would never get her! She is mine! You robbed me of her mother, but her you shall never take from me alive. No, no, not alive!"

As may be easily imagined, the events of the last few minutes had caused no little fright and bewilderment, but these last words of mad Blott at once restored my coolness and self-possession.

"They should not take Sissy from him alive!"

He had declared it over and over again; and it was quite certain that he meant what he said.

There was not a moment to lose.

I had no more doubt of the head constable's hardihood and courage than of Mr. Blott's desperate resolution.

I approached the hole in the roof and looked down.

It was with difficulty that I could make out her little figure, it was so dark.

"Sissy!"

But huddled close by the door, she appeared not to hear me.

"Sissy, Sissy!" Louder this time.

Then she suddenly looked up with a little cry of terror.

"Don't be afraid. Don't you know my voice? It is Joe; you remember Joe?"

"Oh, yes, yes!" she replied, starting up and coming to stand just under the hole through which I was looking down on her. "Go away, pray go away."

"What for? Why should I go away? I'm here to help you if I can."

"Oh, but he said that he would kill you! He's been talking about you, and he says that you are a spy in league with his enemies. Pray go away; if he catches you, he'll kill you!"

"There's no knowing who he may kill, Sissy, you poor little thing," said I, touched by the kind solicitude for me while she herself was in such great danger. "I believe if they goad him he will kill you—anybody. But he shan't, if you will let me help you."

"How can you help me?" she answered, innocently.

"I will try, at all events," said I "But we must be quick. How can I reach you? Is there anything down there that you can stand on?"

"I can't see," Sissy replied, despairingly.

"But you can feel. Grope about the floor with your hands."

Inspired by the unexpected prospect of escape, she did as I bade her, and, feeling about the ground, discovered several loose bricks that had there fallen.

"Place two just below, and put the others on them, straight, and one at a time."

She did so, until she had made a heap two feet high.

"Now climb carefully to the top; steady yourself by holding on to the side wall."

With wonderful dexterity she accomplished this feat, and, next moment, by reaching in at the hole, I was enabled to grasp her wrists in both my hands.

"You musn't mind me hurting you a little, I'm going to try to pull you up."

Whence I derived strength to achieve my object I can only humbly guess.

Suffice it, it was achieved.

In ten seconds Sissy was on the roof beside me.

In ten more we had clambered down the outer wall, and stood free in the open field.

Meanwhile, matters remained within the ruined shed pretty much as they were at the first.

The madman continued to guard the door of the now empty cage, while Mr. Quail and the head constable, by threats and persuasions in turn, endeavoured to gain their purpose.

Bewildered as to what I should do next, I kept close in the shadow of the wall at the back of the building, keeping Sissy close to me.

"The half minute has expired," cried Mr. Leathers. "Make up your mind within there, before I count three."

"I'll smash your head, as sure as it is now standing on your shoulders!" roared mad Blott.

Then came the sharp report of a pistol —once, twice!

It was a revolver; and Mr. Leathers, standing within a yard of the doorway, and having no light, first of all discharged one barrel towards the roof of the hut, so that the flash of it might show him the whereabouts of his game.

This he discerned, and, quick as thought, aimed and fired, wounding Blott in the arm that wielded the hammer.

But though badly wounded, he was not yet conquered.

The bullet from the head constable's pistol had penetrated the fleshy part of his arm, between the elbow and shoulder, causing him to drop his terrible hammer to the ground.

With a bellow like that of an infuriated bull, however, he picked it up again with his uninjured left hand, and renewed the attack.

Not on the besiegers, however.

As he had uttered a cry that was rather of rage than pain, they thought that the shot had missed him, and were, therefore, slow at rushing into the dark shed to complete his capture.

Mr. Leathers had already experienced one narrow escape; he did not care to risk another.

But mad Blott had no immediate designs against them.

He seemed to be convinced that the wound he had received would incapacitate him from protecting his darling charge against those he regarded as her enemies, and he, therefore, resolved to put into execution his oft-expressed and terrible purpose of putting an end to Sissy's life!

The door leading to the narrow space in which he had thrust the little girl had slipped its latch; but mad Blott was not to be baulked; like a blacksmith banging at his anvil, he let drive at the door with his long-handled hammer.

"You have doomed her to death, monsters!" he cried; "her blood is on your heads not mine! But death to her shall be more merciful than was life to her mother. One blow, but one blow, and all her misery is at an end!"

And as he spoke, the battered door yielded with a crash.

"Now, my lamb. Quick, let us make short work of it! Ha! where!—what! —how is this?"

He could not find her.

As we stood huddled against the outer wall, we could hear him groping and staggering about within the narrow space, calling on her to come to him.

But a good foot of stout brickwork stood between the poor little creature and the danger that threatened her.

"Sissy, Sissy! She is not here! They have stolen her from me! They have smuggled her away! Robbers, miscreants, where is she? Tell me what you have done with her?"

But, as the reader already knows, the individuals addressed knew no more of Sissy's escape than he himself did.

But he did not question the fact.

Shrieking rather than talking, mad Blott was rushing out of the hut to settle accounts with the robbers who had stolen away his darling.

"Look out," cried Mr. Leathers. "Keep off with that confounded hammer of yours. I've got a bullet left, and I'll take surer aim this time, take my word for it."

But he was saved the painful necessity.

The raging fury of the poor maniac was his downfall.

Barely had he cleared the threshold of the hut when he flung up his hands, and fell forward flat on his face with a gurgling cry.

When they approached him they discovered that a crimson stream was issuing from his lips, which sufficiently revealed what had happened.

---

## CHAPTER XXVII.

### THE STRANGE GENTLEMAN AT THE "GRIFFIN."

MAD BLOTT, prostrate on his face and bleeding, did not receive that immediate attention his critical situation demanded.

The words he had last uttered bore with them a meaning that banished aught else from the minds of the head constable and his friend, Mr. Quail.

The child had vanished!

In an instant the head constable was within the hut with a lighted match, with which he kindled the wick of his shattered lamp.

At a glance he perceived exactly how the case stood, and was out of the hut again faster than he had entered it.

"Quick! she has escaped from the roof!" he exclaimed. "She can't have gone far in so short a time! She would make for the lights of the village, no doubt, and—why, dash my buttons! here she is, and the boy as well!"

There was no disputing that fact!

There we were, to a dead certainty, not having as yet any time to resolve what to do.

Mr. Quail, with an expression of great satisfaction, caught up Sissy, while the less ceremonious constable inserted two of his knuckles in at the collar of my jacket.

"I can't quite make you out, at present, young gentleman," said he. "I'll take care of you for a little time if you have no objection."

"We had best hurry back," said Mr. Quail, who had secured the poor madman's blouse to wrap Sissy in. "If the messenger made good use of his time, Mr. Harold should be at the 'Griffin' by this time. He'll take no harm till we can send someone to him."

By "he" was meant poor Blott.

"Better make sure," returned the matter-of-fact officer, and forthwith he withdrew from his pocket a pair of handcuffs, and adjusted them on Mr. Blott's passive wrists, and with the leather strap he wore round his waist his legs were secured.

"We couldn't carry him, if we tried," remarked the constable; "the best we can do is to send a doctor to him with all speed."

We were speedy enough.

In less than a quarter of an hour we were in the village and at the "Griffin," the tavern where, in the afternoon, I had bought the wine which Mr. Leathers had drugged.

Evidently the rumour that something uncommon was afoot had gained credence in the village.

At least a dozen wondering men and women were grouped about a private carriage, attached to which were a pair of mud-splashed, panting horses, while within, at the open space before the bar of the "Griffin," there was a second crowd.

Great was the consternation and amazement of the latter, when Mr. Quail hurriedly elbowed his way through them, bearing in his arms the child so strangely enveloped.

"Where is Mr. Harold Hawk?" the valet eagerly asked. "That is his carriage at the door. Where is he?"

"He's upstairs in the best room, sir. He's only this minute arrived. He's in a terrible way, poor gentleman, and enough to make him with that dear child——"

"We will go up to him at once," remarked Mr. Quail, cutting short the motherly landlady's expressions of sympathy. "You had best come up with me, Mr. Leathers."

"It's my duty to do so," returned the head constable, who seemed to think that Mr. Quail was taking rather too much on himself. "Come on, you, sir."

This last observation was addressed to me.

Ever since we had left poor mad Blott, Mr. Leathers had held me by the collar, and the people, remarking my pale face, together with my ignominious position, were evidently impressed with the idea that I was the ruffian who had been guilty of the crime of child stealing. Indeed, I narrowly escaped a malicious box on the ear that one incensed dame aimed at me.

"There'll be no occasion to bring up that boy," said Mr. Quail. "He can wait down here. Lock him in somewhere if you are afraid that he will bolt."

"I am coming up, and he is coming with me," responded Mr. Leathers, decidedly, and up we all went.

In the "best room," as it was called, we found a gentleman anxiously pacing to and fro, and soon as we entered Sissy called out, "Father, father!" and, all entangled as she was in the voluminous skirts of mad Blott's blouse, she wriggled out of Mr. Quail's arms, and the next moment had her arms clasped about the strange gentleman's neck.

But to my astonishment, and, I think, to that of the head constable as well, he did not return the poor little truant's affectionate greeting with over much warmth.

"That will do, Sissy—that will do," said he, disengaging himself from her embrace. "Why on earth, Quail, could you not have her washed and decently clad before you brought her to me? Faugh! her clothes smell as though she had been sleeping on a dunghill!"

"Beg your pardon, sir!" spoke Mr. Leathers, with a touch of sarcasm in his blunt tone; "we didn't think that you'd be patient to wait while she was got up fine and scented; she's had a deal of suffering, I may tell you, sir."

"And I, too, have had a deal of suffering!" remarked the gentleman with knitted brows. "Where is this ruffianly madman? Where was he captured? What had he to say in justification of this monstrous outrage?"

In as few words as possible, the head constable, assisted by Mr. Quail, proceeded to put him in possession of all the particulars that had come within their knowledge; Sissy, meanwhile, continuing trembling at her father's feet, as he sat on his chair.

So the reader may imagine I had not made myself very conspicuous.

On entering the room, I had just stepped aside, and the lamp on the table was so placed that I stood quite in the shade.

Several times in the course of his narrative, Mr. Leathers had occasion to refer to me, but he only spoke of me as "this boy here," and the gentleman in the easy chair had hardly deigned to notice me at all.

But all the time I had been noticing him.

There was that about his hard-looking, handsome face, with its resolute, compressed lips, and its cruel bright black eyes, that had a curious attraction for me.

I felt, somehow, as though I had more to fear from him than from the constable.

Moreover, there was that name that Mr. Quail had used, when he inquired if his master had arrived.

Where had I heard that name before?

Under what peculiar circumstances?

I was aroused from my silent perplexity by the gentleman in the arm-chair, after a brief reflection on what the two men had told him, exclaiming—

"Step forward, you boy."

I would have rather a hundred times have stepped backward—out of the room that is—but Mr. Leathers plucked me by the sleeve, and jerked me forward.

I did not advance more than two or three steps, however, and was still in the shade.

"Then am I to understand that this lad was mainly instrumental in recovering my daughter?" said he, in the same hard, cold voice he had from the first adopted.

Mr. Leathers was prompt enough in his reply, and Mr. Quail was equally eager to back him.

It was that "five hundred pounds reward" they were thinking of.

"Oh, no, indeed, sir," said the head constable, "far from it. Indeed, I am not sure if he shouldn't be prosecuted for aiding and abetting the unfortunate lunatic in what he has done."

"Decidedly!" chimed in Mr. Quail; "he deserves very severe punishment."

But I had a small friend in court they had not reckoned on.

As before remarked, Sissy was crouched at her father's feet, but hearing this last unjust and cruel observation of Mr. Quail, she at once started to her feet, and hurried across the room to where I was standing.

"No, no, no! don't punish him; don't hurt him!" she exclaimed, laying her pale little face on my shoulder. "It was Joe who saved me, papa. He spilled the poisoned wine because I should not drink it. It was him who helped me out at the roof of that horrible shed, or poor cousin Davy would have killed me with his terrible hammer."

But this display of championship on the part of poor Sissy did not have the effect desired on her parent.

Indeed, it seemed to me that the scowl on his face became blacker as he heard the words that Sissy uttered.

"Tut, tut, child! Quail, bring her away from that young ragamuffin this instant. Cecilia, I am amazed at you. Now, boy, what have you to say for yourself?"

Nothing that I was ashamed of, thank goodness.

It would have been acting the part of a cur to hang back after she had spoken for me so courageously.

I stepped forward boldly enough to within a couple of yards of the great gentleman's arm-chair.

"Sir," said I, "what is it that you wish me to tell you?"

But now happened something very wonderful indeed.

He seemed suddenly to have altered his mind, and to have no wish for me to tell him anything at all.

The lamp light was now shining full

on my face, and as he gazed on it he pushed himself back with a violence that made the castors of his chair creak again.

He did not speak ; he only compressed his thin lips the closer, and turned suddenly pale.

Mr. Quail was the first to notice the change.

"Are you ill, sir?" he exclaimed, approaching his master.

"No, no; only a passing faintness," he replied, still, however, with his eyes fixed on mine in so singular a manner, that I was compelled to look away from him ; and then he suddenly burst out—

"Who is this boy? What—what is his name? Confound you, you idiots, can't you tell me? Where did you find him, I ask?"

He asked these succeeding questions in a voice so strangely altered and harsh, and, moreover, with such a singular expression in his flashing eyes, that it was no wonder if Mr. Leathers began to suspect that the malady exhibited by poor Mr. Blott ran in the blood of the family.

"Speak up for yourself, you young scoundrel," whispered the head constable to me; "where did you come from, eh?"

"From London," said I.

"London is a biggish place; what part of it?"

"The south part of it," I replied, resolved not to be too circumstantial until I knew what was the purport of this questioning.

"And how did you get a living there? Who is your father, and how does he get a living? P'r'aps that is what the gentleman wishes to know?"

I verily believe that Mr. Leathers, the head constable, asked this last question in perfect innocence.

But to the ears of the gentleman in the arm-chair the tone in which it was asked gave some subtle force to the words themselves.

"How dare you, sir!" exclaimed the latter, starting to his feet, with his lips whiter than the ashes in the fire-grate. "You grossly exceed your duty in presuming to insinuate that—that——"

And then, as though suddenly conscious of his own rash impropriety, he abruptly paused, and continued, with constrained calmness—

"You must excuse me, sir; my over-whelming grief and misfortune must plead for me."

And he pressed his hands to his head.

"No offence, sir, not in the least," returned the accommodating Mr. Leathers. "You will be better after a night's rest, sir, and more of a mind to talk over this unpleasant business. Do you stay here to-night, sir?"

"Yes—no—that is, I think—— No, I shall not stay here to-night," he replied, with decision. "I shall hurry home with my little daughter at once, and—you can take train and come to me in the morning."

"And this boy, sir? I don't suppose, sir, he has done *much* harm. I suppose we may let him go, sir?"

"Go—go where?"

It was remarkable with what startling abruptness Sissy's father asked the question.

"Oh, it don't much matter, sir; he's of that sort that will be sure to fall on his feet, however he's pitched about."

If the words that Sissy's father muttered under his breath were not "that's true, curse him!" my sharp ears were singularly at fault.

I am afraid that it was a vision of a fair share in the sum of five hundred pounds rather than a friendly spirit towards me, that inclined Mr. Leathers to let me go.

"Look here, young fellow," said he, addressing me, "you may thank your lucky stars that this kind gentleman here is likewise a merciful gentleman. You have had a very narrow escape of being sent to prison. I hope the lesson will not be lost to you. There's the door ; you may go about your business."

But while he was delivering himself of the lenient sentence, Sissy's father had been rapidly revolving in his mind what course would be the best to pursue.

The conclusion he finally arrived at was a startling one for me, at all events.

"No," said he, "he shall go with me."

"With you?"

"Yes," continued her father, "it would be unfair—un-Christian to let the service he has rendered my little daughter pass unrecognised. For her sake I—I feel an interest in him, and would keep him within reach for a few days until I can decide what may be done for him."

"'HOLD ON TO THE COLLAR OF MY JACKET,' SAID HE."

Sissy fairly clapped her hands now, and both Mr. Quail and the head constable murmured something about it being very kind of him; but truth compels me to confess that I did not quite think so.

I could not forget the strange look with which he regarded me when the lamp gave him, for the first time, a full view of my face, nor his muttered exclamations when Mr. Leathers spoke of people of my sort always falling on their feet.

But I had no voice in the matter.

By this time it was announced that those who had gone to fetch in the man who had broken a blood-vessel, and who was left lying in the shed in the brickfield, had returned.

He was still insensible. It was doubtful, the doctor said, whether he would live many hours.

"Would you like to see him, sir? He is lying in a room below," the landlord remarked to Sissy's father.

But Sissy's father evidently had a very decided objection to doing anything of the kind.

Indeed, the bare suggestion was enough to make him hurry his departure, and in less than a quarter of an hour, for the first time in my life, I was riding in a carriage, bound I knew not whither.

---

## CHAPTER XXVIII.

### I AM MADE A PRISONER—THE PEBBLES AT MY WINDOW—GUY FOSTER AGAIN.

I RODE with Mr. Quail on the seat behind, and not one word passed between us during that long, dark, midnight journey, though whether a brief interview that discreet valet held with his master had anything to do with the cautious silence of the latter is, of course, more than I can say.

Finally we arrived at a house—a large, dismal-looking house—that stood in the midst of its own grounds, and there, with my heart beating with wonder (with which, I must confess, not a little fear was mixed), we alighted.

That night I saw no more of either Sissy or her father.

The bedroom to which I was introduced though only that of an upper servant, was, to my ragamuffin eyes, so splendid that it was a long time before I could make up my mind to avail myself of the tempting accommodation it offered.

As for the bed, it seemed quite a sin that only one boy, and that of my small size, should occupy it. Many a time ten of us had rested under the "Dark Arches," on a bed of shavings, not a bit bigger.

And while I was tossing from side to side, and in vain endeavouring to go to sleep, what was Sissy's father about?

He was ill, he had declared, and quite upset by the tormenting anxieties he had endured during the past few weeks.

Nevertheless, he had not retired to bed.

He remained up when all the rest of the household was quiet, pacing the room, and then writing.

To whom, does the reader imagine?

To a dead man!

To Samson Tuff! To the Golden Glazier!

That mysterious penitent thief who, in his last hours, had taken so strange an interest in my welfare, and made me his heir!

It was not till long afterwards that I made the discovery, and even had an opportunity of reading the strange epistle.

It was as follows:—

"Either you have basely deceived me or the dead has rose from the grave. Unless I am grown demented and cannot believe the evidence of my eyes, he is here, under my roof with me. He who so long ago you bargained to rid me of for ever.

"The discovery has come on me so suddenly that just now I am incapable of anything but sending you this word of my terrible suspicions.

"There is just a chance that they may be unfounded, but my conscience (I can fancy the devil grinning over my shoulder as I write the name of that bugbear of fools and cowards) tells me otherwise.

"He has the dark eyes, the thin lips, the dauntless bearing, for all his beggar's rags and his beggar's breeding. And, as far as may be judged, his age would agree.

"You alone can explain this horrible mystery; and I beg of you, nay I *command* you to do so without the least delay. You have received your price, and your work, if my conjectures are correct, remains undone and must be concluded. At all events, something *must* be done, and that immediately.

"I shall not be satisfied with your writing to me. Come to Thorpsehill at once. There is a tavern here called the 'Griffin.' To-morrrw evening and the following, I will make an excuse for calling there, and you must be on the watch for me, and follow me when I leave.

"I address you at the old address. I presume that you are no longer a poor man. The magic means with which I provided you, in hands as unscrupulous as your own, must ere this have brought you riches. Nevertheless, I dare say you have not grown to be such a fine gentleman that your old acquaintances are unknown to you.

"Once more, attend to this *immediately*. I am not a man to threaten idly, and I hereby warn you of the consequence of disobedience.

"H.

"*Samson Tuff,*
    "*Care of Mr. Doomstone,*
        "*Dale Street, Lambeth.*"

From which it will appear that at some period antecedent to the commencement of this story, the "Golden Glazier" must have been a lodger at the domicile of my terrible enemy, Mr. Aaron Doomstone.

Little did I dream, as I lay on that strange bed perplexing my head in puzzling what would be the end of my strange adventure, that a mine so formidable was being sprung under my very feet, as it were.

Nor did either my puzzling or my amazement decrease, when, next morning, I discovered (I was too anxious to lay abed beyond break of day) that the door of my room was locked on the outside, and that the key was removed.

Hour after hour passed, till, about ten o'clock, Mr. Quail, softly unlocking the door, brought me a substantial breakfast.

But I was more anxious concerning my liberty.

"How long am I to be kept here, sir?" I asked.

No answer. Only a grin and a shrug of Mr. Quail's shoulders, as he backed towards the door to take his departure.

"I don't want to be kept here," I cried in alarm. "I won't stay here. It's no use your locking the door. If you do, I'll get out at the window."

"Do, and break your neck," returned Mr. Quail, grinning again, and then coolly shutting and locking the door, and carrying off the key with him.

My first impulse was to hurry to the window.

It was neither barred nor bolted, but between it and the ground, was a sheer descent of at least thirty feet, with nothing but a blank perpendicular wall intervening.

It was a small mug of ale that Mr. Quail had brought me, with a liberal quantity of prime baked meat and bread; but the discovery that I was to all intents and purposes a prisoner, left me but an indifferent appetite for eating and drinking.

All through that live-long day was I left by myself, till come the evening Mr. Quail paid me another visit, bringing with him a plentiful repast; but in answer to all my entreaties, he would not answer one word.

So passed the night, and the next day, and the next.

Had I not before suspected it, I should by this time have found out that Sissy's father had taken charge of me for some hidden purpose of his own; and when I thought of his ominous muttering, and the vengeful scowl with which he had regarded me, my heart sank within me, and more than once my despair made me so desperate that a little further urging would have tempted me to take the leap from the window, and chance the consequences.

But on that third night there happened an event that broke the monotony of my imprisonment, in a manner as unexpected as it was startling.

It was so terribly lonesome to sit for so many hours in that pitch dark, perched-up room, that I had, after the first night, begged of Mr. Quail to provide me with a light, and he had kindly complied, bringing me a small lamp, the flame of which, although no larger than that which a rushlight would yield, was vastly better than no light at all.

It might have been about ten o'clock (for I was just about to get into bed and endeavour to forget my sorrows in sleep) when a quick, sharp noise at the window startled me.

At first I thought that it was rain, since all the evening the clouds had looked lowering.

I approached the window and gently opened it. There was no rain; but scarcely had I raised the sash when several small pebbles struck against my face.

I knew that they could come from nowhere but the garden below, but the night was so dark it was no use looking down.

What could it mean?

My head was still out of the window, as I wonderingly asked myself the question; but a voice from the garden—a strange voice that I thought I had never heard before, caused me to draw it in with all speed.

"Look out!" cried the voice.

And at the same moment, something like a white ball came in at the open window, and fell with a noise on to the floor.

First closing the casement, and securing it as well as I was able, in a tremor of hope and fear I carried the white ball to my lamp and there examined it.

It was a stone, carefully wrapped about with white paper.

There was writing on the paper, in a great, plain hand, as easy to read as print.

It said, "A friend. You may save your life and gain your liberty by hauling in the thread, and whatever comes after."

Truly, it seemed my fate to be plagued by mysteries!

What friend had I? It was a woeful reflection, and one that brought a lump into my throat.

I had not a single friend in the world!

And the "thread!"

This last, however, was a riddle more easily solved than the other.

There was a thread.

The end of it had been tied about the white ball; but when the latter bounced on to the ground, the thread had become loosened from it, and so was unnoticed. There it lay, however, just under the window.

Should I avail myself of it?

After all, it was scarcely likely that any enemy I might have would choose such a method of doing me an injury.

There could be no harm in hauling in a bit of thread anyhow, whatever I might decide to do with what might "come after."

I raised the sash again and gently pulled in the thread, for the length of ten yards, or thereabouts.

Then came into my hands a knot and a thicker substance, whipcord, following the thread.

Ten yards of this, and then came a twine.

A stout twine, or laycord rather, with another bit of white paper attached to the knot that joined it to the whipcord.

"At the end of this string is a rope," said the writing; "trust your friend. Make the rope fast to some heavy piece of furniture, and wait and see."

This brought me to a standstill for a few moments.

What was the rope intended for?

But instantly my qualms vanished. What else could it be intended for but to aid my escape?

As for who was my friend was impossible to say, nor did it much matter to a lad in my desperate situation.

I might at least make sure that, whoever he was, he was the enemy of *my* enemy—for how else could I regard him?—Sissy's father.

I tugged at the cord with a will, and at the end of it there was the rope of deliverance.

An excellent strong rope, with knots tied in it, down which any boy might climb.

I no longer hesitated.

The bedstead was the heaviest piece of furniture the chamber contained, and about one of its sturdy mahogany legs I wound and tied my end of the precious cable.

Then I opened the window wider still, and prepared for the perilous descent.

But here I found myself unexpectedly checked.

Thinking it as well to give my unknown friend some warning of my intention I softly called—

"Look out down there! I am coming!"

To which the strange voice replied hastily—

"For your life's sake don't risk it! I am coming up!"

And at once the knotted rope became taut, showing that now a heavy weight was depending on it.

It was a terrible few moments.

Who was it?

It was a stout rope, but hardly such as a man might venture his life on.

Was it mad Blott?

Had he recovered from his injury and escaped from his keepers, and finding out where I was, under pretence of doing me a service was he coming up to work his insane vengeance on me?

I looked out at the window and strained my eyes till they smarted.

Steadily rising through the gloom I could make out a figure.

Not a large figure.

Not so large as that of mad Blott by half.

This was a relief at any rate.

Up, up, up! crawling up the black wall, as it were, like some monstrous insect.

A wheezing, gasping insect, that found the task it had undertaken one by no means easy to perform.

Up, up, still! Now the head of my unknown friend is level with the window-sill.

"Reach out, and get hold on the collar of my jacket!" said he.

Although taken aback, and scarce knowing what I am doing, I instinctively do as I am bid, and the next moment there comes tumbling and sprawling into the room—who does the reader imagine?

My villanous young enemy, Guy Foster?

## CHAPTER XXIX.

### AARON MAKES A FINAL EFFORT TO WREST FROM ME MY TALISMAN—GONE!

HAD it been the Golden Glazier himself restored to life, and so unexpectedly appearing before me, I could not have felt more amazed and terrified.

As the reader may recollect, my last view of my enemy was that of a boy lying bruised, and bleeding, and insensible in a corner, and many times since my dreams had been haunted with the horrible idea that I was a murderer—that the wounds I had inflicted on Guy Foster's visage with the broken handcuff had proved of so serious a nature that he had never recovered from them.

Here he was, however, hale and hearty, and with no other evidence of our fray on his villainous face than a jagged, pinky-white scar over his right eye.

The sudden cry that I uttered seemed to impress him with the idea that I was afraid that his mission was one of vengeance.

He grinned coolly, and held out his hand.

"Don't feel afeared; I ain't the sort of feller to bear malice," said he. "Return good for evil; that's my motter."

"I'm not afraid—at least, I'm not afraid of *you*," I answered, boldly. "What do you want here?"

Guy Foster's face immediately assumed an expression of virtue unjustly suspected.

"Now, there's pooty language to use towards a friend! A cove risks his blessed neck and grazes the skin all off his knees in climbing up to get at another cove, to do him a good turn, and then he wants to know what I want here!"

But the hypocritical fellow had imposed on me once; he couldn't do so again.

"If you don't tell me at once what you want, and who sent you, I'll call out for someone who will precious soon make you," said I.

"Oh, well, if it comes to that," replied Guy, altering his tone; "if you *won't* accept a cove's friendship when he offers it to you, and you *will* put matters on a business footing, I may as well tell you that I found my way here through a friend of yours."

"A friend of mine! I haven't one living, I'm afraid."

"P'r'aps he warn't living," grinned Guy, significantly; "p'r'aps the friend as I'm speaking of isn't living at all, but a dead 'un."

"Who do you mean?"

"Who? Why, Samson Tuff; *he* was your friend, wasn't he?"

"Yes, he was my friend; at least, I think so," I replied, more bewildered than ever. "But—but——"

"But nothing but just this!" interrupted Guy Foster, so proud of the fag end, and of the mystery that had somehow come to his knowledge that he wasn't able to contain it; "somebody sends a letter to the Glazier, not knowing that he had kicked the bucket, and, as a natural consequence, somebody else opens it and reads it."

"Well?"

"Thereby, that somebody gets a clue to where you are shut up in limbo."

"But who could write about me; do you know, Guy?" I asked, eagerly.

"That's mum," replied my young friend, laying a finger on his nose as though he knew all about it, but it wasn't convenient to tell.

"A friend of mine it was who sent it, didn't you say?"

"A friend! Oh, yes, a very nice sort of friend," returned Guy, laughing; "just the sort of friend as would chuck a brick at you if he saw that you were drownding."

"Who was the friend, then—the one who opened the letter?"

"That's nigher the mark!" replied Guy, nodding his head energetically.

"And he sent you here?"

"He came with me," returned Guy Foster, with a grin.

"Came with you?" I repeated, more and more amazed. "Where is he, then? *Who* is he?"

"He's down in the garden. It was him that was stiddying the rope while I swarmed up it."

"But what is his name? do I know him?"

"Can't you guess?" replied the tantalizing villain; "think of the most hamiable indewidual you ever had dealin's with."

I shook my head.

"An elderly genelman, not quite tall enough for a Grannydear he ain't, though p'r'aps he would be if he was mangled out, hump and all; a handsome old person, with a face something like this."

And as he spoke, my artful young friend instantly contorted his countenance to a peculiar expression, and huddled in his neck in a way that left no doubt as to who it was that he was mimicking.

"Aaron Doomstone!" I exclaimed, in a fright. "Do you mean to tell me that *he* is here?"

"Sh-sh; he's down under this ere window," returned Guy, in a whisper; "don't go a-callin' him names now, or you might spile his good intentions towards you."

"*His* good intentions?"

"Ah, it isn't a bad sort of intention to set you at liberty, is it?"

"No, indeed," I replied, eagerly; "there is nothing that I wouldn't risk for it, Guy. I am afraid to stay here. I should have jumped from the window days ago, only that I knew that it was certain death to do so. Will he release me? Did he say that he would? When, Guy, when?"

"Hold hard a bit!" remarked Master Foster. "I don't know nothing of perticklers; them you'll have to settle with him yourself."

"But how can I when——"

"You can when you see him, can't you, you young flat? Listen to me a minute; you won't go to suppose that he gives me orders to jaw about all what I've been tellin' you? I'm only supposed to bring you a message."

"From Aaron Doomstone?"

"Yes. 'I daren't show myself,' ses he, with that kind of considerate way of hisn, which you might have observed; 'I won't drop on the poor boy on a sudden like, cos I know as he has a sort o' hard feeling against me, and he might be frightened. So you shall pave the way to our interview, Guy,' he ses. 'You shall go up to him and ask him just one question.'"

"What question?" I eagerly demanded.

"One that's a puzzler to me," returned my young friend, with a shrug of his shoulders, "though, p'r'aps, you may understand all about it. The question was this ore: 'Ask him if he has still got what I want, and if he is willing to give it up to me if I set him at liberty, and give him twenty sovereigns told down on the nail?'"

Well enough did I know what it was to which the message referred.

In what manner the Jew dwarf had discovered my hiding-place I could not at present in the least make out, but it was quite certain what was the game he so pertinaciously scented.

My sparkling talisman!

As the reader may possibly remember, I had not been neglectful of its careful keeping.

On the morning when mad Davy Blott had been so kind as to buy me a new pair of shoes, I had cut out a little nest for it in the inner sole of one of them, and there, to the best of my knowledge, it still remained.

I say to the best of my knowledge, for the fact is, during the past two days and nights, I had not removed my boots from my feet, nor my clothes from my back, not daring to trust myself to go to bed in that mysterious place.

Now here was a chance of escaping from it!

Could I trust Aaron Doomstone? that was the question.

My experience of the hideous dwarf by no means warranted a reply in the affirmative.

That he was a stony-hearted, unscrupulous ruffian I very well knew, and in the ordinary way of business, it would be but sheer insanity to rely on his word.

But this of mine was not an ordinary business.

There could be no doubt that he was prepared to pay a prodigious price for the miraculous gem he so coveted, and he would no doubt count its acquisition cheap indeed, as costing him no more than a paltry twenty pounds.

Besides, if it came to that, I wanted no money at all.

All that I wanted, all that I had been pining and praying for during the whole weary time I had been incarcerated in that solitary chamber was liberty!

Liberty to return to my old, free, vagabond life, picking up a crust where I could, and sleeping anywhere.

As for the mystic red gem—the Golden Glazier's "priceless fortune," I was infinitely better without it.

What had its possession brought me?

Nothing but misery, and anxiety, and danger, and never a meal or a single penny!

While I was rapidly resolving in my mind what is here written, there came a sound of small stones pattering against the window.

"That's the old 'un," remarked Master Foster. "He's gettin' tired of waitin'. You're a precious long while making up your mind."

"Tell him," said I, "that I have what he wants, and that I will give it up to him if he does what he says he will do."

"That's enough then. I won't say good-night, 'cos I reckon that in a few minutes you'll be doing what you see me doing now. Take a wrinkle from it, Joe. Put out your legs—so—and grip the rope with your feet, and wriggle out till you can catch hold on the rope so—and then down you go."

And down he went, and was speedily lost in the darkness.

I thought, to be sure, that I was to follow, and at once prepared to do so. Indeed, my legs were fairly out of the window, before I was checked.

"Go back, go back, my tear."

It was Aaron Doomstone's voice, and the sound of it sent a shiver of terror through my whole body.

"But I'm coming down· I've got what—what you want with me," I whispered down to him. ·

"Go back, I tell you. You'll preak your neck. You can't get down, my goot poy, unless I'm up there to help you."

And I was at once aware of his weight tightening the knotted rope as it strained with a creak over the edge of the window-sill.

Heavy as he was, his avarice made him twice as active as the boy, and I had scarcely regained the room ere his hideous head was visible, and then he scrambled in at the window.

He wore a black skull-cap made of the fur of some animal, on his enormous head, and this, combined with his scrubby face and his big yellow fangs, and his glistening eyes, made him look like a wild beast.

He bowed to me a low bow of mockery, while, already repenting of what I had done, I retreated to the further end of the room.

"You are a goot child," said he; "a

very goot child; but you are slippery, my tear. Ve have done pisness before, my tear, if you remember; in vich you got the best of it."

And he made a grimace, and snapped his great yellow teeth together, as though, despite all his efforts to appear amiable, the recollection of how he had been taken in still stuck in his throat, as the saying is.

"Ve vill have no mistake this time, my goot leetle lad; ve vill try your goots, vat ve shall barter for."

And as he spoke he withdrew from the breast pocket of his rough jacket a stoutish piece of bright steel, about a foot long and an inch through, and tapered to a fine edge at the end.

It was not at all surprising that a man of Mr. Doomstone's pursuits should be possessed of such a weapon. The "jimmy," as this diminutive crowbar is called, is the burglar's constant companion and familiar friend.

"Vere ish your leetle treasure vat the Glasier gave you?" exclaimed Aaron, impatiently. "Give it me, quick! Let us try it against this leetle bar!"

But this was not according to my views of how the bargain should proceed.

If I gave him up what he was so greedy after, what was to prevent him making off with it by the same means as that by which he had been enabled to enter the room, and leave me in the lurch, and poorer than ever?

So, quickly as I dared, I submitted this view of the case to him.

"I told you the truth," said I, "when I said that I had what you wanted, and that you should have it. So you shall, the moment you set me at liberty!"

"At liberty to vat. To run away as you did before; at liberty to mock me and laugh at me!"

And for the moment, Aaron's face wore an expression terrible to behold. But with an effort he calmed his rising feelings of vengeance, and spoke in his old wheedling tone.

"But ve vill not quarrel, my tear; ve vill act fair by each other, quite fair! But I must first of all see that you have vat I vant. You are a goot lad, but you are slippery. You can't deny that you are slippery, you clever leetle dog!"

"Well, if you are quite sure that you mean acting fair———"

"Quite, my tear, quite," he interrupted in a fever of excitement. "Vere is it? I mean fair, s'help me Abraham!"

"Well, then it is in my boot; and if you will wait a minute———"

But Aaron Doomstone could not wait a minute, not a sixtieth part as long.

He could no more resist acting as he did, than a thirsty man could resist the sight of cool, sparkling water.

Before I could finish the sentence I had began he sprang at me as a cat does when it sees a mouse, and just as easily carried me across the room to where the bed was, and threw me on it.

With his monstrous hands trembling violently, he applied himself to one of my boots, and endeavoured to haul it off.

They were lace-up boots and fastened with a knot.

But Aaron Doomstone could not waste precious time in undoing knots.

With a snarl as though he meant biting my leg off, he bit at the leather knot with his great teeth and nipped it off as though it had been mere sewing cotton.

"Is this the von?" he exclaimed, holding it up that I might see.

Yes, it was the one—the left one, as I have before mentioned.

I was too terror-stricken to speak, however; I could only nod my head affirmatively.

Aaron carried it to the lamp and eagerly examined the boot by its dim light.

He evidently expected to find the tiny treasure wrapped in something and thrust up to the toe of the boot.

Finding his mistake he proceeded to a much more summary method of treatment.

As I lay on the bed afraid to speak or stir even, I saw him take out his big clasp-knife and open it, and next minute my good sound boot that I had taken such pride in was slit and sliced till the sole and the upper leather were completely severed from each other.

He'll find it now! I thought he might have discovered it with half that trouble, and my boot been saved!

But he had not found it.

All his hacking and cutting was in vain, and he dashed down the wrecked boot with a savage growl of rage and disappointment.

I had seen his hideous face under circumstances sufficiently appalling, but it was a mild face compared with that he now turned to me.

He had his great clasp-knife in his hand, and he glared with such devil's ferocity, that I thought that nothing less than that my last moment was come.

I sat up a scream that made the room resound.

But Aaron Doomstone took no heed of it.

He approached closely enough only to grasp my foot that still had a boot on it, and this latter he lugged off with as little ceremony as he had displayed over the other.

"Only a leetle mistake, my tear," he whispered, with his big lips white and tremulous, and his voice hoarse with suppressed fury; "the wrong boot—only the wrong boot, that is all!"

But I knew better.

Half dead as I was with fright, I was quite certain as to this, that the boot he had at first examined was the one that contained what he sought.

As well as though it had happened but an hour before I recollected raising the inner sole at the heel, and digging a little hole in the leather beneath, and therein depositing Samson Tuff's terrible legacy, and yet with all his pains Aaron Doomstone could not discover it.

I knew that it was quite useless him examining the other boot.

He used his knife on it, and carved it up just as he had served the first one; but in the end he threw it down on to the ground with a terrible oath, and turned with a murderous glance towards me.

In the extremity of my terror, I recovered my voice somewhat.

"It is there—in the first boot—the left boot—I put it there!" I gasped; "at the heel part, under the first layer of leather. Give it to me, I will find it."

With his ugly face twitching with rage he hesitated in his purpose, which I feel sure was to make short work of me, and turning to the spot where the wreck of my boots was strewn, he gathered up the fragments, and brought them to the bed, and threw them down before me.

Then with the hand that did not grasp the terrible clasp knife, he gripped me by the collar.

"Find it!" he exclaimed, through his set teeth; "find it—quick! and save your life!"

He meant what he said—his villainous eyes betrayed that but too plainly.

With desperate courage I took in hand the sole of my ruined left boot, and at once fixed on the spot where the Golden Glazier's legacy had been so artfully stowed away.

It was gone!

The hole in which it had lain was empty.

But Aaron Doomstone was too blinded with fury to perceive how genuine was my expression of astonishment.

"Gone! yes, gone! and it's time that you, too, was gone, you devil's imp!" And he threw me back on the bed.

But by strange good fortune at that very moment a voice came through the open window.

A startled, sudden voice, that from its peculiar tones could have emanated from none other than Master Guy Foster.

In an instant Aaron Doomstone was off the bed, and at the window.

But barely had he reached it when the key was turned swiftly in the lock of the chamber door, and a man appeared with a light in one hand and in the other a pistol. It was Mr. Quail.

Then he beheld the open window, the rope about the bedstead, and Mr. Doomstone, with his eyes bloodshot and glaring with rage, and with a knife in his hand, creeping like a panther towards the door.

"Move another step this way and I'll put a bullet through your head!" cried the valet.

Which other way was the dwarf to move?

To have tried to escape by the window would be to deliver himself with a skinful of broken bones into the hands of his enemies.

There was at least a better chance by way of the door.

Full of the desperate idea, he made for a spring at Mr. Quail, with his knife raised to strike.

But the valet was too quick for him.

The dwarf's big head offered a target not easy to miss, and Mr. Quail did not miss it.

There was a flash and a bang, and Aaron Doomstone, with a terrible cry, staggered and fell death-stricken!

## CHAPTER THE LAST.

DEATH-STRICKEN was Aaron Doomstone, but not dead.

How his detection came about, after events will easily explain.

It was that shrill, despairing scream, in my horror of impending death, I had uttered that saved me.

Solitary and apart as was the chamber in which I had been confined, the men attached to the stables in the rear of the garden had heard the sound, and were curious to know from whence it proceeded.

Their first astonishing discovery was that clever young London thief, Guy Foster, in attendance on the knotted rope that hung from my window.

The cry that young gentleman uttered as the coachman suddenly pounced on him was the sound that first alarmed Aaron Doomstone when he was stooping over me, and I lay before him as helpless as a sheep under a butcher's knife.

Acting on the immediate alarm, Mr. Quail, zealous in his master's interest, hurried up to the room where I was; with what result has already been made known to the reader.

But although Mr. Quail was a zealous servant, and to some extent in his master's confidence, on this momentous occasion he acted entirely on his own responsibility.

His master was from home !

Not far away.

No further than the vicinity of the tavern at which, in his letter to him, he had suggested a meeting with the Golden Glazier.

This was the fourth night he had been on the look-out for the man who, according to the terms of that mysterious communication, alone was able to allay certain terrible suspicions that my extraordinary likeness to someone else had conjured up.

Still in ignorance of his death, and cursing Samson Tuff for his dilatoriness, Mr. Harold Hawk made his way home, and arrived at his gate just in time to encounter the doctor, who had been hastily summoned to attend the wounded burglar that Mr. Quail's pistol had brought down.

He was terribly hurt, poor wretch.

The valet had discharged the pistol full in his face, and the sight of both his eyes was destroyed ; and besides this, his head had sustained such injury that his recovery was impossible.

They lifted him up on to the bed I had occupied, and there he lay, a terrible spectacle—blaspheming, struggling with the strength of three men against the many hands that held him, and howling in pain like a tortured dog.

As for me, such was the panic and confusion, that I remained in a corner of the room unnoticed, and I verily believe that I might have slipped downstairs and so out of the house, and no one the wiser.

I don't know what it was that held me back. Nothing could have done so except the same kind Providence that ordained that now my miserable, adventurous, perilous way of life should cease, and a better state of affairs commence.

With a strangely troubled countenance, the gentleman whom I had once before seen—Sissy's father—entered the room, in company with the doctor.

He did not see me, however ; as before remarked, I had taken refuge in a dark corner.

I watched him anxiously, however, and thought that his face brightened as he beheld the poor wretch writhing on the bed.

Possibly, from the confusing rumours he had heard, he expected to discover in the wounded " burglar," as everyone persisted in calling him, no other than his mysterious accomplice in some bygone crime—Samson Tuff, *alias* the Golden Glazier.

" Nothing can be done for him," the doctor whispered, after a long examination of his hideous patient ; " he will be a dead man within half-an-hour."

Despite his agony and his bad physical condition, Aaron Doomstone heard the appalling verdict, and the instant change in his terrified face was curious to behold.

" Who says that ? " he exclaimed, in an awful whisper.

" The doctor says it, you poor man," answered the housekeeper, who was a pious woman, and most assiduous in her endeavours to mitigate the wretched dwarf's sufferings. "Take good advice, and make the most of the few minutes that remain to you to make your peace with your Maker."

But Aaron Doomstone was in no mood to resign himself to death and that awful hereafter, from which his guilty conscience told him he had so small a chance of escape.

With his dreadful blind face distorted with agony and fear, he asked the doctor to come near, and begged him with all the fervour of despair to save his life.

"I have monish," pleaded Aaron, "I have mosh monish. "Don't let me die! I dare not die! Let me be blind—carry me to prison—anything so as I live! Listen, doctor! a thousand pounds goot lawful monish if you vill save me!"

"Were you to offer me the wealth of the Indies it would be impossible," replied the doctor firmly but kindly. "If you have anything to say, any confession to make, you have no time to waste. I warn you!"

But here Sissy's father spoke himself, in tones of alarm.

"We want no confessions here, Dr. Williams; here is the police officer; let him be removed instantly."

The police officer in question was no other than my old friend head-constable Leathers.

"It would be most inhuman to move him, my dear sir," spoke Dr. Williams; "he would die in the arms of those who carried him ere he reached your lodge gates."

"That is neither your affair or mine, sir," exclaimed Sissy's father, harshly; "this is not an hospital for sick ruffians. Carry him off at once!"

Aaron had lain quite quiet while this conversation was in progress. Now he again spoke, though in a voice that betrayed how rapidly he was sinking.

"Whose voice is that?" he asked, feebly.

"It was Mr. Harold Hawk who spoke," replied the constable, "and seeing that he is master here his orders must be obeyed."

"Harold Hawk! the master here!" repeated Aaron Doomstone, his face brightening with malignant satisfaction. "Stay then, I have something to say

that that gentleman had better hear. Vere is the leetle boy?"

As before stated, everyone had forgotten all about the boy, who was no other than the reader's humble servant. But now there was a look round the room, and he was discovered, and in no enviable frame of mind brought forward.

"Here is the boy," said the head constable, holding me by the cuff of my jacket. "What of him? Do you know him?"

"Better than he knows himself," replied blind Aaron, quietly; "he thinks that his name is Joe Sterling, and that he is a friendless orphan; but I know better. Mr. Harold Hawk, who vill not spare me a bed to die on, let me make you recompense. Take your son—your lost son—for whose murder, years ago, you paid so handsome!"

By this time there were a large number of persons in the room, and each one looked in incredulous amazement to hear this startling avowal.

"It is a lie! a monstrous, wicked lie!" exclaimed Sissy's father, in a voice almost unintelligible with rage; "and you, constable, do your duty. Carry this audacious ruffian away instantly."

It was terrible to see the malicious grin that overspread the countenance of the dying man.

"I have vitnesses," said he, "in an inner pocket. Here are the letters—all the letters from first to last that Mr. Harold Hawk sent to his goot friend Samson Tuff. Let him deny his signature if he can."

And hastily unbuttoning Aaron's jacket, there, as he had said, in an inner pocket, was a packet of old soiled letters.

But when with the packet in his hand the head-constable turned to Mr. Harold Hawk, he had vanished from the room.

Search through the house was made for him in vain, and in the midst of this new commotion, Aaron Doomstone breathed his last.

\*     \*     \*     \*

And for that matter so did "Joe Sterling"—for never again was I called by that name.

Bad man as he was, still he was my father, and it is not for me to hold up his memory to ignominy.

His memory, I say, for he is dead. I was but a mere boy when were made the startling revelations that told me who I was. Now I am grown to man's estate, and it was but a few months since that news of the fugitive's death came to me, and with dear Sissy by my side, I sat down to write the strange eventful history of my early days.

As to my identity of that, the letters that were sent to Samson Tuff furnished ample proof. How Aaron Doomstone became possessed of them remains to this day a mystery; unless, indeed, that memorable night when the Golden Glazier came to his miserable end in Rats' Castle, the Jew, while seeking for the "curious talisman," discovered the packet, and according to his cunning nature secured them.

"And what of that same mystic talisman?" asks the reader.

But on this head also I am in the dark.

How Samson Tuff came by it—how it vanished from the boot in which I had hidden it—is to me a mystery altogether inexplicable.

One thing I hope most sincerely, and that is, that nobody ever found it. But of this I am doubtful. Of late there have appeared in the newspapers certain accounts of bank breaking and safe robbing, that almost induces me to think that the ragged fortune bequeathed me by the Golden Glazier has once more turned up, and fallen into bad hands.

Time will show, perhaps.

But there are matters that time will never show, and which, for the reader's sake as well as mine own, I should like to have made clear.

As for instance, by what means it was that my father contrived to win the luckless woman who was my mother, and of whom I have no recollection, from his cousin David Hawk, or as he chose in his madness to style himself, Davy Blott.

Poor Davy is still alive and hearty, I am happy to say, and the happy harmless sharer of the affluence that is now mine and dear Sissy's.

Who else remains to account for?

Only one that I just now remember—Master Guy Foster.

I am glad to be able to account for Master Guy in a manner that I feel sure will give the reader satisfaction.

Guy is quite a reformed character.

At Sissy's intercession, we took him in hand, and after many, many failures, contrived to bring that young fellow to acknowledge that, after all, honesty is the best policy, and at the present writing he is a steady stoker on board of a Hamburgh steamboat, and in his last grateful letter to us says that he is in a fair way to become second engineer.

And now with many thanks, and an expression of my sincere regard to the hundred thousand boys who have accompanied me through my many perils and adventures, I will make my bow and retire.

---

www.ingramcontent.com/pod-product-compliance
Lightning Source LLC
Chambersburg PA
CBHW081155170626
46813CB00009B/3200